#3

THE SUICIDE PACT

DAVID B. LYONS

D1203043

Print ISBN: - 978-1-9160518-2-9

❀ Created with Vellum

PRAISE FOR DAVID B. LYONS

"This year's must-read thriller from this year's must-read author" – No.1 Bestselling author Rob Enright.

"An outstanding craftsman in the thriller genre" – No. 1 Bestselling author Andrew Barrett

"Lyons is a great new voice in fiction" – Critically-acclaimed author John A. Marley

"Outstanding. Truly outstanding" – Books From Dusk Til Dawn

"Utterly clever" – Novel Deelights

"Smart, dark, fascinating" — Reading Confessions

"Clever, brilliant, gripping" – Nicki's BookBlog

"A devastating twist in its tail" — Irish Independent

WANT TO STAY UP TO DATE WITH DAVID B. LYONS'S NOVELS?

Visit David's official website

www.TheOpenAuthor.com

Or

Sign up here to become a David B. Lyons insider and receive exclusive information on his latest novels.

www.subscribepage.com/dblinsider

For me mam

Our Suicide Pact

1. The decision has been made. Neither of us can ask the other if we want to change our minds anymore.

2. Spend our last day at home, saying goodbye to family (without them knowing we are saying goodbye for the last time).

3. Meet up at 7:30, visit the people we love the most to say goodbye (without them knowing we are saying goodbye for the last time).

4. Get back to Rathmines at Midnight.

5. End our lives.

19:00

Ciara

WHAT ARE YOU SUPPOSED TO SAY TO YOUR MAM WHEN ONLY you know it'll be the last time you ever speak to her?

I mean... she doesn't know it's the last time. She doesn't know anything. She's an idiot. But I know when I leave this house in twenty-minutes time that I will never come back; that I will never sit in this squeaky leather sofa again, that I'll never see my mam's nose get any redder than it's already gotten, that I will never hear my dad tut at me again.

I thought he'd be here today. But it's no surprise that he's not. In fact, it's appropriate that he's not here, I guess... because he's never been here for me anyway.

I place my glass of Coke down on the side table and wonder what I can say to her that won't give the game away. She's shuffling round in the kitchen, probably wondering who my dad is out with this evening. A lot of their shouting seems to be about him not telling her where he's going and who he's going to be out with. They make being an adult look really difficult. I can't bear the thought of growing up.

I stare at the back of her as her shaking hand lifts the glass to her mouth. Any time I think about my mam, I

1

imagine her in this *exact* position; sat up on one of the uncomfortable high stools at our kitchen island with a bottle of red wine open in front of her. Sometimes there're two bottles. And she's either swirling the wine glass around in her hand or she's lifting it to her mouth.

I tried it once. Wine. Yuck. I don't know how she does it. Every day. I heard her telling Auntie Sue one time that it helps calm her down. That made me laugh a little. I don't think my mam knows what calm means exactly. I've never seen her calm. Ever.

I walk towards her, tiptoeing across the tiles of our kitchen and when I get close she spins around, holding her hand to her chest.

'Jesus Christ, Ciara, you frightened the shite outta me. Don't sneak up on me like that!'

I hold my eyes closed and hear my own breaths as she swivels back around on her stool, back to her wine. She holds that glass much tighter than she's ever held me.

'Sorry,' I whisper as I stare down at my feet.

She doesn't react; doesn't turn back around to accept my apology. She just stays on her stool, swirling her glass, staring out the double-doors at nothing. I wonder what she thinks about every time she stares out there. I'd love to know what goes on inside her head.

I fidget with my hands a bit, each of my fingers taking turns to tap against my thumb and then I curl my bottom lip downwards. I'm stuck. I really don't know what to say to her. And I've had all day to come up with something.

'Where's Dad?' I ask.

I don't know why I call him Dad... or her Mam. I should just call them Michael and Vivian. They don't deserve to be called parents.

'You still there?' she says without turning around. Then she lets out that deep bloody sigh she always lets out. I've

2

heard this sound a million times before. I hear it a hundred times every day. 'I don't know where he is. Working late again, I s'pose.'

I know that's a lie. Everything's a lie. He's lying to her. She's lying to me. Our whole family lives in a house full of lies. And I'd know. Because I'm about to lie to her right now.

I clench my hands so that all of my fingers are in a ball and no longer fidgeting. Then I look around the kitchen, as if the words I want to say will be written somewhere for me to read from.

'I'm gonna stay in Ingrid's tonight, Mam. We're studying for our exam. Mrs Murphy said it's okay.'

She holds the hand that's not gripped to her glass up and swirls it in the air.

I almost laugh; a short snort shooting out of my nose. What a bitch! Maybe I should just go... go now... head out the door. That way when they find my body in the morning, this moment will haunt my mam forever: the time she had the chance to say goodbye to her only child and she couldn't even bring herself to turn around. So I do. I spin on my heels, grab at my tracksuit top and then look back at her and realise I have to do this. There's no way I can risk ending up like her.

There was a tiny part of me that hoped this evening would give me some sort of relief. When I thought about the final goodbye to my parents, somewhere in the back of my mind I hoped they would see right through me. That they'd know what I was up to. That my dad would sweep me into his arms and cry. And tell me that he's sorry. That he knows he's been a terrible dad. That he won't be a terrible dad ever again. Then my mam would join in; a big family group hug that we'd hold for ten minutes before my mam would make her way to the kitchen to pour every one of her bottles of wine down the sink.

I stare at the back of her head. Then check the clock. It's not even ten-past seven. I told Ingrid I'd knock for her at half-past. I'm way too early.

But there's not much else for me to do. Dad's not here; Mam's too busy cradling her wine to even turn around and look at me, let alone talk to me. I slip on my tracksuit top and, without even thinking, I pace across the kitchen tiles again, wrap my arms around my mam's waist and snuggle my head into the lower part of her back. I couldn't help it. I couldn't let a swirl of her hand be the last conversation we ever have. But maybe I should have. Because as soon as my hands are around her, I hear that bloody sigh again.

'Jesus, Ciara, I nearly spilt me wine. What are ye doing?' She unwraps my hands from her waist then turns around on her stool. 'What do you want from me?'

I just laugh. A full, proper laugh that seems to roar through my nose. And my mouth. I literally laugh in her face. Take that! Let that be the last conversation we ever have. Me laughing at you. I tried to hug you; I tried to say goodbye, but you were more worried about your bloody wine than me.

I zip my tracksuit top all the way up, so it's tight under my chin, then turn on my heels and — as I'm walking away from her — I raise my hand in the air and swirl a goodbye.

19:05

Ingrid

I STAND ON MY BED, STRETCH ONTO MY TIP TOES AND KISS Gary Barlow's face. I'll miss Take That the most. People always say that early Take That were the best; that when they had Robbie Williams in the band they had better songs. But I like the Take That now more. Then I kiss Howard. Then Jason. Then Mark. I touch at Mark's lips as I sink back down to my heels... I guess I'm not going to grow up and marry him after all.

I hop off my bed and look around my room. I'll miss my teddy bears, even though I haven't played with any of them in years. I haven't even touched one of them in years. But it's always been nice to know that they were there if I ever needed a hug.

I guess I need one now.

I walk towards them, grab them all up in to a bunch and hold them against me.

'I'm gonna tell you a secret,' I whisper. 'Me and Ciara, we're gonna die tonight. We hate our lives.'

Then I smile. And drop them all back down on the chair

DAVID B. LYONS

they normally sit on. I'm going mad; talking to stuffed animals as if I'm three years old again.

I spin my head round my bedroom to stare at it for the last time and then decide I've gotta leave before some memory in here makes me change my mind.

My bedroom kinda lies. It doesn't look as if I'm a sad girl at all. It's filled with magazines and posters and books and toys. Lots of things my parents bought for me. But that's exactly one of my problems. They think it's *things* that'll make me happy. They've no idea things mean nothing. Not to me anyway.

'Bye room,' I whisper through the crack in my door as I close it and walk out. I find myself on the landing, my eyes shut, my hands sweating.

I open my eyes, stare at my digital watch. 19:09. Ciara will be here in about twenty minutes. I need to do this now. I need to say my last goodbyes.

I edge closer to the stairs and stop at the top of them. I really don't want to go down there. How am I supposed to say goodbye for the last time without actually saying goodbye for the last time? I'm a terrible liar, too. I'm worried all three of them will see right through me. That they'll know where I'm going. What I plan on doing.

I take one step down and move my ear closer, to hear if they're saying anything about me. All I can hear is *Heartbeat*. Of course. *Heartbeat*. Mum watches reruns and reruns of that every Sunday night. Not sure why she watches that stuff. Anytime I see bits of those soaps she likes to watch there's normally somebody looking miserable in it. When I watch TV it's to get away from real life. Not to drown myself in it. Though I get the feeling Mum doesn't realise her life is just like those in the soaps. She thinks she's bigger and better than them. She doesn't realise she has drama in her life. She'll know better in the morning.

None of them look at me when I get inside the living room. Mum's glued to the TV, Dad is looking over his notes for his show tomorrow. He'll be going to bed soon. Around eight o'clock. He's got to be up early; early enough to talk to Dublin as they make their way to work. I used to think his job was really cool. But it's not. He just talks into a microphone for four hours and that's it. I remember a time thinking I'd like to be a radio DJ when I'm older. But I'm not quite sure I can think of a more boring job. It doesn't matter anyway. I'm not going to be older. So thinking about stuff like that is kinda pointless.

I don't know what to do. I look at the back of my dad's head, then the side of my mum's face. A lot of people tell me I'll be just as beautiful as her when I grow up. I don't think so. Then I look at Sven curled up on the floor with his action figures. So I sit down beside him and pick one up.

'Who's this?' I ask. He snatches it from me, then gets back to his make-believe without talking. I don't know what to do next. How do I say goodbye to my little brother? I rub the back of his head and he shakes it and groans until I take my hand away. Then he continues to pretend he's GI Joe or whoever it is he's playing with. I can't blame him not wanting me to join in. I never join in. I haven't been a great older sister. Not since we were really young. When he was a baby, I used to help look after him; I'd hold him, cuddle him, kiss him. But I'm not sure when I last cuddled him, when I last kissed him. Years ago, maybe. What relationship is a thirteen-year-old girl supposed to have with her eight-year-old brother anyway? How am I supposed to know that? It's not something they teach at school.

I stare around at my parents again. Neither of them have moved. Then I look back to Sven and blow him a quiet kiss before I get to my feet. I walk, slowly, to the sofa and plonk myself beside Mum. She looks at me, gives me a tiny smile and then gets back to *Heartbeat*. I place my hand on her knee and she places her hand on top of mine. We sit in silence for ages; her staring at the TV, me staring at the big clock above the mantelpiece. Ciara will be here in fifteen minutes. I don't have long to say my goodbyes.

I snuggle into Mum; resting my ear on her chest. Her boobies are really hard. Much harder than they've ever been. They've been that way since she came home from hospital last year after spending a day in there.

'Hey, what's with you?' she says.

'Just fancy a hug.'

She grips me tighter.

'Well, I'll take that,' she says. 'I remember hugging you so tightly on this sofa when you were a baby. I never wanted to let you out of my sight. Now look at you… feels like you're out of my sight way too often.'

I look up at her and feel a bit of pain in my belly. I think it's guilt. I bet it's guilt. Then the stupid music to *Heartbeat* plays.

'Fancy an ice-cream and a wafer?' she says.

I smile that half-smile thing I do when I want someone to think I'm happy but am really feeling sad inside.

'Me, me, me,' says Sven, throwing his action figures behind him.

'Terry?' Mum says.

Dad removes his head from his notes.

'Huh?'

'Fancy an ice-cream and a wafer?'

'Sorry,' he says, shaking his head. 'I'm just too busy here.'

Mum unwraps her hands from around me and gets up off the sofa.

'Not for me, Mum,' I say. 'Ciara's coming soon, we're gonna go back to her house to study for that exam.'

'Oh yes,' she says. 'Big one, huh?'

I nod my head. And as she leaves for the kitchen, I realise I will never hug her again. And it makes me sad. Really sad. I can feel the sadness in my belly. I turn to Dad and swallow.

I'm not sure I'll miss Dad so much. He's not the worst dad in the world. He's not as bad as Ciara's. None of my family are. But he's not a great dad either. I bet if I asked him what my birthdate was right now he wouldn't know the answer. He's too into his work. Actually, it's not work he's that into. It's fame. He used to be more famous; used to have his own show on TV. But now he just does radio. His days as a proper celebrity are gone, though I know he'd do anything to get them back.

'Busy show tomorrow?' I ask him.

He looks up at me, over his glasses and nods. Then gets back to his notes.

Fair enough.

I move towards him… not sure what to do. I can't just hug him like I hugged Mum. He'd definitely know something was up. So I just place my hand on his elbow.

'You okay, Ingrid?' he says to me, staring over his glasses again. I open my mouth to answer, but nothing comes out. Then the doorbell rings.

'Ingrid, Ciara's here,' Mum calls out.

Ciara? Already? She's early. That's not like her. Maybe she's changed her mind. I hope she's changed her mind.

Twenty-two years on, it still infuriates Helen when she isn't privy to the discussions being held in Eddie's office. They're all in there now… well the important ones anyway: Neil, Cyril, June, Patricia.

Helen can tell something major's going on. She'll just have to wait to find out what it is though. A lot of years have passed since she was among the first in line to be handed the juicy information. And waiting can be tortuous for somebody as impatient and nosey as Helen Brennan.

She folds the sheet of paper on her desk into thirds, slots it into a brown envelope and then licks the flap before running her thumb over it. If she was given a euro for every envelope she licks on a daily basis, she'd almost be earning the same money as Eddie. The same money she was destined to be on had her life not come to an earth-shattering stutter over two decades ago.

When she first started working here, way back in November of 1982, Helen had eyed that pokey office. She wanted to lead this station, not fucking stuff envelopes at the front desk. Sometimes, on days like this — when all around her is buzzing, yet she is sat still — Helen blames Scott for the mess her life has turned into. Then she stops herself and mumbles into her chest, as if she's asking somebody for forgiveness. Who she's asking for forgiveness would be news to her, though. She doesn't believe in any spiritual being. Fuck that shit. There ain't no spirit guiding her life. Unless that spirit's some sort of sick sociopath.

'Wonder what's going on in there,' she says to Leo as he passes her desk. He just shrugs his shoulder, takes another sip of his plastic cup of tea and then strolls on by.

Helen doesn't much care for Leo. The little prick has only been here for less than six months and already has the audacity to treat her as if she's insignificant. The only saving grace he has, as far as Helen can see, is that he looks mighty fine in uniform — as if it was bespokenly stitched around his muscular frame.

Helen looks around herself, to see if anyone else in the station noticed Leo's abruptness with her. Nobody. So she tucks her chin back into her chest and begins to fold another sheet of paper, mumbling to herself as she does so.

When she finally hears Eddie's office door open, she swings around in her chair so quickly that her eyes have to take a moment to focus before she can make out the individual faces. She eyeballs Cyril. Nothing. Patricia. Nothing. June. Nothing. She doesn't bother to look at Neil as he makes his way towards his messy desk. That gobshite doesn't share any information with her anyway. Never has. She chews on the nail of her thumb, wondering who she can infiltrate the quickest. Cyril's already talking to Leo. He must be filling the uniform in. So Helen stands up, flattens down the creases on the front of her grey trousers and then casually walks towards the two men. She always walks as if she's on stilts, does Helen; her entire five foot eleven inch frame as stiff and as straight as it can possibly be. She damaged the herniated disc in her lower back as a teenager; has been walking like a robot ever since.

Cyril is talking in hushed tones as Helen approaches but she hears mention of the name Alan Keating and already knows the matter is serious. Keating's been running the streets of Dublin for years. The cops can do fuck all about it, though. The clever bastard keeps his nose way too clean.

'What about Keating?' she says, leaning her face over Leo's shoulder to stare at Cyril.

Cyril looks left and then right before answering.

'He's up to something. We've just had an anonymous call that's trying to put us off the scent.'

'Content of the call?' Helen asks, tipping her chin up and then down, as if she's ordering Cyril to fill her in.

Cyril looks left, then right again. But even when his head has stopped moving, he doesn't answer. He just sucks on his teeth.

'Some kid saying two girls have agreed to commit suicide tonight. They've made a pact,' Leo says turning around.

Helen watches as Cyril stares at Leo, his eyes widening, his teeth clenching.

'Jaysus, it's alright, Cyril,' she says, tutting. 'It was twenty-two years ago. You think I can't ever hear that word the rest of my life?'

Then she spins on her heels, paces as quickly as she can and then snatches at the handle to Eddie's office door.

He looks up when she enters, his forefinger and thumb immediately stretching to the bridge of his nose.

'What makes you think it's Keating?' Helen says.

Eddie sighs.

'Jesus, Hel, you never did lose any of your Detective skills huh? You can get information out of anyone in seconds. They've only just left my bloody office.'

Helen takes one step back, pushes the door closed, then

strides forward, leaning her fingertips on to the edge of Eddie's desk.

Eddie arches an eyebrow, then leans back in his chair.

'It's one of Keating's hoax phone calls to get us chasing red herrings. I've just been on to Terenure Garda station, they've had the same phone call made to them. We've looked into it; it's Keating alright. He wants our officers concentrating on something else tonight. Wants us distracted. You know how he operates.'

Helen takes one of her hands from the desk and swipes at her nose.

'What did the phone call say?'

Eddie holds his eyes shut and then sighs out of his nostrils. He uses the same tics every time Helen sticks her nose into something that shouldn't concern her at work. He uses the same tics the odd time at home too... when she infuriates him by talking while he's trying to watch television.

'Helen, c'mon... you know you're not supposed to be privy to investigative insight—'

'What did the call say?' Helen interrupts.

Eddie peers through the blinds, into the open station at his officers and Detectives beavering away, then turns back to his wife.

'It's... it's an awkward one for me to say to you,' he says, sighing deeply out of his nostrils again. 'Some young guy, maybe a boy, rang in to say two girls have made a pact to die by suicide tonight.' Eddie swallows. 'I'm sorry, Hel.'

'Whatcha sorry for?'

Eddie looks down at his lap. He doesn't answer. He can't answer.

'Anyway,' he says, 'I must get on with this investigation. I've got to organise some uniforms to call out to Keating's house. We need to get a whiff of what's going on. So if you don't mind...' Eddie points his whole hand towards his office door.

Helen looks back at it, then towards her husband again.

'What about the two girls?' she asks. 'I assume somebody is looking into that?'

'Helen, if you don't mind... I'll be running this investigation. We have every reason to believe this is a Keating distraction call. I've got information I just can't share with you. You already know much more than you are supposed to. Anyway...' Eddie says twisting his left wrist towards his face, 'it's almost half seven, you should be heading home now. Relaxing. Forgetting about work.'

Helen squints at Eddie as her breaths begin to grow in sharpness. Then she spins on her heels, snatches at the door handle and marches out of his office.

'Who's been put in charge of looking into the girls?' she says as she approaches Cyril, interrupting him as he was about to instruct two members of his team.

'What girls?' he asks. Cyril often feels uneasy around Helen; especially when she's trying to extract information out of him about work. The lines between them have always been blurred. She used to be *his* boss. Now he's many ranks above her.

'The girls who are planning to die by suicide.'

Cyril stares over his shoulder, towards Eddie's office, and when he realises he's not going to get any support, he holds his palm to Helen's shoulder.

'We don't believe anybody is going to commit suicide. It's a hoax call; Keating trying to distract us.'

Helen brushes Cyril's hand away from her shoulder.

'So nobody is looking into the girls, nobody's going to at least investigate that angle?'

Cyril re-shuffles his standing position, so he is face on with Helen.

'Helen, there are no girls, it's just a—'

'A hoax fucking phone call,' Helen says slowly into his face. Then she storms off to her front desk, grabbing at the top sheet of paper from her pile, folding it into thirds and then stuffing it into an envelope.

She looks at the digits on her phone. 19:27. *Coronation Street* will be starting in three minutes. She hates missing *Coronation Street*. But she ain't leaving yet. Not until Eddie delivers the team briefing.

'Okay, okay,' Eddie shouts out as he claps his hands twice.

Helen spins in her chair and watches as everybody in the station stands to attention; the ritual they normally go through when the Superintendent shouts and claps. There was a time Helen used to stand for briefings too.

'We've had a phone call saying two unnamed girls are planning to die by suicide in the local area tonight. Terenure have had the *exact* same call. We have it on good authority these were hoax calls, the type of call Alan Keating has used in the past as a red herring. Patricia... I want your team to tail Keating's closest confidants, find out where they are this evening and keep your nose up their asses. Cyril, ring around our grasses, find out anything you can — and keep me informed of your progress. June, can you rally some uniforms in the city and put them on red alert? I'll fill you in later on what they should be looking out for. Neil, as I mentioned to you in our meeting, I want to see your patterns on Keating again, can you give me all the paperwork you have and—'

'What about the girls?' Helen shouts over everybody's head.

All in front of her twist their necks to stare at her. She has her legs spread, is swivelling side to side slowly in her chair.

Eddie holds his eyes closed in irritation, then sighs out of his nostrils. Again.

'Hel, thank you for your input but I can assure you all is under control.'

Helen hisses a tiny laugh through the gaps in her teeth.

'I'm sure they are, Eddie. I'm sure you all believe this is a hoax call and that Keating is up to something — and if that's the case, no better station in the country to have that investigation under control.' Helen holds both of her hands up, her palms facing the team of people staring at her. 'But just in case — *just in case* — the call isn't a hoax, who is out there looking for these two girls?'

Murmurs ripple from the team. She knows what they're whispering about. She's aware that they'll all be thinking this subject is far too sensitive for her to handle.

'Hel, I've been assured by Terenure Garda station that they have somebody treating the phone call as legitimate and will be looking into that line of enquiry.' Eddie claps his hands again. 'Now, if everybody else can—'

'Who?' Helen shouts, interrupting her husband again.

Eddie holds his hands together, as if in prayer, then creases his face into a sterile smile.

'I eh…' he, says, 'I don't know who exactly, but I've been assured all is in order in that regard. Now, if you don't mind, Hel, we have some investigating to do. It's half-past seven, shouldn't you be thinking of lying flat out on the couch, watching your soaps by now?'

Helen stands up, stares at Eddie long enough to make everybody in the office cringe a little, and then turns back around to swipe her leather coat from the back of the chair. She folds it over her arm, stares again at her husband, and then storms towards the exit.

19:25

Ingrid

I DON'T WANT TO LOOK AT THEM. ANY OF THEM.

Ciara hasn't stopped talking; about her mam, about school, about me. As if her life is all rosy. It's mad how well she's hiding it all. Though I shouldn't be surprised. Ciara's always hidden her sadness well. She hid it from me for years.

'You're hilarious,' my mum says, laughing at something Ciara said that I didn't listen to because I was thinking... thinking about leaving this house for the last time ever. I'm standing in the middle of the room, staring at my shoes, making a small laughing sound every now and then just to pretend I'm listening.

'You right then?' Ciara says, nudging me. I stare up at her, offer my best half smile and then nod my head. I decide not to look at *them*. Dad won't notice anyway, he's too busy studying his notes.

'Okay, you two, enjoy yourselves. And don't come back too late, Ingrid. School in the morning,' Mum says as she holds her hand to my shoulder. I pause, just for a second, and place my hand on top of hers. And then it's gone. I don't say anything. I just zip up my tracksuit top up and head towards the door, passing Sven without looking at him. We were supposed to spend our last day at home with our family. But I just stayed up in my bedroom for most of the day.

I close the door slowly, still only half-believing that I'll never set foot back in that house again; that I'll never see my mum. My dad. Sven. But I know deep inside my own heart that this is for the best. They don't want a mopey, depressed teenager living with them. Once they're over the shock, they'll be okay. They might even be happier without me. I'm pretty sure I'm a burden to them all anyway.

'What did you say to your parents?' I whisper to Ciara as we walk down my garden path.

She puffs a small laugh out of her nose.

'Nothing. My dad wasn't in all day — surprise, surprise. My mam was… go on have a guess, where was she?'

'Sitting at the kitchen island drinking a glass of wine.'

'A bottle. That's what we say, Ingrid. A bottle!'

I sniff a laugh out of my nose this time. It's so weird knowing what we are up to and still feeling as if I want to laugh. Maybe I feel relaxed enough to laugh because I know we've made the right decision. Or maybe I'm laughing because I don't think we'll actually go through with our pact. I've been changing my mind all day. Though most of the time I've been thinking the right thing to do is to end it all. I don't enjoy living. I really don't. It's my thoughts. They keep getting on top of me. Dad. Mam. Sven. Stitch. Ciara. Every time I'm alone and thinking, I realise my life is really sad. Too sad to continue with.

'So what did you say to her?'

'I hugged her.'

'You wha'?' I say, hearing the thick Dublin in my accent. I never sound thick Dublin. My family are way too posh. They kicked all of the Dublin out of me.

'Don't know what I was thinking. I just told her I was

going to your house and she didn't even turn around to look at me. She just threw her hand in the air and kinda waved it. Bitch. I shudda just left then and there, but I couldn't. So I stood in the doorway of the kitchen, staring at the back of her head as she drank her wine. Then I just ran towards her, threw my arms around her waist.'

My mouth opens. I can feel my bottom lip hang out.

'Sure, you're not supposed to give it away. No suspicion, that's what we agreed to.'

'Don't worry. She didn't have any suspicion. She doesn't think about anyone but herself.'

'What did she say when you hugged her?'

'She gave out that I nearly spilt her wine.'

I laugh. There it is again. Me laughing… as if everything is normal.

'Then what?'

'I walked away from her, threw my hand in the air and waved. Two minutes later I was ringing your doorbell.'

'You were early. Thought you were coming to change your mind.'

'None of that!' Ciara says, giving me an angry look. 'We don't talk about changing our minds. It's part of the pact.'

I hold my hands up, purse my lips and then stop walking.

'Ciara. I'm one hundred per cent in,' I say. 'I can't… I don't… I don't want to live anymore. It's… it's…' I shake. Not just my head, my whole body.

Ciara steps towards me, wraps both her arms around my shoulders and drags me in close. Our noses are touching. As if we're about to kiss.

'I know, I know,' she says.

Of course she knows. We talked about nothing else all last night.

One thing's for certain, Ciara won't change her mind. She's been suicidal a lot longer than me. In fact, I think she's just been waiting on my sadness to catch up with hers so we could do this together. I didn't say that to her last night. But I've thought about it a lot today. It doesn't change anything, though. I think I still want to do it. I really want my mind to turn off. I know now how Ciara has been feeling for the past couple years. It's horrible. Really, really horrible. It feels like such a heavy weight on top of your head. There's only one way to lift that weight off. Stop the mind from working. Stop thinking altogether.

'Ready for the last supper?' I say.

Ciara's eyebrows twitch. Then she laughs.

'Been looking forward to it all day,' she says.

She throws her arm through mine, swivelling into me and we link as we turn from Castlewood Avenue onto Rathmines' Main Road.

'It's going to be really tough isn't it?' I say. 'The whole saying goodbye without saying goodbye thing.'

Ciara turns to me, then shrugs her shoulder.

'Once we know that we visited them for the last time and kinda gave them all one last hug, that's enough. It's why we're doing it, isn't it? So they know that they meant something to us. We just need to act cool, as if we're just… y'know… dropping by. We're the only ones who'll know it's our last goodbye. They won't know a thing.'

'Just dropping by to Miss Moriarty's house?' I say. Then we both laugh again. This is mad.

'We discussed last night what we'd say at Miss Moriarty's house. Y'know… that we happened to be in the area she lives in so thought we'd knock on her door.'

I poke out my chin.

'Guess so,' I say. 'Gonna miss her the most probably.'

'Yeah, I kinda love Miss Moriarty. That's why she's on our list of last goodbyes though, isn't it? I'll miss either her or Debbie the most. Or you.'

We stop walking to stare at each other and hold hands. Both of them. I can feel tears come up behind my eyes. I've no idea if Ciara is feeling the same. She doesn't cry. Ever. I've done enough crying for both of us over the years.

'I'm gonna miss you too. So much.'

Then we hug. Really tightly. I know we'll hug again before we finally do it. But this feels quite final. We've been walking and talking for ten minutes now. Neither of us are backing out. Neither of us have let the day change our minds. This hug tells us everything. We're both ready for this. Our pact won't be broken.

'Tell ye what I'm also gonna really miss,' Ciara says.

I laugh before I answer. Because I know the answer.

'Macari's chilli chips.'

She drags me in close, kisses my forehead and spins me so that we're both linking each other again. Then we head straight towards the chipper; towards our last supper.

19:35

Greta

'THAT WAS WEIRD.'

'What was, love?' he says, squinting over his glasses at me.

'They're up to something.'

'Who, love?'

'What d'ye mean *who*? Those two. Ingrid and Ciara.'

He just pushes back his glasses on the bridge of his nose and looks back down at his paperwork. Course he does.

I sit back in to the sofa, pick up the wafer I'd left on the side table and lick at a melting drop of ice cream as I sink into my thoughts.

'She couldn't look at us going out that door. Lying, she is. Saying she's going over to Ciara's house.'

Terry looks over the rim of his glasses at me again, then back down at his notes.

It's not like Ingrid to lie. I knew she would eventually. I guess turning thirteen is the ideal time for little girls to start lying to their parents. I used to lie to my parents all the time as a teen. Couldn't let them know I was off doing modelling shoots. They'd have killed me. Swedish households are much stricter than here in Ireland. Certainly much more strict than our house. Terry's way too laid back as a father. Especially in comparison to mine. Even had he known I'd grow up to be a successful model, my father still wouldn't have let me do the shoots back then. He was way too conservative.

That could be what Ingrid's doing. Modelling shoots. Same lie as I had when I was a teenager. She certainly has the looks for it. Not sure why Ciara'd be going along though. Maybe for some moral support.

Nah.

That can't be it. I bet they have boyfriends. It's probably boyfriends. Ingrid would be starting to attract boys now. They'd love her long golden hair and golden eyebrows. She certainly got a lot more of my Swedish genes than the Irish genes of her father. Both our kids did. Sven's hair is practically snow white.

I wonder if Ciara's got a boyfriend too. I love Ciara. She's a great character and I'm delighted Ingrid has such a close bond with a girl who only lives down the end of our avenue, but she's not the prettiest. She's slightly overweight and I'm not sure the sharp bob haircut does much to hide that. If anything, it makes her face look even plumper.

'Bet it's boyfriends,' I say, before licking at my ice cream again.

Terry stares over the rim of his glasses.

'Better fuckin not be,' he says. That's about the extent of his parenting. Laying down the odd opinion without so much as doing anything about it. I guess he's used to it; giving opinions and then doing sweet fuck all about them. It's what he does for a living.

'Who's on the show tomorrow?' I ask.

He removes his glasses this time. That's the only way I can ever get real engagement from him; ask him about his job.

'We've got the transport minister on. Have to try and

catch him out over these plans for the M50 upgrade,' he says.

'No better man,' I reply, then take another lick.

'Yeah — I want to get him to admit live on air that he's blown the budget, that he's overspent. Just trying to think of the best way to go about it.'

I'm not really that interested. Terry thinks he has the most important job in the world. So I play along. Would never admit that I don't think he's as much of a major player in society as he thinks he is. I used to love that he was a famous broadcaster. If he wasn't, we never would have bumped into each other. We met at the Eurovision Song contest in Sweden seventeen years ago. He was doing a backstage broadcast for RTE. I was there as a guest of the promoters. Jaysus, I used to be on the guest list for everything back then. I don't miss it. Not really.

Terry's still talking interview tactics with me when I tune back into his words. When he stops talking, I nod my head.

'Yeah good idea,' I say.

That usually works; telling him that his plans are A-Okay.

I twist my neck and look over my shoulder at Sven playing with his action figures on the floor. Where else would he be?

'Ten more minutes, Sven,' I say to him. He doesn't look around. Poor thing. I don't know what he hears and what he doesn't hear. I've researched his condition so many times but still can't find definite answers to the questions I need answering.

'Do you hear me, Sven? Ten more minutes.'

Nothing.

So I lick my ice cream again and think about my daughter. I wonder who her boyfriend is. She was at a birthday party last night. I bet she met somebody. That's why they're snooping around. Ah, sure I shouldn't be worrying. I'll leave them to it. Didn't we all snoop around at that age?

HELEN DRUMS HER THUMBS REPEATEDLY ON THE TOP OF THE steering wheel any time she's impatient. Which is somewhere close to always when she's driving. She automatically hates the stranger in the car in front of her, no matter who they are. She'll find a reason readily; perhaps because they're driving too slow, or maybe they forgot to indicate properly at a roundabout. Sometimes she'll decide to hate them simply because she doesn't like the colour of their car. No matter the reason, if you happen to be driving in front of Helen Brennan, you're bound to hear her car horn blast every couple minutes.

'Fuck sake,' she mutters under her breath as she stops at another red light. She picks up her handbag, roots inside and pulls out a small tub. She's staring up at the Rathmines Clock Tower, snarling at it as she always does, as she tries to pop open the lid. But the light turns green before she can, so she just throws the tub back into her bag, the pills rattling, and then steps on the accelerator. She wheel spins the car, turns on to the canal road and makes her way to Terenure Garda Station.

She's still mumbling to herself in frustration when she steps out and paces — in her own unique robotic way — to the entrance, not hiding the sigh she produces when she steps inside to see a young woman struggling to contain her two children at the front desk. The young woman's trying to get information on a boyfriend. Something about a raid at their flat this morning and his subsequent "unfair" arrest.

Helen shuffles her feet from side to side, her attempt to get the attention of the officer dealing with the woman — and her two snotty little brats.

One of the kids turns around, drops his bottom lip open when he stares at the vision behind him. Helen sure does look intimidating to a child. To anyone really. Her upright posture makes her stand out, but more so because she always tries to hide it under a long leather overcoat. The coat falls all the way down to her ankles; just her red Converse sneakers on show under it today. And her hair doesn't help blend her into the crowd either. She doesn't have the patience to allow her brown hair dye to soak into her greying strands for the full hour as is recommended on the bottle. It means her short bob is a streaky shade of rusty oranges.

She stares back at the kid, his face smudged with stickiness, and then scoffs.

'Sorry,' she says eventually, taking one large stride forward. 'I'm Helen Brennan; Detective from Rathmines Garda station,' she lies. 'I'm here to talk with the Detective looking into the phone call that was made about two eh...' she stops herself, looks at the young woman and her two snotty little brats, then leans forward to the officer behind the desk and whispers, 'the eh... hoax suicide call.'

The officer raises his eyebrow.

'Let me buzz you through, Detective Brennan,' he says, reaching under his desk. Helen hears the double doors to her left release and then pushes through them without even turning to thank the officer who opened them for her.

When she steps inside, she gasps. Terenure Garda station is a helluva lot more modern than Rathmines. Rathmines has barely changed in the thirty-seven years she's known it. Aside from maybe the office chairs. They needed to be updated to comply with modern health and safety requirements a few years ago, but the desks are still the same old-school oak desks she sat at on her very first day.

Here, though — in Terenure — the desks are a modern white. As are the walls. They look as if they've just been painted. She can't remember the last time anyone painted the walls at Rathmines Garda station. They're supposed to be magnolia, but time has turned them dirty yellow.

She stops a young plain-clothed officer who was about to walk past by holding up a hand.

'Detective Helen Brennan from Rathmines,' she lies again. 'I need to speak with the Detective who's looking into the two girls reported to be planning suicide tonight.'

'The hoax call?' the woman says.

'No, well… I want to find the Detective looking into the two girls. As if the call is legitimate.'

'Oh,' the young woman says, tugging at her ear. 'It's not a Detective looking into that. This is definitely a hoax call. So eh… Charlie, I think… yeah Charlie Guilfoyle is taking care of that.'

Helen raises both eyebrows and then shrugs her shoulders.

'Who?' she says.

'Oh, he's eh…' the woman looks around the room. 'That guy there; the spikey hair.'

'The uniform?' Helen says, all high-pitched.

The woman huffs out a small snigger as she nods her head, then walks on.

Helen sucks her lips, making a pop sound before she strides towards the spikey hair. She can't believe her eyes as she nears; the face below the spikes is way too fresh. Way too young. There isn't a trace of even light stubble on it. Plenty of acne, but no hair.

'Charlie Guilfoyle,' she says standing over him. 'I'm Detective Helen Brennan from Rathmines Garda station. Believe you are looking into the phone call.'

Charlie swallows a lump down his throat when he sees the woman hovering behind him, then he coughs into his hand.

'Yeah... well, kinda... yeah.'

'Kind of?' Helen hisses.

'Well, I'm just, well eh...' he looks down at his lap, then back up, 'all the intel leads us to believe this is a hoax call, right? Alan Keating.'

'Intel?' Helen says, nodding her head sarcastically.

'Well, Keating's done this before, hasn't he?' Charlie says. 'Besides, who would report a suicide attempt and then just hang up without giving us any names? It don't make no sense.'

Helen wipes her face with her hand and then she squints at the young man sitting in front of her. His ears stick out below his black spikey hair, his nose slightly upturned and pointy at the nub end, making him look like some sort of human-rodent hybrid.

'How old are you, Charlie?' Helen asks.

He creases his brow. 'Twenty-three.'

'Twenty-three? You look ten years younger than that.'

Charlie's brow creases even more. He's not sure if what he's just heard was a compliment or not. It wasn't.

'Well,' Helen says, pulling at a chair from the desk beside Charlie's and wheeling it behind her so she can drop into it. 'I've been asked to look into the suicide angle for Rathmines station. What have you got for me so far?'

Charlie coughs into his hand again, then turns back around to his desk and begins to fidget with his mouse. After a couple silent seconds, he turns to Helen again, the palms of his hands facing upwards.

'I eh… don't really have anything yet. Telephone network can't tell us where the phone call was made from. It was too short… only lasted eighteen seconds.'

'The two of em?' Helen asks.

'Sorry?'

'Did both phone calls last eighteen seconds?'

'Both calls?'

'Yes, Charlie. Two calls were made. One here, one to Rathmines.'

Charlie makes an 'O' shape with his mouth and as he does so, Helen tuts.

'Listen, if two girls commit suicide tonight, you're gonna take a serious amount of time getting over it, d'ye hear me?' she says. 'You and I both. We're gonna find them, we're gonna save them.'

Charlie creases his brow again.

'Do you… eh… do you really think the phone call is legit?' he asks.

Helen looks around herself, swivelling ever so slightly on the chair.

'It's *your* job — *and mine*,' she says, pointing at her own chest, 'to take this phone call as legit. Everybody else, here, and at Rathmines, is treating it as a hoax and getting their knickers in a twist about Alan Keating. But me and you; we're the ones who owe it to these girls to save them. If the call is legit, we can be heroes. If it's not… well, fuck it, there's enough of the force looking into what it might be.'

Charlie offers Helen a smile that makes him look even

younger. He stands up, readjusts his navy tie into his sky-blue shirt by repositioning his tiepin and then holds his palm towards Helen.

'You wait here a second, Detective Brennan. I'll go find out what the latest is with tracking the call.'

'It's eh…' Helen says holding her hand out in front of him, 'it's Helen, call me Helen. And,' she looks around again, 'don't tell *anybody* I'm looking into this with you. I'm off duty, but I can't live with the guilt of two girls dying by suicide. I need to be looking into this, whether it's legit or not. Besides, you can use a helping hand, right?'

Charlie smiles again, then winks before pacing to the back of the station. Helen stretches her legs wide apart and swivels side-to-side in the chair again, her fingers forming a diamond shape just above her naval. She's popping her lips with impatience when the pocket of her coat begins to vibrate. She reaches inside, grabs her mobile phone and then winces when she notices who's calling.

'Hello.'

'Hel, listen, I'm so sorry. I shouldn't have talked to you like that. It was…' Eddie doesn't want to finish his sentence, but Helen's silence forces him to continue. 'It's just, we're pretty certain this is Keating. Fucker's done this to us before, had us running around all night looking for two missing girls when… well… you know. I just wanted to ring you to apologise for being… for being short with you.'

Helen sighs.

'Apology accepted,' she says. 'How's the investigation going?'

There's a slight pause on the other end of the line before Eddie finally speaks up.

'We've got guys all over Keating and his cronies, but God knows what's going on. Chances are they aren't going to be the ones carrying anything out, ye know how Keating operates. So, I guess all we can do is gauge things as we go.'

'But what about the calls that were made... any progress tracking them?'

Another pause.

'Yeah... one phone network gave us an approximate area — somewhere along the Grand Canal between Inchicore and Drimnagh, but no specific number. Anyway...' he says, 'nothing for you to worry about. I'll fill you in in the morning. How about I treat you to breakfast — Bark about ten-ish in the morning?' Helen nods her head. She loves a breakfast at Bark. Best Poached Eggs in Dublin.

'Okay,' she says.

'Good. So... did you get home safe?' Eddie asks.

Helen looks around herself, taking in the cleanliness of Terenure Garda station, noting it in comparison to the one she and her husband work in.

'Yep, all curled up on the sofa... watching *Coronation Street*.'

The line falls silent. For way too long.

'Good... good,' Eddie eventually says. 'So I'll see you, okay? I guess you'll be asleep by the time I get back tonight... we'll do that breakfast when we wake up, huh?'

Helen doesn't answer, she just takes the phone from her ear and presses at the red button. Then she clicks into her news feed; just to see if there have been any oddities reported by the national media recently; something that might offer her some sort of lead. It's rare that the media would be a step ahead of the cops... but it still doesn't stop Helen from checking. She scrolls. And scrolls. Nothing. The media are just running with the same story they've been running with all day: the two Dublin guys who've been arrested in Rome for stealing from American Central Banks last year. She clicks out of her news feed and places her phone back into her pocket. Then she stands and peers down at Charlie's desk. A framed picture of a pretty girl, way too pretty for Charlie, smiles back at her. She picks it up, puts it back down. Then she picks up a bunch of keys and turns them over in her hand before placing them down. Then an open bottle of Coke. Then a notepad. She's flicking through it when she hears him breathing behind her.

'Charlie,' she says, turning around and dropping his pad back on to his desk, 'whatcha got for me?'

'Don't think anybody's been able to determine where the call was made,' he says, sitting back into his chair. Helen rolls her eyes. 'But I do know it was made — to this station anyway — at six forty-nine p.m.'

'That it?' Helen says.

'Nope,' Charlie responds, shuffling his chair back into his desk. 'I have it here.' He slips a USB stick into the side of his computer screen, then fiddles with his mouse. Helen reaches for the chair she had been sitting in earlier, wheels it closer and plonks herself in it.

'Terenure Garda station, how can I help you?'

'Two girls from my school are going to commit suicide tonight...' the voice sounds panicky. *'I heard them talking about it. They've made a pact. Please help them. They're good girls. Just misunderstood.'*

'Thank you for your call, Sir,' a female voice says. *'Can you give me your name to begin with and then I can—'*

A dead tone pierces through Charlie's computer.

He turns around and stares at Helen.

'Can't be legit. Who'd ring in a suicide warning without giving us the names—'

'Replay that,' Helen says, interrupting him, 'the bit where he says "please help them".'

Charlie's brow creases, but he turns back to his computer and drags at his mouse again.

'They've made a pact. Please help them.'

'There, hear it?' Helen says.

'Hear what?'

'The Luas. The chiming of a Luas tram.'

Charlie drags at his mouse again.

'Oh yeah,' he says listening to the same two lines over and over. 'The call musta been made somewhere close to the Luas tracks. But sure that could be anywhere.'

'Red Line, between Inchicore and Drimnagh,' Helen says standing up. 'Let's go.'

'Huh?' Charlie puffs out of his mouth, before turning back. He swigs from his bottle of Coke then throws his navy Garda jacket on and follows Helen towards the exit.

'How the hell can you tell the call was made between Drimnagh and Inchicore?' he asks.

Helen doesn't answer.

19:40

Ciara

I LOOK UP INTO THE CORNER OF THE CHIPPER AND NOTICE THE CCTV camera staring down at us. Then it hits me. I bet this footage is going to be shown on the news over the next few days. Our last movements. How the two girls who committed suicide in Rathmines looked happy and were laughing in the local chipper just a few of hours before they ended it all. But I don't mention it to Ingrid. I don't want to take her out of her thoughts. She's more likely to change her mind than I am. In fact, I'm one hundred per cent certain I won't change my mind. I'm going to do this. *We're* going to do this.

I've thought about this day so much over the past two years. I'd have done it two years ago if it wasn't for Ingrid; if it wasn't for the beautiful friend she is. I have the best mate in the whole world. She'd do anything for me. Including kill herself.

'What you staring at?' she says, twisting to look over her shoulder.

'Nothing, nothing. Just thinking.'

'Here ye go, you two,' Marjorie says as she plonks our fries in front of us. 'Enjoy.'

We don't waste time even thanking Marjorie. We just pick up our wooden forks and dive straight in.

This has been our favourite meal for years. We pop in here every Friday after school for chilli chips. I think the secret is in how they melt the cheese on top of the chips before they pour the chilli over. Ingrid thinks it's all in the sauce. It doesn't really matter. Every mouthful is bleedin' delicious.

'I'm gonna miss this,' Ingrid says, her mouth full. She half smiles, then drops the smile. I know how she's feeling. She's excited because she knows her suffering is almost over. But then the suffering hits again. It's a roller coaster of feelings. Up and down. Up and then deeper down. Up and then really, really low down. So low down you can't even be bothered going up again. Just keep me down, get me down. Six foot down. Inside a wooden box.

I've thought about my funeral lots of times. My mam will be sobbing; will probably have to have two people either side of her to hold her up in the church. She'll make it all about her, of course. How my suicide was *her* loss. How my suicide affected *her*. I think my dad'll keep a straight face as usual. He'll pretend to be holding it all together. Or maybe he will be holding it all together. I'm not sure my death will be a huge loss to him. Perhaps it'll be a weight off. Something less for him to care about. I don't think he likes caring. About anyone.

'Penny for em?' Ingrid says.

'Huh?' I refocus my eyes and realise that as I was thinking about my funeral I almost finished my chilli chips.

'Penny for your thoughts.'

I dig my fork into the last of my chips, leave it standing there and then suck at my lips.

'Was thinking about my funeral. How much my mam will be sobbing. She'll probably roar the church down.'

Ingrid's eyes roll upwards. Then she leans back in her chair and folds her arms.

'Bet they'll play a Take That song for me. Probably *Pray*, whatcha think?'

'Defo. A hundred per cent. It'd be madness if they don't play *Pray* at your funeral.'

'Think I'd kinda like to be there… at my own funeral. I want to see who turns up.'

I laugh a little, then pick up my fork again and take another bite.

'Ohhh,' Ingrid purrs.

I look up; my heart beating a little faster. I really don't want her to change her mind. She can't change her mind.

'What's wrong, Ingrid?'

'My last bite. Ever.'

I smile. I think it's from relief more than anything.

'Hold on,' I say. 'My last bite too. Let's do it together, okay?'

We both scrape the bottom of the tin tray our chilli chips came in, so that we have all of the mince, all of the sauce, all of the cheese and all of the chips that are left and then hold the fork up.

'Let's do it,' Ingrid says. And we do. We stuff our mouths with Macari's chilli chips for the final time; both of us holding our eyes closed so we can suck down the deliciousness of our last supper.

'It's fucking delicious,' Ingrid says after she swallows. It always makes me laugh when Ingrid swears. She's so posh that any time she says 'fuck' it sounds as if she uses an 'o' instead of a 'u'.

I rub my belly and then tilt my head sideways. I don't enjoy much in life. That's why I want to end it. But I do enjoy these chilli chips. And now I know I'll never have those tastes in my mouth again. But I genuinely don't mind. We're doing this. Life is not worth living just for a ten-minute taste thrill at Macari's chipper every Friday evening.

'Don't be sad, Ciara,' Ingrid says, placing her hand on top of mine. I'm not sad. In fact I'm happy; happy that she's encouraging me as much as I'm encouraging her.

'I'm not sad,' I reply. 'I'm ready to do this.'

'What do you think it's gonna feel like?' she whispers over the table to me, her fingers tapping on top of mine.

I blow out my cheeks.

'Oh — it won't hurt. We'll be dead before we even know it,' I whisper back.

'Nah, not the actual suicide itself... death. What do you think death feels like?'

I squint at her. How can she be asking such a stupid question? She knows dead means dead. Neither of us are that thick. Even if we are only thirteen. We're not dumb enough to believe we go anywhere after we die. We don't *want* to go anywhere anyway. We don't *want* another life. We want to die because we want to stop all of the horrible thoughts that we have. We spoke about this before we wrote out our suicide pact on the park bench last night.

I place my other hand on top of hers, so her hand is sandwiched between my two.

'Y'know what it feels like before you were born?' I ask.

She looks at me funny.

'Before I was born? Course I don't. I didn't feel anything. How could I?'

'Exactly,' I say.

Her brow points down. Then her eyes widen.

'So, we won't feel anything? Just like before we were born. We only feel when we are alive?'

I nod my head slowly at her. I thought she knew all this.

Maybe she just needed reminding. Confirmation. Isn't that the word?

'And that's why we're doing it, isn't it? So we don't need to feel again,' I say, clapping her one hand between my two. She nods back at me, then holds her other hand into our little hand huddle and we both sit there, gripping each other as tightly as we can.

It makes sense she'd have all these questions. I've thought all this through over the course of two years. She's only been suicidal for less than a day.

'I'm not gonna change my mind,' she says shaking her head. And I believe her. She won't. She has never lied to me. I don't think Ingrid is capable of lying. 'Okay, so we're visiting who first? What's the timetable again?' she asks.

I purse a tiny smile back at her and then release one of my hands to hold my finger to my bottom lip.

'So it's Debbie's house first, then Harriet's, then Miss Moriarty's.'

Ingrid nods her head.

'Then what?'

'Then… then we do it.'

She bends a little backwards in her chair so she can see the clock in the middle of the menu behind the counter.

'So we'll be dead around midnight, right?'

I nod my head slowly.

'About that time, yeah.'

19:45

Vivian

IT'S A SORRY SIGHT. I KNOW.

I know because I stare at it every night.

My reflection.

In the windows of the double doors that lead out to our back garden.

I'm fuckin sick of this. Yet it's all I do. Sit here, a glass of wine swirling in my hand, staring at a blurry image of myself.

I take another sip. Taking in my reflection as I do so.

What a loser.

Yet, I know tomorrow evening I'll be doing the exact same thing. And the evening after that. And the one after that. Probably be doing this for all the evenings I have left. Another forty years of sipping wine. That'll take me into my early eighties. Isn't that what they say the average age to die is? Seems like a long way off to me.

I pick up the bottle of wine, pour it into my glass, shaking every last drop out of it, and then huff because it didn't fill my glass enough. So I place both forearms across the kitchen island and lay my forehead on top of them.

'Fuck sake!' I grunt into my elbow. I lift my head slowly, swivel on my stool and slide off it. I drag my slippers as I walk across the tiles and reach up into the cupboard to grab at another bottle of Chateaneuf-du-Pape. Then I drag my slippers over to the slide drawer for the corkscrew and wrestle with the horrible red wrap of film that covers the top of the bottle. I've opened two bottles of this shit every night for the past seven years and I still struggle with the process every time. Opening the second bottle is always more difficult than the first. It'd probably make sense for me to open the two of them when I'm sober and leave them in front of me. But making sense has never really been my thing.

'Fuck!' I say when the sharp point of the corkscrew pinches at the top of my thumb. Then I finally release the film, and am faced with the task of popping the cork itself. I've let one or two bottles slip out of my hands over the years during this part of the process. It should be a helluva lot fuckin easier than this in this day and age to open a bottle of wine. How have they not come up with something better than a bleedin' corkscrew? Sometimes I can nail this in one go. But most times I have to spoon out lumps of cork from my glass after I've poured it.

'Come on, you bitch,' I say to the corkscrew as I yank at it. Pop. Done. Decent job.

I fill my glass, then sit back into my stool and stare at the blurry image of myself again. I often wonder if I stare at this reflection because it hides the lines in my face and makes me look younger. Then I turn my face to notice the time on the oven. 19:50.

What a prick. Why can't he be home with his family? Then I realise his family aren't actually here. Ciara's out too. Where'd she say she was going? I can't remember. Didn't she try to hug me? What the hell was all that about? Silly child. She *is* gone out, isn't she?

'Ciara. Ciara.' I shout it so that I can be heard as far up as the loft. Sometimes she likes to hang out up there. I don't know what she does be doing.

No answer.

She must be gone out. Probably in Ingrid's house.

She'd rather be there than here. I don't blame her.

I envy the Murphys. They've got it all together. A proper family, they are. Terry's as successful professionally as my Michael, but at least he's man enough to stay loyal to his wife and kids. Even if one of the kids is a bit retarded. I'm not sure what his condition is. I keep forgetting. Some new-age made up mental illness that begins with an 'A'. I'm sure it begins with an 'A'.

Maybe it's easier for Terry to stay at home with his family because he has a mental son. Or perhaps it's just easier because his wife's an ex-model. She's beautiful, is Greta. Tall. Slim. Blonde. I'll never be tall. Never be slim. I tried blonde once. Just to see if Michael would like it. He tutted. Said I looked like a tart.

The Murphys have invited us to have dinner in their house loads of times over the past few years. They want us to be closer because our girls are best friends. But we've never taken them up on their offer. That'd be Michael's worst nightmare. A double date with the neighbours. Jesus, could you imagine?

Besides, I'm not that keen myself. Even if by some miracle Michael did agree, I can't really be relied on to do socialising. I'm too... what's the word... too nervy, too anxious. I'd be over-conscious of my dependence on wine. They probably wouldn't want Ciara to pal around with Ingrid anymore if they found out I was a borderline alcoholic. And she needs that friendship more than anything. It's Ingrid who looks after my Ciara. Especially now that Debbie has gone.

I stare at my reflection again and take another sip. Sometimes I swirl the wine around in my mouth to get a sense of whether or not I can taste it anymore. I'm numb to it by now, I think. But I'm not numb to the effect. I need it. I need the alcohol to take the edge off. Couldn't live without it.

I turn my face to look at the oven again. 19:54.

Where is this prick?

I place one foot down, then the other, holding a hand to the edge of the kitchen island for balance, then I drag my slippers across the tiles again, the swish-swash of them irritating me as if my hangover has settled in already. I find myself in the hallway, picking up the telephone and dialling one; the quick dial for Michael's office. He has one of those new fancy mobile phones, but the bloody thing is never switched on.

The tone rings. And rings. Then cuts off.

I blink my eyes so I can become more conscious to my thoughts. What time was it when I looked at the oven clock again? Jesus. I can't remember. I shuffle my way back down the hallway, down the one step that leads to the kitchen tiles and then cock my head so I can see the microwave. 19:56. Yeah. Almost eight o'clock. That's what I thought. I'm sure he's still in the office. He's normally there till ten-ish, even later sometimes. So I shuffle my way back up the hallway and pick up the phone again, dial one and hold the receiver to my ear.

It rings out.

'Fuck sake!' I yell, slamming the phone back down on its receiver.

Then I remember.

'It's a fucking Sunday, isn't it?'

I blow out my cheeks and shuffle my way back to the kitchen. Back to the island. Back to my stool. Back to my wine. And back to my blurry reflection.

THERE WAS A STRANGE SILENCE IN THE CAR, EVEN THOUGH energies had somewhat heightened.

Charlie had already felt as if he'd asked too many questions before they even started the engine. Or at least the same question too many times. So he just concentrated on his driving while Helen stared out the side window of the passenger seat as they made their way towards Davitt Road.

There was no doubt Charlie was intimidated by the lanky woman he thought was a Detective from Rathmines Garda station. Yet he seemed somewhat excited. When he was offered the task of looking into the phone calls as if they were legitimate, he assumed he was put in charge of an insignificant case again; the type nobody else in the station could be bothered looking into. It'd be nothing new for Charlie to be doing a whole lot of nothing for his entire shift. But now that he'd been partnered with a Detective from another station, his mood seemed to be shifting. Adrenaline was threatening to pump inside of him.

'How long you been a cop?' Helen asks, just as they reach their destination.

Charlie indicates left, slots his car into one of the tiny parking spaces outside the Marble Arch pub and then pulls up the handbrake before answering.

'Eighteen months.'

Helen stiffens her nostrils.

'Enjoy it?'

'I will.'

'What ye mean you will?'

'Soon as I'm outta this,' he says, lifting up the flap of his tie and letting it fall back down.

Helen opens her door, stretches her long legs out, and by the time she has walked around the other side of the car, Charlie has done the same. He's zipping up his navy Garda jacket when Helen places a hand on his shoulder.

'What… you want out of uniform already? Wanna be a Detective?'

Charlie nods, then stares down at his clunky black shoes, his jaw clenching. Perhaps he's said too much already.

'You got balls, Charlie? You willing to play the game, not the system?'

Charlie's brow creases. Every time he does this, Helen notices that his nose gets even stubbier.

'Whatcha mean by that?' he asks, looking back up at Helen.

Helen doesn't answer. She steps off the path and, in her own unique stiff way, strides across the road towards the tram stop.

Charlie waits, hands in his pockets, his mind swirling, before he jogs after her.

He observes Helen as she stands still at the tram stop. He's intrigued, not just by how she seems to be going about her job, but by every nuance of her character. Her coat looks, to him, as if she is trying to dress for a role in a cheesy TV series. And her hair? Well… Charlie could barely keep his eyes off it. Is itching to ask her what colour it is. But there isn't a chance that question will ever come out of his mouth. He knows that odd face would offer him a strange stare. And no answer.

'Whatcha looking for?' he asks, his rural accent thick.

'See that?'

'What?'

Charlie's gaze follows Helen's. Right up into the corner of the shelter of the tram stop.

'CCTV.'

Charlie holds his eyes closed, then grinds his teeth. He feels like an idiot. He should have known that's what she was staring at.

'Lights are on. It's working. All along the stop the CCTV seems to be working.' She flicks her wrist, stares at her watch. 'It's eight o'clock. Call was made at six forty-nine you said… over an hour ago.'

Helen huffs out a sigh from her nostrils, then pivots her head left and right, all the way up and down the straight stretch of the Grand Canal.

'No point in us being here, then,' she says. 'We need to go up to the Luas HQ, up to the Red Cow roundabout.'

'To get the CCTV footage from six forty-nine?' Charlie asks.

'Good boy, Charlie.'

He creases his brow again. Then realises Helen is already halfway across the road, heading back to the car. He jogs again to catch up with her.

'Do you mind if I ask you a question, Detective Brennan?' he says.

She doesn't answer as she opens the passenger door and swoops her way inside the car.

When Charlie gets in to the driver's seat, buckles up his belt and ignites the engine, he turns to her.

'How did you know the call came from here, from somewhere along the tram tracks between Drimnagh and Inchicore?'

Helen stares straight out the windscreen.

'You've already asked me that… five times.'

Charlie squirms a little before he shoves the gear stick into reverse and pulls out of the parking space.

'Sirens,' Helen says.

'Really?' Charlie's brow creases again.

When he doesn't get an answer, he flicks the button next to the steering wheel that allows a loud blare to sound from the car and suddenly the speedometer jumps from twenty miles an hour to sixty in the space of five seconds.

'It's just… if I wanna be a Detective, I'd love to learn from you,' he shouts over the sirens.

Helen turns her face and looks him up and down before taking her gaze back through the windscreen. 'You will,' she shouts back.

Charlie smiles to himself. His first smile of the day. He's been frustrated with life. Had become an insurance broker straight from school; working at a small brokers called Fullams before realising he hadn't one Goddamn care about insurance in any capacity. It took two-and-a-half years for him to realise that. When he noticed the Gardaí advertising for new recruits, he assumed a life solving crime would take him out of the boredom of office work. But after landing a job in Terenure Garda station straight after his graduation, he was longing to be back helping people renew their car insurance policies. He hates being a cop, is sick of every colleague at his station talking down to him. The egos he has come across as a Garda stagger him. He can't comprehend why those trusted the most to be as impartial as possible in society possess such vanity. But perhaps he was about to catch a break. If he were to assist Helen in solving a case everybody else was poo-pooing, he might buy himself some credibility. Maybe he could become one of them; somebody who didn't have to wear a fucking tie.

When the siren dies down, so too does Charlie's smile. He leaps out of the car, fixes his hat to his odd-shaped head and makes his way to the front office of the Luas headquarters without even looking back at Helen. He's feeling determined now; transfixed on earning that credibility.

He holds the door open for Helen who scoots by him without thanking him. Then she holds an open palm towards the young woman at the front desk.

'Detective Brennan and Officer...' she turns around, stares at Charlie.

'Guilfoyle,' he says.

'We need to speak with the person in charge of your CCTV.'

The young woman gulps, eyeballs Charlie's uniform and then picks up her phone.

'Can you tell Larry I have two police officers in the reception please.'

'He's coming straight away,' she says to Helen after placing the receiver back down.

Helen takes one step backwards and stands straight and tall as she waits, her arms shovelled deep into her coat pockets. Charlie looks around the pokey reception area and begins to read the work notices on the board. He feels he should look busy, as if he is investigating. He wants to impress Helen. Though he hasn't one darn clue what he's looking for. He's hardly going to solve the mystery of the anonymous phone call by reading staff notices about a new training initiative for tram drivers. After cringing a little, he steps back towards Helen and stands as straight as he can to at least try to match her for height.

'What the fuck were you doing?' Helen whispers.

Charlie turns his head sideways, stares at the unusual face beside him and then shrugs his shoulders. The door flying open saves him from his discomfort.

'Officers, I'm Larry Hanrahan, how can I help you?' says a tall, skinny bald chap in a purple shirt.

'We need to view the CCTV footage of your Drimnagh and Goldenbridge stops between six thirty and seven o'clock this evening,' Helen says.

Larry nods his head once, then holds the door he had just come through open, waving both Helen and Charlie through.

As the three of them pace down an overly warm corridor, Helen taps Larry on the shoulder of his purple shirt.

'I assume, Mr Hanrahan, judging by the fact that you haven't said anything, no other officers have come to you today to view this footage?'

Larry's eyes widen a little.

'No,' he says shaking his head. 'Why, what's going on?'

'Police inquiries, Mr Hanrahan. The case is confidential right now, but there are two separate teams looking into the same case today — two different lines of enquiries. So I assume we won't be the only team calling by this evening.'

Larry purses his thin lips.

'Whatever you guys need,' he says. Then he pushes down on the handle of a heavy door and heaves his way through to a tiny room packed with computer screens.

'Kristine,' this is eh... this is...'

'Officer Guilfoyle and Detective Brennan from eh... well, I am from Terenure Garda station, Detective Brennan here is from Rathmines,' Charlie says.

Kristine stands and stares at Helen as if she was staring a creature from another planet.

'They need to view footage from the Red line, the CCTV from Drimnagh and Goldenbridge stops please,' Larry says.

He approaches Kristine's desk, scribbles some notes on

her yellow post-it pad and then stands back a little. Helen strides forward, standing beside Larry and watches as Kristine stabs her chunky fingers at her keyboard.

'Kay, so between six thirty and seven, hmmm…' Kristine mumbles to herself. 'Right, this screen here,' she says slapping a monitor to her left, 'is footage from the Drimnagh stop from six thirty onwards and this one here,' she slaps at the monitor to her right, 'that's Goldenbridge from the same time.'

Helen eyeballs Charlie, then nods her head towards the screen on the right. Charlie steps forward and stares at it. And then Helen does the same on the other side.

'S'what we looking for, Detective Brennan?' Charlie asks.

Helen stares at him almost cross-eyed, making him feel like an idiot again.

'What do you think, Charlie? C'mon, you said you wanted to be a Detective when you grow up. What do you think we're looking for?'

Charlie's shoulders shrink. He looks down, straightens his tie, even though it doesn't need straightening, and then gulps.

'A eh… a young man making a phone call from a mobile phone?'

'Bingo,' Helen says.

'Isn't it mad to think nobody knows where we are, that nobody's looking for us? I almost feel... what's-the-word?'

'Free?' Ciara says.

I nod my head. Yeah. I think that's the word I mean. *Free*. In control. As if we don't have to answer to anybody for the first time ever. I'm actually enjoying this. But I know I only feel free because of what we're about to do. If we weren't gonna kill ourselves in a few hours time then I wouldn't feel like this. If I had to go back home and wake up and go to school tomorrow then there's no way I'd be feeling this... what's-the-word... content. Yeah, that's it. I feel content. Maybe it's because I know we've made the right decision. I bet that's why we've been laughing and joking a lot. We're happy with the decision we made.

I turn my face back around and look out the window as the bus shakes its way down the canal road. Ciara just seems to be staring into her lap. She's gone a little quiet. In fact we've both been quiet since we left the chipper about fifteen minutes ago.

'I feel free too,' she whispers. I turn to look at her, grab her hand and clench it really tight. Then I bring her knuckles towards my face and kiss them.

'I love you, Ciara Joyce,' I say.

She smiles at me.

'I love you Ingrid Murphy, ye mad thing,' she says.

We both laugh. And then both sigh after we're done laughing.

I return my stare out the window and look into the darkness. Stitch keeps coming into my mind, but I don't want to let him in there. He's been in there way too long and doesn't deserve it. The words he said to me last night keep repeating over and over and over. I need to stop thinking. Maybe I should continue talking to Ciara. The silences will just drive me mad. Even if I do only have about four hours left of the madness.

'It's only two more stops, isn't it?' I ask.

'Yup,' she pops out of her mouth,

'So, do you know what you're going to say to her?'

Ciara sticks out her bottom lip, then shakes her head.

'It's just about… y'know… her realising that I called by to say goodbye, even if I don't—'

'Actually say goodbye!'

She huffs out a small laugh, then looks up at me again and smiles. I'm used to this; Ciara's moods being up and down. I'm never really certain when I knock for Ciara in the mornings before we go to school just what Ciara I'll be walking to school with. Some days she's buzzing; laughing and joking all the way there. Other days she just has her chin resting into her chest, staring down at her clunky shoes as she walks. She's been like that for years. Is never going to change. Some days she's a cross between both moods; can be buzzing one minute, staring at her shoes the next. I've tried to work out what it would feel like to be depressed, but only last night did it really sink in. Then I think of

Stitch again and I have to shake my head to get rid of his words.

'What you shaking for?' Ciara asks.

'Nothing. Just eh… just looking out the window here, staring at all these houses.'

'A lot smaller than our gaffs aren't they?' she says.

I nod.

'Yeah. Imagine living in one of them. They're tiny.'

'Bet they have better lives though. I bet the kids in those houses aren't going to kill themselves tonight are they?'

I stare at Ciara and hold my lips tight together. She's right. Dead right. I mean, we have everything we could possibly want. Both of us live on a lovely street, in massive big houses. Ciara's gaff has six bedrooms, ours has five. And we don't even need them. Neither of our families do. There are literally rooms in our homes that we never walk into; that we never use. Ciara's dad is stinking rich. He owns about ten different accountancy and insurance businesses. My parents aren't poor either. My dad's been a big name in broadcasting for about twenty years. I don't know whether I'd call him rich, but we're certainly not poor. Dad drives a brand new Mercedes. Black it is. Mam has a red Mini Cooper. He's got to be doing well. Having your own show on RTE radio must pay good money, I guess.

We're lucky, Ciara and I. Or at least we should be lucky. But I guess our lives prove it: money can't make you happy. There are kids at our school who go around in ripped runners and who live in tiny little gaffs like these and they're a hundred times happier than me and Ciara. It's always annoyed me when people at school say they want to be surgeons or lawyers when they grow up because they want to be rich. Having a big job that pays lots of money isn't a good ambition. My dad barely listens to me because he's too busy planning for his show. Ciara's dad doesn't listen to her because he's never home. If I was going to grow up I wouldn't want a big job. My ambition would be to pay my children as much attention as I possibly can. That's being a proper parent. A proper adult. I wouldn't care if I was earning a hundred pound a week or a thousand. I'd only care that I was loving my children. Anyway. It doesn't matter. I'll never be a parent. Will never need a career. And that's all fine by me. Cos I don't want any of that stuff.

'Here we are,' Ciara says standing up. She presses at the bell and suddenly the bus is pulling in for us.

'Thanks, mister,' Ciara says to the driver. I just nod my head at him and offer a half smile.

We both leap off the step and then turn left, towards Debbie's. I've never called to her house before but Ciara has pointed it out to me. It's a tiny little gaff; the type of house happy people live in. Debbie is really nice. She practically raised Ciara until sometime last year when, because Ciara was going to secondary school, her mum felt she no longer needed a nanny. Debbie minds three other children now, in Rialto I think it is. That hurts Ciara. I know it does.

'It's that one there with the blue door isn't it?' I say.

Ciara nods her head and then pushes at the gate that leads us into Debbie's tiny garden. It's no bigger than the small room under our stairs that mum keeps all the cleaning stuff in.

Then Ciara holds her finger to the doorbell and we wait until we see Debbie's figure through the frosted glass.

'What the hell are you two doing here?' she says when she answers.

20:05

Ciara

I skip from one foot to the other as I wait for her to answer the door. Haven't seen her in ages. I'm a little excited. I think I am anyway. I've never really been able to tell exactly how I'm feeling. I've always been like that.

'What the hell are you two doing here?' she says when she finally answers. My heart sinks. I thought she'd be delighted to see me.

I look at Ingrid then back up at Debbie.

'I eh... I...'

She opens her door further and stands to the side.

'C'min, girls. But you can't really stay long. I have a friend coming soon. Thought you were him.'

She shuts the door, and I stare at her. She's barely dressed. She only has a black bra and a pair of matching knickers on. They're pretty knickers; they have a little pink bow on the front of them. She must have been getting dressed when we knocked. Maybe that's why she was a little bit upset at first.

Then she holds her arms wide for me and I walk into them. I smell her perfume as we hug, then I rest my chin on her shoulder and try to stop myself from crying.

'Long time no see,' she whispers into my ear.

'Hey, Ingrid,' she says as she releases me. She offers Ingrid a high five and then takes a step back, her hands on her hips. She looks… pretty. *Really* pretty. Like one of those girls you see in magazines. I've never thought of Debbie as pretty before. When she used to mind me she'd wear some oversized jumpers in different colours; normally dark colours like grey or black. Or navy. Mostly navy, I think. And she never wore make up. She seems to have lots on today.

'S'wot you two doing here?'

'We eh… we…' I look at Ingrid.

'We were just in the neighbourhood. I have a friend who lives close by and Ciara said she'd love to pop by to see you… as a little surprise,' Ingrid says.

Debbie takes one step to the side and leans to look through to her sitting room.

'Well, it's lovely to see you. I eh—'

'We won't stay long,' I say. 'Just wanted to say hi and that I miss you.'

Debbie smiles. I miss that smile. I used to see it every day. Now some other snotty little kids get to see it every day.

'I miss you too. Course I do. I think about you all the time.'

Then I smile. At Debbie first. Then at Ingrid. Ingrid will know just how much it means to me that Debbie told me she thinks about me all the time.

The three of us stand smiling at each other in Debbie's hallway. Then the silence goes on a little bit too long. I don't know what to say. I'm here to say goodbye without saying goodbye. Where do I even begin?

'How about a quick glass of squash, then?' Debbie says. 'I'm sorry, but yis can't stay long.'

'Have you blackcurrant squash?' Ingrid asks.

Debbie turns around and walks into her kitchen. We both

follow. It's tiny in here. You wouldn't even fit the island we have in our kitchen in this entire room.

'Don't you eh... want to finish getting dressed?' I say as Debbie roots around in a cabinet.

'Yes!' she says turning around. 'I do have blackcurrant.' She holds it up and then looks down at herself. 'Yeah... tell you what, the glasses are there drying by the sink. Fill one for yourselves and I'll be back in a second.'

Ingrid reaches for a glass and begins to run the tap.

'She seems different,' I whisper when Debbie has left.

Ingrid looks back at me, nods her head once. Then she picks up the bottle of squash and pours some into her glass before downing it all in one go.

'Those chilli chips sure are salty,' she says. 'You having a glass?'

I shake my head.

'Nah, I'm alright.'

I feel weird. Really weird. Though maybe I'm supposed to feel weird, seeing as me and my best friend are going to kill ourselves tonight... but I didn't feel this weird on the bus coming out here. There's something odd about Debbie.

I turn and head towards the sitting room to wait for her. Ingrid follows me.

'We shouldn't stay long, not if she has a friend coming over,' Ingrid says to me.

Then I gulp. That's why I feel weird. I know I'm going to say goodbye to Debbie in just a couple minutes for the last time ever. I love Debbie. *Of course* that's why it feels weird... I think. I didn't feel weird saying goodbye to my mam because I really don't care about her. But Debbie... Debbie's different. I love her. She's always been good to me. Like a mother. Like a mother should be. I'm so jealous of the kids she minds these days. Jammy bastards.

Ingrid's eyes widen. As if she's just seen a ghost.

'What?' I ask. But she doesn't answer because we hear Debbie run down the stairs.

'Did yis get a drink?' she says, tightening the belt of her bathrobe around her waist.

'Thought you were getting dressed?' I say.

She puffs out her cheeks.

'I eh… I'm waiting on my friend, then we're gonna decide what to do.'

Ingrid shuffles her way in front of me, her eyes still wide.

'We need to go,' she says, grabbing at my hand.

Debbie gasps a little, as if she choked on her breath.

'Well, out of this room anyway,' she says sweeping both of her arms towards the hallway.

I feel bad again. Weird. It really seems as if Debbie doesn't want us here. As if she is done with me; has moved on to other kids and would rather forget that she ever helped raise me. I'm old to her now. Too old for her to care about. It's only kids she likes.

Then the doorbell rings and Debbie looks at us as if she's annoyed; as if we've done something wrong on her.

'I just wanted to say goodbye,' I say, wrapping my arms around her. She pats me on the back.

'Hey, why don't we meet up soon? I can take you to that park you like in Harold's Cross. We can buy ice-cream, hang out for the day.'

She's said that to me a few times over the past year. We still haven't done it. Then she releases me from my hug and walks towards her hall door and opens it.

'C'min, Gerry,' she says. 'Don't mind the girls. They're just leaving.'

An old man walks in and stares at me and Ingrid. He looks older than my dad. How the hell is he friends with Debbie?

'Okay, girls, out ye go,' Debbie says, almost shoving at the two of us.

My heart sinks. I can't believe this is the last time I'll ever see her and she doesn't even want to know. She doesn't have time for me anymore. Fine. She'll miss me in the morning.

'Goodbye then,' I say.

'Bye,' Debbie calls out without even looking at us. Then the door bangs shut and we're out in the tiny garden, standing right next to the stinky bins.

'What the hell was all that about?' I say.

Ingrid doesn't answer, so I turn to her. Her eyes are still wide.

'Ingrid!'

'Oh my God,' she says holding her hand to her forehead, 'did you see what I saw… in the living room?'

Larry continues to breathe heavily behind Helen. She's turned her cheek in his direction three times now, just to let him know she'd rather he fucked off. But the poor fella hasn't copped her irritation.

'Nothing yet?' Charlie asks.

Helen stares over at him, one of her eyebrows raised.

'Don't you think I'd tell you if I saw something?'

Charlie swallows, then returns his gaze to the screen in front of him, his nose just inches from it.

'If we're gonna see anything we'll see it now, right?' he then says. 'According to this screen it's 6:48. The call to Terenure will be made in one minute. Fingers crossed it's caught on camera.'

Helen doesn't answer. She moves her face nearer to the screen, stretching and then blinking her eyes to relieve some of the strain.

'How old you reckon he is?' she asks.

Charlie takes one step to his left, stares at the figure Helen's pointing at.

'About fifteen,' Larry says.

Both Helen and Charlie look over their shoulder at the bald head behind them. Larry takes one tiny step backwards and sinks his neck into his shoulders a little, finally becoming aware of his insignificance.

'Yeah, about fifteen, I s'pose,' Charlie says as he and Helen return their gaze to the screen. 'Think it's him?'

Then the figure on the screen lifts the phone he had been holding in the palm of his hand towards his ear.

Charlie stares at Helen; his stubby nose a little too close for her comfort. She balks away a bit, all the while staring at the black and white image. She watches as the figure hangs up the phone, before he flips it in the air and catches it.

'It *is* him, isn't it?' Charlie says a little high-pitched. He's beginning to let his excitement pour out of his mouth.

'Well… that call was made at bang on 6:49 and it must've lasted the same eighteen seconds as the call you played for me earlier,' Helen says. She rolls her tongue around her mouth. 'The direction this figure is walking to,' she says turning to Larry, 'he's going towards the next stop, what is it?'

'Suir Road,' Larry says. 'You want me to call up that footage?'

Helen nods her head, then places her hands in to the deep pockets of her leather coat.

'This is so cool,' Charlie says.

Helen stares at him, until he realises what he had just said was rather *un*cool.

'Kay, here we go,' Larry says, tilting another screen towards both Charlie and Helen. 'This is the Suir Road stop from 6:49 onwards.'

'How long does it take to walk from Goldenbridge stop to Suir Road?'

'Two, three minutes. Straight down the canal,' Larry says.

The three of them stare at the screen while Kristine, who

had been tapping away at the keyboard on her desk, stops and turns to look at them. She watches their faces, waiting on a moment of realisation to drop on one of them. But it doesn't come.

'It says 6:53 now on the screen, he hasn't walked this way, he'd be here by now.'

Helen spreads both of her lips open, so that her clenched teeth are showing. Then she slams the palm of her hand against the top of the screen.

'Bollocks,' she says.

'What's it matter?' Charlie says. 'We got a shot of him. Isn't that enough to go on?'

Helen holds her eyes closed in annoyance and then lets a sigh slowly exhale its way out of her nostrils.

'I wanted to see what direction he was walking in next, Charlie. It might help us catch up with him.' She nods her head and stretches her brow sarcastically as she says this. Charlie sinks his neck into his shoulders. Helen has an incredible ability to make men do this. It's why she initially fell in love with Eddie; because he never shied away from her. He was her perfect match. Always has been.

'He could have gone anywhere after the Goldenbridge stop, right? Over Goldenbridge itself into Inchicore. Across to Drimnagh past the Marble Arch pub? Onwards down the other side of the canal towards... Jesus, he could have splintered off in any direction after that, right?'

'Yup, on towards the hospital or perhaps Kilmainham. Could have even headed up towards Rialto.'

Helen allows another sigh to shoot through her nostrils. Then she chews on her bottom lip as Kristen answers a ringing phone.

'Larry, two more police officers at the front desk looking to view CCTV,' she says.

'Ah, must be the friends you were telling me about,' Larry says to Helen as he makes his way towards the door.

'Hold on, hold on, Larry,' Helen shouts out, 'Charlie, take out your mobile phone, get a clear picture of the best still of that young boy we have. Kristine,' she says as if she's an army major barking out orders, 'can we make this image any clearer?'

Kristine rises from her desk, begins to tap away at a keyboard right next to Charlie.

'Shall I go get your colleagues—'

'No, hold on!' Helens says, holding the palm of her hand towards Larry.

He creases his brow, begins to wonder what the hell is going on.

'That's as clear as I can get it,' Kristine says.

Helen nods towards Charlie, ordering him to take a picture with his phone.

'Kay let's go,' Helen then says, cupping his shoulder.

'Larry you can go get the other officers... is there a eh... Ladies room you can show me to on the way?'

Larry nods slowly. 'Yeah, there's one just here, down this corridor.'

Charlie and Helen leave with Larry, forgetting to thank the only person who was actually helpful to them while they were in the control room. Kristine doesn't mind. Is used to not receiving praise for the mundane tasks she carries out.

'Through there,' Larry says pointing at a door.

'You come with me, Charlie,' Helen says.

Charlie stops walking. 'What? Sorry? You want me to go to the Ladies with you?'

Larry stops walking too, but when Helen turns to face him, he gets the gist and then heads towards reception to allow the other offices through. Helen strides to the door and holds it open to allow Charlie to enter before her. He scratches at his forehead, wondering what the fuck Helen is up to, inviting him into this pokey, smelly cubicle.

'Let me see the photo?' she says, still holding the door ajar. She peeks through the crack of the door, then back at Charlie. After he's handed her the phone, she peeks through the crack again, notices Cyril and Leo from her own station being led to the CCTV control room.

When they're inside, the door closed behind them, Helen pulls at the toilet door and walks out. Charlie doesn't know what to do; whether or not he should follow her. So he stands still, waits on instruction.

Helen brings his phone closer to her nose, refocuses her eyes to the image of the boy. He looks blond, though it could be brown hair. His face isn't really clear. Could be anybody, really.

'Fuck sake,' she mumbles to herself. Then she pivots her head left to right. 'What the fuck?' she says. She turns around, strides in her own unique way towards the toilet and pushes the door wide open.

'What the hell are you doing? Will ye come on?' she says.

Charlie opens his mouth to respond, then thinks better of it, so he just follows Helen like a trained puppy dog back down the corridor, past the reception and out towards his own police car. He's still wondering what the hell just happened when he presses at a button on his key ring, allowing Helen — who is still a couple yards ahead of him — to swing the passenger door open and sweep her tall frame inside.

He scratches at his head again, then opens the driver's door and gets in himself.

'Eh... sorry, Helen, but eh... what was all that about?' he says.

'What was what about?' she says as she reaches for her seatbelt.

'Why eh… why did you invite me into the toilet?'

'Oh, that?' Helen responds. She sniffs her nose. 'Normally lights in toilets are more clinical…. to stop people from shooting up in them. You can't find a vein if the light is clinical. Did you not know that?'

Charlie creases his brow at her, making himself look as young as the boy he took a photograph of just a few minutes ago.

'Public toilets in bars and restaurants maybe, but not a bloody office toilet,' he says. Then he shrinks into his chair a little, in fear of what way Helen will react to him questioning her.

She swipes a sleeve across her mouth, wiping up some of the moisture under her nose.

'Yeah, you're right. There was no clinical light. Just thought we should give it a go,' she says.

Charlie's brow hasn't uncreased and his silence makes Helen look at him for the first time since they returned to the car.

'I just wanted to see what other Detectives were looking into the CCTV footage, wanna know who's on the job, okay?' she says, relenting.

'Why?'

Helen shrugs her shoulders.

'See who we might need to lean on later if we need anything.'

Charlie scratches at his head again, the lines in his brow still wedged deep.

'But why the secrecy, why didn't we just tell them we had a visual of the boy who made the phone call?'

Helen whistles, a slow piercing whistle. 'Wow, young Charlie, you've a lot to learn about this Detective business,' she says. 'Now; given the information we have, where d'ye think we should go next? If you were leading this investigation, where would your next port of call be?' she asks, changing the direction of the conversation.

Charlie sits more upright, grabbing the steering wheel with both hands, then makes repeated bop sounds with his lips as he thinks through Helen's question.

'Well,' he says, 'we don't really have anything, do we? A grainy picture of a boy who looks to be in his mid-teens. We don't know where he went after the call... so eh...' he scratches his forehead again, 'I actually don't know.'

Helen allows a small snigger to creep its way from the corner of her mouth.

'You're right,' she says. 'That *is* all we have. One grainy picture of a boy. A boy whose friends are going to commit suicide in about four hours. It's not much to go on. But we can't sit here and wait for those two girls to tie nooses for themselves. We have to act. *Think*. Where could we possibly get information from about the boy in this image?'

Charlie brings his fingers to his mouth and begins to tap away at his bottom lip.

'Sorry, Detective Brennan. But I actually don't know. Walk the streets, show young people the image, ask if they know who he is?'

Helen nods.

'Not bad, Charlie,' she says. 'We could do that. But that'd take an awful lot of time. Time we don't have. What about the school next to that Luas stop, the one on the Drimnagh side of the canal.'

'Yeah, Mourne Road school. What about it?' Charlie asks.

'That'd be the place to start wouldn't it? Rather than ask a hundred teenagers on the streets of Inchicore and Drimnagh if they know this youngfella, we can ask the Head of the school. He's bound to know every teenager in that whole area.'

'Ahhh,' Charlie says as he places the key in the ignition.

Then he pulls the car out of its parking spot and heads towards the Naas Road.

'But hold on a minute,' he says, 'the school'll be closed now. It's half eight in the evening.'

Helen flicks her eyes towards him.

'Jesus, Charlie... you do have a lot to learn.'

She takes her mobile phone out of her pocket and begins to flick her fingers across its screen.

20:25

Ingrid

THE DOORBELL RINGING FRIGHTENS ME, TAKES ME OUT OF THE shock I'm in. I can't believe it. Debbie?

My eyes are wide when an old man walks in, wearing a suit. He must be fifty, sixty even? I don't know. I'm not good with ages.

He stares at me and Ciara as if he's never seen two teenage girls before.

'Kay girls, out ye go,' Debbie says. She holds both of her arms out, almost pushing us to the door. That's fine by me. I want to get out.

'What the hell was all that about?' Ciara says when we're standing in Debbie's tiny front garden.

I don't answer her. I'm too busy thinking about Debbie. I think I'm in shock.

'Ingrid!' Ciara says.

'Oh my God,' I reply. I still haven't decided if I want to tell Ciara. It'll break her heart. 'Did you see that... in the living room?' I ask. Ciara's face goes all scrunchy. She does that when she's confused. 'Cocaine,' I whisper. 'Loads of it on a little mirror. I know. I've seen cocaine in films.'

Ciara's face is no longer scrunchy. She's making an 'O' shape with her mouth. Her eyes are kinda making the same shape too. She knows I'm not making this up. I've never lied to Ciara. I've never lied to anyone. Not until tonight. Not until I told my mum I was going to Ciara's to study.

Then Ciara swallows really hard.

'Debbie? Drugs?' she says. 'That doesn't make any sense.'

Ciara blinks then twists her head left and right. I know Ciara inside and out. I know she wants to go back in there. She'll have to know the truth. So I hold my hands to the back of both her shoulders and try to lead her out of Debbie's gate, back to the bus stop.

'C'mon,' I say. 'We've got to go say our goodbyes to Harriet and Miss Moriarty.'

But Ciara bends forward a little, places her hands on both of her knees and begins to breathe a bit heavier.

'C'mon, Ciara, let's go. You've said goodbye to Debbie. Two more stops. Then we can finally get ourselves away from all these thoughts. Please. C'mon… let's go.'

She stands up straight, blows a large breath through her lips and then heads straight for Debbie's door, pressing her finger against the bell and holding it there until Debbie snatches the door open.

'Whatcha playing at, Ciara?' she says. She seems to have lost her bathrobe; is back in just her bra and knickers again.

Ciara storms by her, heads straight for the living room. I don't want to follow her in. But I kind of have to. I have to be by my friend's side.

When I get to the living room I see the old man with his shirt all open, lipstick marks on his chest. Ciara is pacing around the living room, looking for the mirror I told her had cocaine on it. When she looks up at me I nod my head to the corner of the room, where a nest of tables sit. Ciara walks over to it, picks up the small mirror and then stares at Debbie.

'Ciara Joyce, that is none of your—' but before Debbie can get her full sentence out, Ciara holds the mirror above her head and throws it as hard as she can against the wall. She walks over to Debbie and I can see her jaw moving in circles, like it does when she gets really angry. I blink my eyes, because I think I know what's going to happen next. Ciara raises her hand, slaps Debbie across the cheek and then turns to me.

'Let's go, Ingrid,' she says. And we do. We run out of the house, out the garden gate and down the avenue. After a while we are both out of breath. Both hunched over, holding on to our knees.

'Whew,' Ciara says, before she starts laughing. 'That was mad.'

I look at her in shock. Though I don't know why I'm in shock. I know Ciara better than anyone. I know she can be really angry one minute, laughing her head off the next.

'What did you do that for?' I say.

She stops laughing and looks up at me.

'That bitch is doing drugs,' she says, pointing back to the avenue Debbie lives on. 'She was supposed to be one of my best friends. Like a parent to me. The only adult I thought cared for me.'

Ciara takes steps closer, waving a finger at me as if it's all my fault. But I catch her as she continues to rant, and wrap both my arms around her. I let her cry on my shoulder. Again. This is nothing new. Though it was quite the opposite last night.

'But… but Debbie has her own life outside of being your nanny,' I say, as if I'm protecting Debbie. I don't know why, though. I'm as shocked and as disappointed as Ciara is.

'Debbie? Drugs?' she says, wiping at her nose after she's lifted her head from my shoulder.

I just shake my head a little. I want to tell Ciara that I think she overreacted; that she didn't need to smash Debbie's mirror; that she didn't need to slap her across the face. But I won't. I'll just keep her close by me, my arms wrapped around her waist until she stops crying.

'This will all be over soon,' I say, stooping my head a little to catch her eyes. I want her to stare at me. 'We want out of this life, right? Look, we can't even say goodbye to the people closest to us without getting upset. We're just... we're just not right for this life. Time to do this, Ciara. Let's just do it!'

Ciara swipes at her nose again as her eyes stare into mine. She offers me a tiny smile, then nods her head once.

'Okay, let's just do it. Let's do it now!'

'Ciara Joyce. You come over to me right now!'

I look over my shoulder. It's Debbie. She's tightening the belt of her bathrobe around her waist again.

Ciara turns, runs as fast as she can and I sprint after her.

'Ciara! Ingrid!' We can hear Debbie shout, but her shouts are getting further and further away.

'Here's the bus, here's the bus,' Ciara says. We both stop running. Then I see that look in Ciara's eye. She's changed moods again. The tears have stopped.

'Let's run out in front of it, ye ready?' she says, grabbing both of my hands. 'On three. One, two—'

'No! Wait!' I scream. 'I'm not ready. I'm not ready.'

20:25

Michael

I FUCKIN LOVE THIS STUFF. I PINCH AT MY NOSE, MAKING SURE none of it falls back out, then duck my head down again, grab at the rolled up note and sniff.

'Fuck yeah,' I say.

Claudia laughs, then sits up and kisses me, her tongue filling my mouth.

'C'mon, fuck me,' she begs, lying back down on my desk.

She looks fuckin deadly with her blonde hair all sprayed out over my work notes. I hired her because she reminds me of that filthy lookin' bitch who lives up the street from us. The Swedish one. Ingrid's mam. Jesus, I'd love to fuck her brains out. That jammy bastard Terry Murphy gets to bang her every night. That's good snatch he gets to play with for someone who's such a known bore.

I squint my eyes a little, just so Claudia's face turns into Ingrid's mam's and then I slap both of her thighs wide open and shove my dick inside.

I've had tighter pussy. But I didn't know what I was hiring, did I? I could hardly have a go on her before she started working here. That's not how it goes down.

It's the power these chicks are into. You have to exert the power before they'll let you inside them. Once they figure they have opportunity to better themselves in the workplace, they'll do anything. Filthy bitches. I'm riding three birds from the office at the minute. This time last year I had five on the go. That's how it works round here. It's my thanks to myself for building this place up from scratch.

'Yeah, ye filthy slut,' I say grabbing a fistful of her hair. I continue to thrust in and out of her, enjoying each and every one of her little squeals. Then the fucking phone rings. Again.

Claudia lifts her head to stare at it. As if she's never seen a phone ringing before. I yank at her hair and pull her back into position.

'Ignore it,' I say. 'It'll be just my wife.'

Helen puffs out her cheeks, places the phone in the drinks holder next to the gear stick and then turns to face Charlie.

'He lives in Walkinstown. A Mr Patrick Tobin. Balfe Road.'

'Okay,' Charlie replies, swinging the car around. 'D'ye think he'll know the boy in the image?'

Charlie can see Helen staring at him in his peripheral vision and, in that moment, realises the question he asked was quite stupid. How could she possibly know that? 'Sorry,' he says.

Helen looks away, back through the windscreen.

'No need to apologise, Charlie. He's more likely to know the teenagers in this area than anyone. He works with them all day every day. So… there's more chance of him knowing who the boy is in the image than anyone.'

Charlie nods his head. He's glad, more than anything, that Helen didn't snap at him. Maybe she's beginning to warm to his company.

He shifts his ass cheeks, leaning from one to the other, as

he drives, wondering whether or not he should ask her a question that's been burning his mind ever since she first walked up to his desk about an hour ago. He scratches at his forehead, then sucks in a cold breath through his teeth.

'Mind me asking you a question?' he says. He tenses his eyeballs as he awaits the response.

Helen turns to face him again.

'Go on.'

'It's just eh... it's just...' he pulls at his ear lobe, 'every other member of the teams, at Rathmines and at Terenure stations, are eh... well they don't believe the call is legit, do they? They're out trying to stop something major from happening. Why do you eh... why do you think the calls *are* genuine? Do you really believe two girls really are out there somewhere wanting to kill themselves tonight?'

Helen arches an eyebrow, then returns her gaze through the windscreen to allow a silence to settle.

'It's personal,' she says.

'*Personal?*' The pitch in Charlie voice rises.

'Listen,' Helen says, pulling at the strap of her seatbelt and turning side on so she can face Charlie. 'What did they teach you in Temple Moor when you were training as a cop about dealing with phone calls to the station?'

Charlie nods his head once. 'To treat every call as seriously as the caller themselves.'

Helen doesn't say anything, she just opens both of her palms and then closes them.

Charlie shifts in his seat again.

'It's just... it's just, the caller wasn't really serious was he? The youngfella didn't give any names... any location. It just screams as a hoax call to get us out here looking for something that probably isn't happening. Meanwhile, something else is going down—'

'Charlie shut the fuck up!' Helen spits out of her mouth.

'Listen to me, and listen to me carefully. There are enough Detectives and officers out there looking into the possibility that this was a hoax call. Too many if you ask me. I'm actually furious with how this phone call is being considered by both of our stations. A suicide concern is not... *not...* to be taken lightly.'

Charlie glances over at Helen, the emotion in her voice offering the first slither of evidence that there's a heart beating somewhere beyond that leather coat.

He wants to ask more, is repeatedly lifting his bum cheeks from side to side in anticipation of asking more. But he stops himself.

'Sirens,' Helen then says.

Charlie doesn't even look at her to question the instruction. They're not attending an emergency, but he knows matters need to be dealt with as soon as possible. He's not fully convinced, as much as Helen seems to be, that there are two girls out there planning to commit suicide. But if they are, the clock is ticking.

He steps on the gas, overtaking cars with his sirens blaring and heads past Crumlin shopping centre towards Walkinstown; towards the home of the local school's Headteacher.

'If we find the boy, we'll know everything,' Helen shouts over the siren.

Charlie nods his head. He knows she's right. Regardless of whether or not there are two girls out there wanting to end their lives, or whether it's just Alan fucking Keating playing games with the cops, they need to track down the boy who made the phone calls. This is a proper investigation, no matter what way Charlie looks at it; his first proper investigation. Normally he's dealing with domestic disturbance calls, or calls from annoyed elderly neighbours giving out that boys are using their gates as goalposts for their little street football matches. Life as a rookie cop really hadn't lived up to the dramatic hype painted in a lot of TV shows Charlie used to watch.

'D'ye think the other cops will be coming out to this Headteacher's house as well? Think they'll be just behind us?' he asks.

Helen shakes her head.

'Doubt they'd have thought of it this way. They'll be wasting time trying to view other CCTV footage of where they think that boy would have gone to next. They'll be trying to trace his movements. But sure, that was almost two hours ago now since he made that call. He could be anywhere. They're trying to find *where* he is... me and you, we're gonna find out *who* he is. That's because we're better investigators,' she says. She then winks at Charlie. He's not sure how to feel about the wink. It sure looked weird. And came at the end of a very weird comment. But it's more confirmation that she's warming to him; that she's happy to teach him as they go.

Despite his growing confusion, he doesn't say another word as he races the car up Balfe Road, before turning sharply — causing Helen to grip the handle of the passenger door as her body leans towards Charlie.

'What number we looking for?' he asks as he reaches for a small switch that turns off the siren.

'It's that one there,' Helen says pointing, 'look, he's outside waiting for us already.'

As Charlie is pulling in, to park his car across the drive of the man they've come to visit, Patrick Tobin strides towards them.

'Hi, officers,' he says. 'I got your call. I do hope none of my students are in trouble.'

Helen waits until she is fully out of the car, standing

upright and towering over the short, balding man, before answering.

'We believe two of them may be in quite a bit of danger,' she says. 'May we?' She points towards his open front door.

'Please,' he says. He leads them up his modest garden path, into his modest home before closing the door and holding a hand to his forehead. 'Which two students is it?' he asks.

'Well, that was the information we were hoping you could help *us* with, Mr Tobin,' Helen says. 'We have a picture to show you. Can you name this individual? We believe he may be a student of yours...'

Helen looks behind her, her hand outstretched. Charlie's eyes widen.

'Shit,' he says, 'left me phone in the car. Gimme one sec.' He rushes back out the door.

Helen sighs. A deep, frustrated sigh.

'What is it? What's wrong?' Tobin asks, tilting his head. He had initially been annoyed, thinking students had been up to no good. But he's sensed a haunting mood since the police entered his home. This news is bad. Really bad.

'We've had a call saying two young girls are planning to die by suicide locally tonight. At midnight. We don't have much time to save them. A young boy rang in to give us that information, but he didn't leave any names, any locations.' Tobin scrunches up his nose, then squints at Helen. 'We don't know why,' Helen says, answering the question before it could come out of Tobin's mouth.

'Here,' Charlie says, racing back in the door, holding his phone out.

'We are hoping you can give us the name of the individual in this image,' Helen says.

Tobin takes the phone and stares at the screen as he walks towards his green sofa and sits in it. Helen winces a little as she watches his head begin to sway from left to right.

'No, I'm sorry. I mean the image is not very clear but I don't think I know this face. I'm pretty certain he's not a student in my school.'

Helen runs her hand up and down the back of her neck, tossing her orange hair into a mess. She's gutted; genuinely felt she was going to leap yards in front of the other investigation.

'Are you sure, Mr Tobin? Take another look.'

Tobin shakes his head again.

'Sorry,' he says, handing the phone back to Charlie. 'Is there anything else I can help with? I'm willing to help, as much as I can. Course I am. I care for every one of my students. I can't believe... I can't believe two of them are planning on committing suicide. You have to stop them... you just have to stop—'

'We will, Mr Tobin. Rest assured we are doing all we can. We just need to know who they are. If we knew who this young man was, we could get to the girls.'

Helen washes her hand over her face this time, giving herself a quiet moment to think.

'Are there any girls in your school suffering with depression that you know about?' she asks.

Tobin blows out his cheeks.

'Well... yes, we have so many issues with so many students. Depression?' He blows his cheeks again. 'You'd really need to speak with Sana Patel. She's our safeguarding and student welfare officer. Bloody good at her job, she is. Knows every student inside out.'

'Can you get her on the phone for me?' Helen asks.

Tobin stands up, reaches for the mobile phone on his mantle piece and begins to scroll through it.

'Hey, ring her on Facetime... you got Facetime?' Charlie asks. Tobin looks at him as if he has two heads. 'Sana Patel, you said, yes?' Charlie says, taking the phone from Tobin. He scrolls through it, then scrolls through his own phone with his other hand.

'Got her,' he says,' holding his own phone in front of his face as a gurgling tone rings.

'Hello,' a woman answers.

'Ms Patel, my name is Charlie Guilfoyle, I'm a Garda at Terenure station, this here,' he says turning the screen to face Helen, 'is Detective Helen Brennan from Rathmines station and I'm sure you know who this man is.' He turns the screen towards Tobin who holds his hand up to say hello to his colleague.

'Oh my,' she says, with a subtle Indian accent, 'what is going on? Are you okay, Patrick?'

'I'm fine, I'm fine,' he says.

'It's a couple of your students we are worried about,' Charlie says. 'I want to show you a photograph of a young boy. I need you to tell me if you recognise him.'

Charlie fumbles with both phones, mumbling to himself as he does so, then turns the image of the boy on his phone towards Tobin's screen.

'Take your time, Ms Patel, don't come to a conclusion straight away, allow the image to sink in,' Helen says. As she's saying this, she holds her eyes closed in anticipation, her fists clenched inside her coat pockets.

'No. No, sorry. He's not one of our students. I know the picture isn't clear, but I could tell if he was one of ours.'

Helen shows her teeth; her hands tightening into a firmer ball inside her pockets. Then she lets out a huge grunt.

'Okay, Ms Patel. We have one more question for you,' she then says, trying to compose herself. 'Can you tell us of any girls who have come to you with any suicidal tendencies recently.'

'Oh my,' she says 'what is going on?'

'We just need answers to the questions, Ms Patel,' Helen says.

'Okay, okay. Let me compose myself. You have me so worried. Suicidal tendencies. No!' she says, matter of factly.

Helen holds her eyes closed.

'What about depression? Any female students talk to you about feeling depressed?'

'Oh yes, oh yes,' Sana says.

Helen's eyes widen. And when Charlie glances towards her, she winks at him.

'Can you give me the names of those girls?' Helen says.

'Of course. But we'd obviously have to go through the proper procedure in order to—'

Helen snatches the phone from Charlie, pointing the screen towards her own face. She notices Sana balk backwards at the sight of her. Helen's aware she's odd looking. Is used to this kind of reaction.

'Excuse my French here, Ms Patel. But *fuck* procedure. Two students of yours are planning on killing themselves tonight. Two girls. I need access to the list of female students who have ever confided in you about depression.'

Sana's mouth falls open. She doesn't answer. Is too shocked to talk.

'Sana, you have my permission to share the information with these Guards,' Tobin says. 'This is an emergency. We'll deal with all of the red tape tomorrow. Just let these officers do their job as quickly as they can.'

Sana nods her head.

'Wait there,' she says. 'I need to access my computer.'

Helen winks a thank you towards Patrick, then holds a hand on Charlie's shoulder. A breakthrough at last. She's gonna find out who these two girls are. Is gonna save their lives. It'll make up for the fact, somewhat, that she couldn't save Scott's.

'Okay,' Sana says down the line. 'I have my notes here. What do you want me to do, read out the names?'

'Yes. Please,' says Helen.

Sana clears her throat.

'Okay. Jacinta Archer.'

Helen nods at Charlie.

'Elaine Bailly. Anna Barnes. Nicole Casey. Elizabeth Clarence. Sarah Dunne...'

Helen's eyes squint.

'Are you... are you reading these names in alphabetical order?' she asks, bringing the screen to her face again.

'Yes, officer,' Sana says.

'How many girls have you had come to you to talk to you about their depression?'

'This year, officer?'

Helen nods slowly.

'Yes.'

'Eh... lemme see...'

Helen watches as Sana's lips mumble her counting. She looks up at Charlie. Then at Tobin.

'Modern times,' Tobin says, shrugging his shoulders.

Helen holds her eyes closed, gripping the phone as firmly as she can, her knuckles whitening.

'One hundred and sixty-four,' Sana says.

'Ah for fuck sake!' Helen roars.

20:35

Ciara

I'M BREATHING REALLY HEAVILY. I'M NOT USED TO RUNNING SO much. Ingrid's fitter than me. Always has been. She could probably keep on running. But I can't. I stop. And bend over. I can't get the slap out of my head. Jees, that was probably bad. But she deserved it.

Debbie. Drugs.

I can't believe it. But I have to. Because I saw it with my own eyes.

I have my hands on my knees, breathing as heavily as I can to try and get rid of the sharp pain in my chest. Then I hear it. A bus. It's coming down the road quite fast. I can end it all right here. Right now.

I grab both of Ingrid's hands and stare into her eyes.

'Let's run out in front of it, ye ready?' I breathe in and out really heavily. 'On three. One, two—'

'No! Wait!' Ingrid shouts in my face. 'I'm not ready. I'm not ready.'

She releases both of her hands from mine and wraps her arms around my waist, pulling me back as I try to step out onto the road. The bus whizzes by. Beeping its horn.

Wow. I nearly did it then. I nearly killed myself. After years of telling myself I would do it and chickening out every time, I nearly did it just then. It seems a little bit… I don't know… exciting.

'Jesus Christ, Ciara,' Ingrid says, releasing her grip on me and then holding a hand to each side of my face. 'Let's calm down a bit. We have a pact. We have to stick to the pact.'

She's right. We discussed this last night. Then we wrote out a pact that we swore we'd stick to.

She uses her weight to push me back a little until I'm sitting on a small wall outside somebody's house. Then she sits beside me and throws her arm around my shoulder.

'Ciara, how stupid would that have been?'

I nod my head, then look up to the sky and suck up the wet snot that's running down my nose. What was I thinking?

'I know. I know,' I say, blinking away some tears.

'Jesus, we could have ended up in hospital, like vegetables forever.' I nod my head again, swipe my sleeve under my nostrils and then look at my best mate. 'You talked me through this,' she says. 'We spent two hours talking through this last night. There are ways to do it and ways not to do it. Running out in front of a bus is not a way to do it.'

I lean my head onto the top of her shoulder.

'It's just… Debbie. Drugs,' I say.

I hear Ingrid swallow.

'I can't believe it,' she says.

Me neither. I really can't. I've a lot going on in my mind right now. But the shock of Debbie doing drugs is taking over.

'And what the hell was that guy doing there?' I say, taking my head up off Ingrid's shoulder and turning to face her.

Her eyes are all wet. She shakes her head, sticks out her bottom lip.

'Were they… were they having sex?' I ask.

Her lip stretches out further and then she shrugs her shoulders.

'What a bitch!' I say.

'Hey,' she says. 'It's Debbie. There must be some… some… what's-the-word?'

'Explanation?'

'Yeah… explanation, there has to be.'

I shake my head slowly. I really can't think straight.

'There was cocaine on the mirror and she was in only her bra and knickers. That old man's shirt was all open… uuuugh,' I say as an image of the grey hairs on his chest come into my mind. 'He was older than our dads.'

Ingrid closes her eyes. Tight. She's remembering the chest hair too. Some of it had lipstick marks on it.

I rub at my face with both hands. Then Ingrid leaps from the small wall, wraps her hands around my waist and leans into me. I place my cheek on top of her head and just look down the street at nothing. The road is totally silent. As are we. Except for the thoughts that are going around in our heads non-stop. We need to shut them up. Shut them up once and for all.

I'm glad Ingrid stopped me running in front of the bus. Glad we're going to do this right. Just as we had planned. It won't be long. Two more bus rides. Two more houses to visit. Then we're done. For good.

I suck up my nose again, to stop snot from dropping onto Ingrid's beautiful hair. I've always loved her hair. Never been jealous of it though. Ingrid is too nice to ever be jealous of. I've only ever been jealous of her once; when she told me that Stitch asked her to be his girlfriend. I fancied him first.

'If anything, tonight has proved we've made the right decision,' she says, lifting her head. 'Think about it. You tried to say goodbye to your mum, she didn't want to know. You tried to say goodbye to Debbie, she didn't want to know. I know some people love us but…' Ingrid shrugs her shoulder as tears start to fall down her cheeks. She wipes one of them with her baby finger, then smiles up at me. Not a real smile. A fake smile. A pity smile.

'No need for us to cry,' I say, leaping off the wall. 'We've made a decision. There's not long to go, Ingrid. Couple more stops. Soon all this pain will be gone.'

We hug each other, knowing there's probably going to be another fifty hugs like this before we finally do it.

'So… off to Harriet's, then. You know what you're going to say to her?'

Ingrid almost laughs. Then she shakes her head.

'Same problem isn't it? Got to say goodbye without letting anybody know we're saying goodbye,' she says.

I think of my mam again; imagining her crashing to her knees when the police call to the house after our bodies are found. Sobbing her heart out. But she'll only be crying because of herself. Not because of me. Then I think of my dad; wondering how he'll take the news. He'll be put out. He'll have a funeral to arrange. A drunk wife he'll have to try to keep sober until the funeral is all done. He'll be so relieved when it's all out of the way. Then he can get back to doing… whatever the hell it is he does.

'Think your dad will do a show about us?' I say as Ingrid's parents come into my mind.

Ingrid nods her head.

'Definitely,' she says. 'He'll even begin some sort of suicide charity, won't he?'

We stand in silence thinking about that. She's right. That's exactly what Terry Murphy will do. He'll be on every chat show in Ireland talking about us over the next few months. Pity we won't be around to see that. I've thought about that kinda thing a lot over the years. It's quite annoying that I'll never be around to see the aftermath of my suicide. My mam crashing to her knees. My dad rolling his eyes during the funeral as my mam cries into his chest like a baby. The students at our school being given the news at assembly in the morning. The look on the faces of those who will feel most of the guilt.

Jaysus, if only we could turn into ghosts straight after we die and come back and watch all of the carnage we've left behind. That'd be ace.

'Will we go then?' Ingrid says, shivering a little. We've been standing in the cold too long, thinking about stuff we've thought about way too many times already.

'C'mon then, let's catch the bus to Harriet's. I promise I won't try to jump in front of it this time.'

Ingrid puffs another one of those laughs out of her nose, then throws her arm around me as we walk towards the bus stop on the far end of the road. We're strolling, very slowly, when flashing blue lights flicker in the sky.

'Girls,' a voice calls out. 'Stop right there!'

20:40

Debbie

I HOLD MY HAND TO MY CHEEK. JESUS FUCKIN CHRIST DID that hurt. Not just the slap. But her running away, the disappointment on her chubby little face. I haven't seen Ciara's face that purple since she used to struggle to poo into her nappy when I first started minding her. I feel so bad. So guilty.

I shiver as I walk back towards my house, holding my bathrobe closed around my waist. I'm not sure if most of my shivering is down to the cold, maybe it's the guilt; the embarrassment. I pivot my head up and down my street as I walk, hoping none of the neighbours come strolling by.

But I'm not really that concerned about myself. I'm only concerned about Ciara. How the hell would she even know what cocaine is? Surely it just looks like bloody salt or sugar to her. I hold my eyes closed and allow a loud groan to force its way from the back of my throat and all the way out through my mouth. Then I stop walking.

'Oh my God, she's going to tell her folks isn't she?'

I look up to the darkening sky and try to think it all through.

I know she also saw Gerry with his shirt undone and me back in my lingerie. But what could she deduce from that? She's too young. Or am I just being a fuckin idiot; assuming Ciara is and always will be a baby?

I hold my hand to my cheek again to try to rid it of the stinging. Jesus, she gave me a fair oul whack. Come on — get your thoughts together, Debbie. Try to think straight. Ciara and Ingrid came into the house for whatever reason. I rushed them out. Then Ciara came back and saw the coke. Threw the mirror against the wall. Saw a man on my couch with his shirt undone, me back in my lingerie. Shit... this doesn't look good.

She's probably off home right now, to tell Michael and Vivian that I do Class A drugs.

I let out another groan. Then squelch up my nose and shake my head.

Fuck Vivian and Michael. Sure they probably do coke themselves. I'm certain Michael has always had the glazed eyeballs of a coke user. And Viv, well, I'm not sure Viv does coke. She wouldn't take her nose away from her glasses of wine long enough to sniff a line. They probably won't give a shit if Ciara runs home and tells them. Sure, why am I even worrying about Michael and Vivian Joyce? It's not them I give a shit about. It's Ciara. I wanted her to be a part of my life forever. I know I haven't seen her much lately, but I just assumed she'd always be there; like a little sister to me. I fuckin raised her. I can't just let her go out of my life.

I head towards my garden gate and as I do so, I decide I'll ring their house in the morning. To make sure I explain myself. Tell her I wouldn't even dream of doing drugs. That it's not my thing. I'll take her out somewhere nice next weekend. Treat her. I've been meaning to spend more time with her anyway. I've missed her.

I push at my door and walk into the living room to see Gerry man spreading on my couch.

'What the fuck is going on?' he says.

'Sorry, Gerry… that little girl, the chubby one, I helped raise her. She's like a little sister to me. I feel awful that she saw the coke.'

'What t'hell did ye have them in here for, anyway? Ye know I booked this time with you.'

I eyeball him. All of him. His horrible saggy neck, the matted grey hairs on his chest, his huge belly hanging over his yellowing Y-fronts. What the fuck am I doing with my life?

I've asked myself that question loads of times over the past year or so. But I need this. It's only one hour. One hour every Sunday night for a hundred quid. It increases my income by twenty-five per cent. I'd barely be able to afford food for myself if I didn't do this. The Joyces paid well… the Franklins just don't pay the same. I need the extra income. So I signed on to be an escort. It's not as if I'm out on the streets every night waiting on anyone to ride me for a few quid. I'm part of an elite escort agency that sends a man — mostly fat fuckin Gerry — to my house every Sunday night for one hour. They pay one-hundred and fifty quid for that hour and I ship fifty of it to the agency.

'They just knocked on the door, Gerry. I thought it was you. I couldn't just throw them back on the street, I invited them in for a drink until you came, and when you did, I kicked them out. What more do you want me to do?'

'I'll tell you what I want ye to do,' he says, opening his legs even wider. Jesus, the fuckin state of him. 'Do a line.'

I huff, then tut.

'I don't do fuckin drugs, Gerry, how many times do I have to tell ye? It's your fuckin coke. And that's the last time you leave it in my house, d'ye hear me?'

I unwrap my bathrobe, sit beside him on the couch and then sigh. 'You do a line yourself,' I say. 'Then do me. Let's get this over with.'

HELEN IS STILL PACING UP AND DOWN PATRICK TOBIN'S TINY sitting room, her jaw clenching, when Charlie stands up and winks at her.

'Okay, got it,' he says.

Helen nods her head, then strolls over to Tobin.

'Think it through, Patrick,' she says. 'And ring us if anything comes to mind.'

Tobin mumbles a worried 'yes' to her, then Helen cocks her head sideways to motion to Charlie that it's time for them to leave. As they're heading for the door Charlie scrolls his finger down the screen of his phone.

'There's a hundred and sixty-bloody-four names here, Helen. How the hell are we gonna find out which two are the girls we're looking for?'

Helen makes a sucking noise with her mouth, then pops her lips.

'We'll find em.'

They both pace towards the police car; Helen still stewing their next move. They have a list of girls' names that's been emailed to Charlie's phone, all of whom have been noted by the school as having symptoms of depression. And — of course — they have an image of the teenage boy who made the phone calls that started this whole investigation. It wasn't a bad start, not by any means — and Helen was secretly quite chuffed that she hadn't lost any of her investigative nous — but it was only a good start if they had time to investigate. With the clock ticking towards midnight, Helen and Charlie had it all to do. They didn't have the time to trawl through the list of girls' names; didn't have time to go door-to-door asking the community if they knew who the young boy in the grainy CCTV image was.

'Sirens?' Charlie asks while both of them are pulling at their seatbelts.

Helen narrows her eyes then sucks her mouth again.

'What would you do, Charlie? If you were the lead Detective in this case, what would your next move be?'

Charlie gently drums his two index fingers against the steering wheel as he stews his answer.

'Ye think the two girls are on this list?' he says, nodding his head towards the phone he dropped in the cup holder beside the gear stick.

Helen scrunches up her face.

'Can't be sure of it,' she says. 'I just... ugh... we just need more time.'

'Let's ask the local teenagers about the boy in our image,' Charlie says, there's a football club who play their games around the corner here. St John Bosco they're called, there's always lads hanging around that clubhouse.'

Helen swallows, then nods her head.

'Okay. Let's do it.'

'Sirens?' Charlie asks.

Helen shakes her head this time.

'Not if you still want the teenage boys to be hanging around when we get there.'

Charlie holds his eyes firmly closed as he cringes a little. He should have known. That was quite an amateur question.

He drives off, rounds the first bend and by the time he's approached the roundabout, both he and Helen can see a group of lads sitting on a small wall next to the dressing-rooms of the football club. Some of them stand, bracing themselves to run as the police car edges up beside them. But when Helen gets out, her hands held in the air as if to call for peace, they all seem to relax.

'We're only looking for a bit of help,' she says as she inches towards them; her hands now back in her pockets, the leather coat open, making her look like a character from *The Matrix*.

'Need you to identify a boy of your age. He's not in trouble, we just need to find him.' She looks behind her at Charlie fumbling with his phone, then rolls her eyes because he's not prepared. He was supposed to show the image bang on cue. Now she thinks he's made her look uncool to the boys. As if her leather overcoat and orange hair hadn't already done that.

'C'mon, piglet, hurry up,' one of the boys shouts to a ripple of laughter. Helen offers the boy who yelled a stern gaze. He just stares back.

Then Charlie holds his phone towards the pack and they circle in.

'Ah yeah — that's Mike Hunt,' one lad says.

An ounce of excitement forms in Helen's stomach, until she hears the rest of the boys laughing again. Mike Hunt. My cunt. She should have copped it; had been fed that fake name a few times when she used to do routine beat work back in the day.

'Boys, lemme ask you this,' Helen says, stepping in to the middle of the group. 'Any of you got sisters?'

One boy cocks his head up, a couple others mumble a 'yes'.

'You,' she says talking to the boy who cocked his head. 'Your sister younger or older than you?'

He swallows.

'Younger.'

'So about… twelve, thirteen?' Helen asks.

The boy cocks his head again.

'Well let me tell you this.' Helen takes her hands out of her pockets. 'Two thirteen-year-old girls are planning to die by suicide tonight, somewhere in this area. We don't know who they are or where they are. We just know they are alone, and they want to end their lives. The boy in this photograph is the only person who can lead us to the girls. Guys… they're only young. Same age your sister. Please,' she says, holding her palms out, 'no more messing; we need you to be serious. Do you know who the boy in this image is?'

Charlie stretches the phone closer to the boys and they shuffle their way for a closer look.

Helen winces when she notices the beginning of a Mexican wave of heads shaking from side to side.

'Sorry,' the boy who had called Charlie a piglet says, 'we don't know him. He's not from round here anyway; we'd know.'

Helen spins on her heels, pivots her head backwards and offers a silent grunt towards the sky.

'Thank you, boys,' Charlie says, before he trudges after Helen and into the car.

Helen is snarling as they both reach for their seatbelts again.

'We've enough information to find these girls, don't we?' Charlie says as he repeatedly knocks the butt of his phone off his bottom lip. 'It's just we don't have enough to find them before midnight tonight. We'd need a team of officers, wouldn't we? Calling around houses, showing neighbours this image. Calling around each of the girls' homes that are on our list.'

Helen nods her head slowly as she stares out of her passenger window.

'Yep,' she says. 'If we were to take the time to ring each girl's home on that list, and spent just two minutes on each call, that'd take us over five hours.'

Charlie digs the phone into his lip, then looks over at Helen.

'It's stupid that it's just the two of us out looking for these girls. The rest of em are all obsessed with tracking down whatever it is they think Alan Keating is up to.'

'Uh-huh,' Helen says, still staring out the passenger window.

The evening has turned to darkness; the moon forming full in the navy sky. Not a good sign for Helen. She believes in all that quirky shit; is convinced bad things are more likely to happen when a fuller moon makes an appearance. She's also one of those who believe that the horoscopes printed in the *Irish Daily Star* every day are genuinely accurate. This morning's horoscope suggested she should be looking at taking every opportunity by the scruff of its neck as it will lead to a brighter future. She's now wondering whether the horoscope meant she could get back on the force if she were to save these girls' lives. That'd certainly offer a brighter future for her. Though maybe the future the horoscope was referring to was the future of these two girls. If Helen can stop them, she can turn their lives right around. And that'd mean more to Helen than getting her job back. Saving people from the brink of suicide would be a lottery win for Helen Brennan. A goal she wishes she could have achieved twenty-two years ago.

She moves her head for the first time in a couple minutes

to snatch Charlie's phone out of his hand and then presses at the screen to view the time.

'It's almost nine o'clock,' she says. 'We need to get a move on.' Charlie looks at her, his eyes squinting. 'You're gonna have to ring your SI; tell him that you need more men to carry out door-to-door enquiries,' Helen says.

She hands the phone back to Charlie and notices him swallow hard as he grips it.

'He'll just laugh at me, Helen. I'm just... I'm just—'

'You are a police officer doing his job properly,' Helen says. 'Put him on speaker phone. And remember... don't mention you're with me. I'm supposed to be off duty.'

Charlie holds his eyes closed in frustration before he scrolls at his screen.

A ringing tone eventually sounds and both of them cock their ears towards the phone Charlie has held between them.

'Yello,' a voice says.

'Superintendent Newell it's eh... Charlie, Charlie Guilfoyle.'

'Ah, howaya, young Charlie, Everything alright?'

'Yeah... it's just, I was asked to look into the possibility that the anonymous phone call made earlier about the suicides was well... well...' he pauses, looks at Helen. Helen nods her head, then waves her hand in a motion that suggests he should just get the fuck on with whatever it is he's trying to say. 'Eh... well, I've been asked to look into the phone call as if it was legitimate and I've found something interesting.'

A snuff of a laugh crackles down the line.

'Y'know the call's not legitimate, young Charlie, yes? It's that fecker Keating playing games with us.'

'Yeah... yeah, I know,' Charlie says, looking at Helen again. 'It's just... my job was to look into the call as if it *was* legitimate and well... I have a list, a list of girls in the vicinity who suffer with symptoms of depression. I got them from the local school's Headteacher.'

Charlie stops talking, then squints his entire face in anticipation of a response. But no sound comes down the line.

'Sir,' he says, reprompting Newell.

'Well, I'm glad you are taking your work very seriously, Charlie. And that is... that is fine investigating indeed. Really impressive outside-the-box thinking. But ye know... this *is* Keating. We're one hundred per cent certain of it. I've got five Detectives sniffing their noses around — so do Rathmines station — and we really need to get back to the invest—'

'Sir, I need help. I need more manpower to try to locate the two girls from this list. I'm sure the two girls who are planning to die by suicide are on it.'

As the line cackles with laughter Helen grinds her teeth, itching to get in on the conversation. But she manages to bite her tongue. If her husband found out she was investigating behind his back, that could spell the end of their marriage. It's surviving on such tenterhooks as it is. They've been sleeping in separate bedrooms for the past fifteen years; Eddie accepting that they will stay with each other forever, but their marriage — in a traditional sense — well and truly ended the day Scott died. Helen's been waiting on Eddie to retire, so that they can move to Canada. He promised her — on the evening before Scott's funeral — that they'd both retire to Toronto when the time was right. That dream is the only thing that's kept Helen going over the years. She's desperate to move away from Dublin; desperate to move on from Scott's death. She nags Eddie about his retirement on a regular basis; but has a horrible feeling the move will never happen. She thinks Eddie loves his job a little more than he loves his wife. She couldn't be more wrong.

'Listen, young Charlie, you keep following up your leads, I'm glad you are taking the role you've been given as seriously as you can, but… I've gotta go.'

Charlie stares at Helen as a dead tone echoes through the car.

'The cunt!' Helen yells. 'Why are all Superintendents a bunch of fucking cunts?'

She clicks at the buckle of her seat belt, then opens her car door.

Charlie inches forward in his seat and watches as Helen screams into the sky.

'Did the two girls kill themselves missus?' one of the boys they had been speaking to a few minutes ago shouts over.

Helen doesn't answer him; she pinches at the bridge of her nose, then tucks her chin into the collar of her leather coat. After forcing in and out three deep breaths, she takes her own mobile phone out of her pocket.

'Guess I'll have to make a call,' she says to herself. She presses at the screen a couple times, then brings the phone to her ear and, as she does so, she walks slowly away from the car.

'Hey,' Eddie says. 'We're crazy busy here at the minute, what's up?'

20:50

Ingrid

'C'MON THEN, LET'S CATCH THE BUS TO HARRIET'S. I PROMISE I won't jump out in front of it as it's coming,' she says, smiling. Typical Ciara. Running out in front of a bus one minute, joking the next.

So I smile too, pretending I'm not scared. And then we both walk, arms wrapped around each other, towards the end of the road where the bus that'll take us to Harriet's house stops.

Harriet is the only one I really want to say goodbye to. Apart from Ciara, she's the one person who speaks to me like I'm me... not as if I'm somebody she wants me to be. My parents talk to me as if I'm another person altogether; like a daughter they wished they had instead of me. I feel like I'm bothering them anytime I have to ask a question.

My teachers don't talk to me at all. Most of them don't even know my name. I'm just another face in a room full of faces to them. In primary school, our teachers were great. I love Miss Moriarty with all my heart. But in secondary school it seems as if they don't care. A little part of me was excited when we were getting old enough to go to secondary school. But I've felt so sad ever since we've gone there. I never wake up happy in the mornings. Secondary school has been such a let down.

We're walking in silence when blue lights flash off the windows of the houses in front of us. Then I hear a car pull up slowly and I turn around to see a policeman with his head sticking out of his window.

'Girls — stop right there!'

I look at Ciara's face; wondering if she's going to make a run for it and thoughts of whether or not I should run with her go through my mind. Running from Debbie is one thing, but running from the police... well... But Ciara doesn't run, she just stands still beside me as the policeman approaches us.

'Girls, a bus driver has just stopped me up the street there and said two girls fitting your description almost ran out in from of him.'

He frowns his forehead. His wrinkles are really deep. Like an old man's. Only he isn't really that old.

'No... don't be silly,' Ciara says laughing. 'I just nearly walked out in front of the bus by accident... my friend here pulled me back. I just wasn't looking where I was going.'

He looks at my face, back at Ciara's, then at mine again.

'This true?' he asks me.

I nod my head. This isn't good. I'm lying to policemen now. He reaches into his back pocket and takes out a small notepad.

'You two girls from around here?' he asks.

Ciara nods her head before I have a chance to speak. Which is fine by me. I don't even know what to say. I'm half scared, half-relieved that a policeman has come to save us.

'Well, not far from here. We'd need to get a bus home,' she says.

'What're your names?' He clicks on the top of his pen and rests it against his pad.

'Emma Brown,' she says as quickly as she can, 'and eh… Mel Bunton.'

I hold my eyes closed. The last thing I want to do is laugh. But I know exactly where she plucked those names from… it's a mix up of two of the Spice Girls. Typical Ciara. Thinking on her feet. Making everything up as she's going along.

The policeman looks at me when he's finished scribbling.

'Are you okay, Mel?' he says. 'You look a bit eh… ashen-faced, if you don't mind me saying.'

I slowly nod my head, unsure what ashen-faced means exactly.

'She's not ashen faced. She's just pale. Always has been. Has Swedish blood, don'tcha, Mel?'

Ciara nudges me.

'Yes… yes, Sir.' I say. I can hear the fright in my voice. I try to swallow it down, deep in to my stomach before I speak again. 'Yes. My mother is Swedish. I got her pale skin, her blonde hair.'

The policeman doesn't react; no words, no nodding of his head, no scribbling of his pen. He just shifts his eyes from my face to Ciara's and then back to mine again.

He clicks at his pen, then stuffs his notepad into his back trousers pocket.

'I'm concerned that the bus driver had to stop me. He got a big fright, said he had to swerve to miss you and he has about twenty passengers on that bus. Nobody was hurt, thankfully.'

Ciara reaches her arm around my shoulder and gives it a squeeze.

'We're sorry, officer. It was an innocent mistake. I just didn't look where I was going. We wanted to cross the road and — silly me — I tried to cross it without using the Green Cross Code and then... last second, Mel here dragged me back. She saved my life.'

Ciara squeezes me tighter.

I don't do anything, except stare at the ground in front of me. I want to stare at the policeman's face. I'd love to know what's going on inside his head. But I can't bring myself to look up.

'And you can get home safely now, yes?' he asks.

He's going to leave us alone. I'm not sure if I feel relief or fear go through me.

'Yes, officer,' Ciara says. 'We're just walking to the bus stop now. Heading straight home. Promise.'

He nods his head once.

'Kay, look after yourselves, girls. And watch what you're doing when you're crossing the road, young Emma, yes?'

Ciara giggles.

'Course I will, officer. I won't make that mistake again.'

He looks at her face, then at mine. I don't think he's buying all of this. But he seems done with us. Is almost turning to go.

'One thing I don't get,' he says, holding a finger to his lips. 'If you were crossing the road, why haven't you crossed it since?'

I feel my mouth fall open. I look at Ciara. She seems lost for words... for once.

'Well?' the policeman says.

'Changed our minds,' Ciara says.

He stares at both of our faces again, shifting his eyes back and forth as if he's watching a bloody tennis match.

'Girls... I'd like you to come with me,' he says. 'Into the car please.'

I'm popping another Malteser into my mouth when I realise the second episode of *Heartbeat* is about to end. That flew in quick. I look up at the clock. Almost nine.

My two men are in bed. No idea where my little girl is.

I chomp on the Malteser, wait on the stupidly addictive *Heartbeat* theme tune to play over the credits and then sit up straight on the couch. She was only here a couple hours ago, cuddling into me. It's not unusual she'd be in Ciara's house, but — I don't know whether it's mother's intuition or what it is — I just have a feeling all is not right. It was something about the way she held her face as she was leaving. She didn't want to look at me. She was holding something back.

I shuffle my feet into my slippers and make my way to the hallway. Then I flick my way through our little phone book until I see the Joyce's number and I proceed to dial it.

'Hello.'

'Vivian, it's me… Greta. The girls at your house, yes?'

There's a silence.

'Oh, sorry. I thought you were going to be Michael. I'm expecting him to call.'

Another silence.

'Vivian... the girls with you? Ingrid said they were going to your house to study.'

I hear her sniff her nose.

'No. Eh... I'm sure Ciara said they were going to your house.'

Shit. Something *is* up. I bloody knew it!

'Little rascals are up to something. Y'know, I knew it as soon as they left the house. Ingrid looked... she looked as if she was hiding from me.'

Vivian sniffs again.

'They're probably down in Macari's eating chips,' she says.

I sigh. I can't imagine that's what they're doing. They only go to Macari's on a Friday evening. Nah... something else is going on.

'It's just they were at that party last night. I'm wondering if something happened at it.'

'Ah... they'll be fine. They'll be fine,' she says; almost as if she doesn't care.

'Well eh... if they come back to yours, tell Ingrid she has to come straight home. She's in trouble. They shouldn't be lying to us.'

'Ah, we all lied to our parents when we were teenagers,' Vivian says. I hold the phone away from my ear and stare at it as if I'm staring at Vivian, my eyes narrowing. 'But yeah... I'll send Ingrid back when they get here.'

Then she hangs up.

She really is a crap mother. Always has been. So bad, she had to hire a nanny even though she didn't even work herself. I know it must be nine o'clock, but I still look up at the clock over the fireplace when I stroll back into our living room to make sure. Maybe they did sneak out for some Macari's chips. But it seems too much of a coincidence that they've gone AWOL the night after they've been to a party. I bet they're meeting boys. I get it. We all start fancying boys at that age… it's just, I can't stand the thought of Ingrid lying to me. I love Ciara, but her character is probably becoming too influential on Ingrid. I don't want Ingrid to grow up. Not yet anyway. I love that she's quiet. Love that she's shy. Because it means she'll never really get herself into trouble. Though that may be wishful thinking. I read a book once that said parents never truly know their own children, because children act differently at home than they do outside the house. But I always assumed that was a bullshit theory when it came to my two. At least I know Sven will never lie to me. He's not capable.

I suck on my lips and then find myself taking our stairs two at a time, clinging on to the banister as I go. I peak around the door of Sven's room and stare at his face; his mouth open, his nostrils whistling a little snore like they always do.

I walk, almost on my tiptoes, into my own bedroom. Terry's not snoring, but I can tell by his heavy breathing that he's already fast asleep. He'd hate it if I woke him. He's got to get up at five a.m., needs to get into the radio station for six. But maybe I *should* wake him; our daughter's a hell of a lot more important than his little show.

I tip-toe back towards the bedroom door, and shut it behind me. Tight. Fast. Then I hear him… shuffling under the duvet before he lets out a groan.

'For Christ sake, Greta,' he says, 'you've just fuckin' woken me.'

I blink my eyes and feel a little relief wash itself through my body.

'Sorry, dear,' I say, turning around to re-enter the bedroom. 'Door slipped out of my hand as I was closing it. I eh… I'm glad you're awake though. I'm eh… worried. About Ingrid. And Ciara. They've gone missing.'

20:55

Ciara

He presses at the top of my head as I get into the back of his car, then does the same with Ingrid.

I feel frightened. Though I'm not sure why. He's hardly arresting us for walking out in front of a bus, is he? He's just worried for us. Is doing his job to protect us. But he won't. There's nothing he can do that'll save our lives. Even if he delays it by an hour or two, even if he calls our parents to come pick us up from some police station, me and Ingrid will eventually get around to doing what we want to do. I try to slow my breaths, reminding myself that there's no need to be frightened.

When he shuffles his way into the driver's seat, he reaches for a button that turns off the blue lights. Then he turns around to us, his hand resting on the top of the passenger seat.

'No need for you to take the bus, I'll get ye home,' he says. 'Where is it ye live?'

I feel Ingrid about to speak up, about to rattle off her address, so I place my hand on her knee; my sign to her that she should leave the speaking to me.

'Connolly Gardens, in Inchicore,' I say. 'Number fifty-one.'

The officer winks at me, then turns around and starts the car.

I feel Ingrid turn to face me. I'd bet any money her eyes are wide. But I don't look at her. I don't want to give the officer any clues that we have lied our asses off to him ever since he started asking us questions. So I just stretch my fingers towards hers and grip on to her. I can feel the sweat on her palm. Bet she can feel the sweat on mine too.

'How old are you girls?' the officer asks, staring back at us through his mirror.

I cough before I answer.

'Eh... thirteen, both of us.' That's the first answer I've given him that isn't a lie.

'Does eh...' he says nodding his head in the mirror, 'does Mel not talk, no? Cat got your tongue?'

I squeeze Ingrid's fingers.

'She's just quiet is all,' I say.

'That right?'

We don't answer and the car falls silent as we turn onto the canal road.

The officer made me forget what happened back at Debbie's house for a few minutes. It starts to play at my mind again. That slap. But to hell with it! I can't let what Debbie does affect me. I thought she was bigger and better than doing bleedin' drugs though. But I guess I don't really know her as well as I thought I did. I can hear the slap over and over in my head as I stare out the car window and every time I do I feel the sting of it inside my hand. She deserved it though, I s'pose. And besides, that's only a tiny bit of pain compared to how she'll be feeling in the morning when she's told the news. I don't really wanna hurt Debbie by dying, though. I don't want to hurt Miss Moriarty either and Ingrid sure as hell doesn't want to hurt Harriet. That's why we were visiting them this evening, to let them know that we called by to say our final goodbyes. We wanted those three to know they meant something to us. But instead of a long hug to say goodbye to Debbie, I ended up slapping her across the cheek. And now here we are — both of us — in the back of a bleedin' police car.

I squeeze Ingrid's fingers again and then we both turn to face each other. I wink an 'it's all okay' at her and she gives me that half smile thing she does. She seems to be taking being in the back of a police car better than I ever thought she would. She's not crying, anyway. Unlike last night. Jesus, she could have filled a swimming pool with the amount of tears that came out of her eyes.

I twist her wrist a little so I can look at her digital watch. 20:59. Just a few hours until all of her pain is gone away. And mine. We're almost there. As soon as this officer drops us off, we'll be back on track.

'I love you,' I mouth to her. And as she does the same we squeeze each other's fingers even tighter.

'What school do you go to, girls?' the officer asks.

I think quickly.

'Goldenbridge.' I'm so good at lying. It's almost as if the lie comes to my mind before the truth does. That seems to be how my brain works. I'm sure I got that skill from my dad. I knew I had to say the name of a school that was close to the wrong address I gave him. I know Harriet goes to Goldenbridge. She's actually in her last year this year. Is doing her Leaving Cert in June.

'Ah… I know it well. I went to Junior Infants in Goldenbridge. Grew up in Inchicore until I was seven meself,' he says.

Neither me or Ingrid say anything back to him. We both just turn our heads to look back out of the side windows.

Hopefully he gets the message. We don't wanna talk. We just want you to drop us off.

The streets are too dark. I can't quite make out where we are, though this area is a bit unfamiliar to me. Ingrid would know it better than me. She hung around here a bit when she was younger. I assume we're in Inchicore by now. It shouldn't have been that long a drive.

'Okay, so which one is Connolly Gardens?' he asks, eyeballing me in the mirror.

I turn to Ingrid. She coughs.

'Eh... next turn right and then it's the eh... I think it's the second turn after that,' she says.

I look at him in the mirror, notice his brow go all wrinkly again. Shit. I hope he isn't getting suspicious.

'Yeah, this turn here,' Ingrid says.

Now I know where we are. I've been here a few times with Ingrid. It's a quiet little cul de sac. The type, I'm sure, no drama happens in. Not like the road we live on.

'That house there,' I say. And then I unclick my seatbelt.

He turns around to us after he stops the car.

'Ye want me to walk ye up to the house?'

'Oh... no thank you,' I say. 'I don't want to give my dad a fright. It'd be his worst nightmare if I showed up at the door with a policeman.' I reach my hand towards his shoulder and pat it gently. 'Thank you, officer.'

Then I open the door and hop out.

I can sense him watching us as we stroll towards the house and push at the gate that leads us into the tiny garden.

He's pulling away slowly as we knock at the door. I know he's waiting to see if anybody answers. It doesn't take long until he gets what he wants.

'Wha' you two doin' here?'

'Ah, Uncle Brendan. We just wanted to see Harriet. Is she in?'

Ingrid's uncle pushes his door wider to allow us to walk in to his hallway. And as we do, I turn back and offer a wave of my hand to the police officer.

'She's inside watchin' the tele. Your mother know you're here, Ingrid?' Brendan says.

Ingrid turns to face her uncle and then nods her head slowly.

'Course she does,' she says, her cute little smile wide on her face. But I know that will have hurt Ingrid a bit. She hates lying.

21:00

Terry

So I'll just cut to the chase, Terry. The reason we called you in here was not to marvel at your successes so far, and not to meet you and see that big, handsome smile of yours. We asked you here for a very specific reason. We need a new Saturday night prime time entertainment show on RTE television, something that'll get the entire nation tuning in. And, we know of no better man to front that show than the great Terry Murph—

My eyes shoot open. I let out a groan.

'For Christ sake, Greta, you've just fuckin woken me.'

It's not like her. She's normally very careful when I'm sleeping. So I know she closed that door with a bang on purpose.

I turn my face to look at the clock. 21:01. Jesus, I've only been asleep an hour.

She pushes the door open and looks around it sheepishly at me.

'Sorry, dear. I'm glad you're awake though. I eh... I'm worried. About Ingrid. And Ciara. They've gone missing.'

I try to clear my mind of the annoyance by squeezing my

eyes closed. I fuckin hate being woken. Then I rub a hand over my face.

'What do you mean missing?'

She perches her butt on the end of the bed and looks over her shoulder at me, her arms crossed.

'Ingrid said she was going around to Ciara's house to do some studying for that exam they have coming up. But I've eh… I've just rung Vivian and they're not there.'

I rub my face again with my hand.

'What did Vivian say?'

'She eh… she said Ciara had told her they were coming around here to study.'

I sigh as loudly as I can and then sit up in the bed, leaning the back of my head onto the top of our wooden headboard.

'Something's going on, Terry. I know it. I said it to you as soon as they left the house this evening. Ingrid could barely look at me as she was going out the door. That's not like her.'

I hold each of my forefingers to my temples; not so much to think through where Ingrid might be, more to stop the annoyance of being awake from scratching through my mind.

'She'll be back soon. She knows she has school in the morning,' I say.

I scoot myself back down in the bed, until my head is resting on the pillow again.

'Call it mother's intuition or whatever Terr—'

'Jesus, Greta. She'll be home soon. And when she walks through that door you'll be annoyed with yourself that you woke me up for no fuckin reason.'

I sit up sharpish. Because I know that was a little harsh.

'Sweetie, it's Ingrid. She's incapable of doing anything wrong.'

'Except for lying.'

Greta's standing now, her hands on her hips.

'What do you mean lying?'

'Well, lying about where she was going.'

'Ah,' I say, shaking my head. 'That's a little white lie. She's thirteen now. Isn't that what teenagers do?'

'I hope it's just a boyfriend or something. They probably met boys at that party—'

'It fuckin better not be boys,' I say, sweeping the duvet off me. I take one step over to our window and pull at the curtain so I can stare up and down our street. Then I look back at my wife.

'Jaysus, I always loved that Ingrid was really pretty, but now that she's a teenager, I wish she had a face like the back of a bus.'

Greta shoots a little laugh out of the side of her mouth. That'll do me. She's obviously not as concerned as she seems to be letting on.

'Sweetie, she'll be back in a while,' I say, tossing her hair. 'Don't worry about it. I'll talk to her when she gets home from school tomorrow. If she's messing around with boys, she'll have an awful lot of explaining to do.'

I jump back into bed and pull the duvet nice and snug around me again.

'Now,' I say, turning on to my side. 'I've got a big show in the morning… Close the door gently this time.'

THE KIDS ACROSS THE STREET ALL COCK THEIR HEADS UP AGAIN at Helen as she strolls away from the police car, the phone to her ear.

'I know you're crazy busy, won't keep you long, Eddie. I was just, y'know, lying here on the sofa and thought I owed it to you — owed it to our marriage — to be totally honest and up front with you.'

There's a hesitation on the other end of the line.

'Go on,' Eddie eventually says.

'You *did* hurt me earlier. So much so I've been crying. I thought what you said was really insensitive… about me needing to go home to watch the soaps. In front of everybody.'

There's silence again, but Helen is aware Eddie will be rolling his eyes.

'I'm sorry, Hel… it's just I'm under so much pressure here and… well, yeah… there's no excuse for me saying that in front of everybody. Please accept my apology once more and we'll speak in the morning, yeah?'

Helen fake-coughs down the line, is not really sure where to take the conversation from here.

'Yeah, yeah — I know you didn't mean it. It just hurt is all, and I didn't wanna just lie here getting angry with you, so thought I'd call so I can just put it all behind me. I know you're mad busy... how's the investigation going?'

'Frustrating,' Eddie says. Helen smiles to herself. Is aware her husband has fallen into her trap. 'We're certain Keating is up to something. He's keeping well away, for sure. We know he's in Spain. Again. Same place he always is when he's pulling off something big. None of his main men seem to be doing anything, but we'll get to the bottom of this. We have to before it's too late. I'm not letting this fucker give us the run around again.'

'You'll sort it. I'm sure you'll figure it out. Did you eh...' Helen looks over her shoulder, 'did you trace the caller? Y'know; if you get the caller, you'll almost solve this thing.'

'Yeah. Call was made near the Drimnagh Luas stop, we managed to get CCTV footage of the boy making the call. He looks about fourteen, maybe fifteen. The type of young recruit Keating normally uses to carry out a little bit of the dirty work for him.'

'Track him down yet?' Helen says, nibbling at the edge of her thumb. She stops walking, awaits the response.

'No. We've no name. Just an image. That and the fact we know he walked to Harold's Cross after making the call. We tracked him on CCTV all the way up the canal. He turned off at the main Harold's Cross bridge. No sight of him after that. We're closing in.'

Helen grabs some air with her fist, chuffed that her little mind game of pretending she was upset soothed Eddie into opening up to her. She spins on her heels and begins to pace back towards the car.

'Interesting... interesting,' she says. 'Eh... apology

accepted. We'll do that breakfast after we wake up tomorrow, yeah?'

'Helen, you okay?' Eddie asks. But Helen barely heard; was too busy bringing the phone back down to press at the red button. She places the phone in her coat pocket and begins to quicken her pace as she gets nearer the car, wiring her finger around as if to signify to Charlie that it's time to get going.

'Here, yis aren't gonna find the two girls if you're just gonna leave that car parked there all night,' one of the teenage boys roars towards her. She doesn't pay him any attention, nor any of the other boys who decide to laugh at his silly statement. She just snatches at the door handle, folds her tall frame into the passenger seat and instructs Charlie.

'Harold's Cross.'

He stares at her, then turns the key and speeds off, staining the road with tyre marks.

'What's going on?' Charlie asks.

'The young boy, in our image… he's in the Harold's Cross area now. Walked there after making the call.'

'How do you know?' Charlie asks as he reaches for the siren switch.

As the sound blares out from the car, Helen sucks on her lips and then says nothing; as if Charlie hadn't just asked that last question. She's trying to remain mysterious; as if she's operating at a different level to Charlie. It seems to be working. He has no idea that his low rank as a recently-recruited uniformed beat officer makes him her senior.

Charlie chicanes out of the narrow streets of Drimnagh and finds his way back on to the canal road. He's a decent driver, is Charlie. Was given the share of a car with another beat officer who works a different shift pattern to him about three months ago. For the minimal admin work they do, as well as the odd walk beat they take, they barely need the wheels. But there was a car left over at the station. And Charlie was chuffed with the offer. It almost felt like a promotion to him.

'So, what we gonna do? Door-to-door?' Charlie shouts over the siren.

Helen has the nail of her thumb held between her teeth.

'Same again,' she shouts. 'Let's contact the local school Headteacher. He'll know every teenager in that area. What's the local school in Harold's Cross?' she asks.

Charlie answers by picking up his phone and handing it to her.

Helen clicks into his Internet browser history, Googles 'secondary school Harold's Cross' and finds her answer in a matter of seconds.

'St Joseph's CBS,' she says. 'The number's here.' She holds the phone to her ear; hears a tone ring twice before an answer machine kicks in.

'The school office is currently closed. We operate between the hours of eight a.m. and five p.m., Monday to Friday. Please leave a message after the tone or — alternatively — call our emergency site team on 01 5333873 in case of an emergency.'

Helen holds her eyes closed, soaking in the number just read out to her, then she swipes at the screen of Charlie's phone and punches in the digits.

Another answer machine.

'Ah for fuck sake!' she says before the beep sounds.

'This is Detective Helen Brennan from Rathmines Garda station,' she yells down the line, 'ring me back on this number as soon as you possibly can!'

Then she hangs up, places Charlie's phone back in the cup holder and screams into her hands.

'Supposed to be a fuckin emergency number that!'

Charlie continues to speed up the canal road, swerving past cars that pull over for him.

He looks at Helen, then back at the road in front. He does this numerous times. Is itching to ask her another question, but he can sense her frustration and isn't quite sure now's an appropriate time.

'Helen,' he says tentatively.

She doesn't hear him.

'Helen!' She opens the hands from around her face, looks over at Charlie. 'I eh... I can see why you are a brilliant Detective. You take things really seriously, but do you eh... do you normally get this animated during an investigation?'

Helen stares straight ahead.

'I take every case as seriously as the last one,' she says.

Charlie can just about hear her over the siren. His fingers begin to fidget on top of the steering wheel.

'It's just,' he shouts again, 'you said earlier that this one was personal...'

Helen looks over at him, arching one of her eyebrows. Then she lets out a long sigh.

'Just do lights,' she says.

Charlie reaches for a button near the ignition and clicks at it. The sound of the siren stops but the blue lights remain flashing, bouncing off the car bonnet and back into their faces.

Helen sits more upright in her seat and then fixes the seat belt around her so that it runs at a straighter diagonal across her chest.

'Somebody very close to me died by suicide,' she says.

Charlie turns his face towards her and purses his lips. But she doesn't notice. She's just staring at the light show on the bonnet.

'Sorry to hear that,' Charlie says.

'You've nothing to be sorry for.'

The car falls silent, except for the noise of tyres zooming down the canal road.

'My son,' Helen then says, still staring straight ahead. Charlie offers another purse of his lips. 'Similar age to these two girls, I suspect. He'd only just turned fourteen. Y'know… I still don't know why. What I wouldn't give to know *why*. Ye know what my husband says to me all the time? "Helen, you will *never* know why." As if it's that easy to just forget about it.'

'I'm so sorry,' Charlie says, 'I can see why you are so passionate about saving these girls. Suicide… it's … it's such a waste of life—' Charlie holds his hand up to his mouth. 'Oh, I'm so sorry. I meant… I meant, if only they could be stopped…'

'I know what you mean, Charlie,' Helen says, taking her stare away from the lights. 'And you're right. I think how much of a waste of life suicide is every single day of my life. That's been every day for twenty-two years.'

Charlie winces a little as he clicks down the gears to turn off the canal road; at the Harold's Cross junction.

'It was the same as these two girls… him and his friends, they must have made a pact.'

The vibration of Charlie's phone ringing in the cup holder halts Helen. She reaches for it and without even looking to see who's ringing, presses at the green button and brings the phone to her ear. Then she stretches across Charlie, flicking at the button that makes the sirens blare up again.

'Hello, Detective Helen Brennan speaking,' she shouts, holding one finger to her opposite ear.

'Detective Brennan, my name is Trevor Halpin, I am the site manager of St Joseph's CBS… I just received your voicemail, is everything okay at the school?'

'Trevor, I need to speak with the school's Headteacher right away, I need you to give me his contact details.'

'Brother Fitzpatrick is his name,' he says. 'Is everything okay, sounds like something bad has happened.'

'Nothing bad has happened *yet*, Trevor, and only Brother Fitzpatrick can help stop something bad from happening. We need him to identify a school student as soon as possible. Tell me, Trevor, where does Fitzpatrick live?'

'Jesus, Mary and Joseph,' Trevor says, 'I hope the student is okay. Eh… hold on for a second. He doesn't live that far from the school. I have his details in my phone… gimme a sec.'

Helen winks over at Charlie, then waves her hand up and down, signalling that Charlie should slow his driving.

'Parkview Avenue, number one-three-six,' Trevor says. 'A little cul de sac, y'know those old Victorian style houses off the main road?'

'Gotcha, Trevor. Thanks for your help.'

Helen hangs up the call, then taps into the Maps app and punches in the address that had just been read out to her.

'Do a U-turn, Charlie, then it's the second left.'

Charlie causes the wheels to smoke as he swings around.

'He's got to know him. If the kid lives around here, the Headteacher of the school *has* to know who he is. We just had the wrong area when we spoke to the first Headteacher.' Helen slaps her palm off her knee, excitement beginning to grow inside of her.

'One-three-six, one-three-six,' she repeats as Charlie inches the car down Parkview Avenue, switching the sirens off. 'There it is,' Helen says, pointing. She clicks at her seatbelt, jumps out of the car whilst it's still moving and sprints — in her own unique way — across the street. Charlie doesn't even bother parking; he leaves the car — lights show still on — in the middle of the road and paces after Helen;

catching up with her just before she presses at the doorbell. No one comes to the door.

'Brother Fitzpatrick,' she shouts as she bangs at the knocker. 'I am Detective Helen Brennan, I need to speak with you as a matter of urgency.'

She stands back, takes in all of the windows.

'Bollocks,' she whispers over her shoulder to Charlie when she realises nobody's home.

Charlie rubs at the back of his head as Helen makes her way to the window, clasping her hands either side of her eyes to peer into the darkness.

'Not a sign of life. Fuck it,' she says, turning around, to be met by the face of an elderly woman, waiting at the gate.

'Ye won't find him at home, not at this time o' the evenin',' she says.

Charlie takes a step towards the woman.

'Where would we find him, ma'am?'

'Same place as always,' she says. 'The Horse and Jockey.'

'A pub?' Helen asks.

'Yep, not far from here. It's on the other side of those houses. Better off walking. If ye take the car, you've to go round the Wrekin… but there's a lane way over there ye can cut through. You'd be there in five minutes.'

Helen walks towards the woman and places the palm of her hand on her shoulder.

'Thank you, miss.' Then she turns to Charlie. 'Park the car up. We're going for a little walk.'

21:05

Ingrid

HARRIET LOOKS HAPPY. SHE *ALWAYS* LOOKS HAPPY. I REALLY don't know why though. She's had so much pain in her life. Much more pain than I've ever had. But she seems to be able to get over it. She's got a strength I know I will never have. I've tried. I've tried to be strong like her, but it's not me. I guess everybody just has different minds, even if they do share the same blood.

'Hey, good to see you two,' she says as she hugs me. Then she hugs Ciara. She knows Ciara a bit. Not that well. But whenever Harriet has hung around in my house, Ciara is normally there. Me and Ciara often talk about Harriet; we say how cool it would be to be just like her. And we both agree that we never will.

She has a hooped nose ring that we know would look stupid on us. If we walked into school trying to dress the way Harriet does, we'd be laughed at until we raced out of the classroom with embarrassment. She wears clothes like Indians do. Not Indian people that live in India. Indians that live in America. She always seems to have a poncho on over her shoulders; a different coloured one almost every time I see her. Today it's brown with light blue stripes. And she's wearing long trousers that are so wide at the end that they cover her shoes. Mum says those type of trousers used to be big in the seventies. They have a name, but I can't remember it.

'Great to see you too,' I say. 'We just thought we'd pop in to say hello.'

Harriet gives me a big smile, then points to the sofa; right next to where Uncle Brendan is sitting.

'Take a seat,' she says. 'Can I get you anything?'

We both shake our heads and plonk ourselves on the sofa. I'm not really sure what to say. Here we are, trying to say goodbye to somebody we love without letting them know we'll never see them again. It seemed like an easier thing to do when I came up with the idea last night. It was me who added it into our pact; I felt I couldn't end it all without paying the people I love one final visit.

'Don't you two have school in the mornin'?' Uncle Brendan says taking his eyes off the tele.

I sit more forward on the sofa so I can look at him.

'Yes, we do. But we were visiting a friend of Ciara's who lives nearby and said we'd pop in to see Harriet. To see you both.' Uuugh. I hate lying. But maybe I'm getting good at it. That's about my fourth lie today.

Uncle Brendan nods, then looks back at the tele. I'm not sure what it is he's watching.

I feel sad for Uncle Brendan. Always have. Aunt Peggy died when I was just three. It must be coming up to ten years now. Cancer she had. I don't really remember her that much. If it wasn't for the photos I don't think I'd have a face in my mind for Aunt Peggy at all. Harriet was only eight when her mam died. That's why it confuses me that she's always happy.

'Where's your friend live?' Harriet asks Ciara.

'Eh...'

'Up in St Michael's Estate,' I say, jumping in. Lying again.

'Jaysus, I don't want you two up there in that estate at this time of the evening... are yis mad?' Uncle Brendan says. He doesn't look away from the tele this time. He's just sitting there, slouched into the sofa, his two hands on top of his big belly. 'Yer mammy and daddy know you were there?'

'We eh... we were with my mam. She just dropped us off here so we could say hello to Harriet,' Ciara says.

I feel a bit of relief in my body. Ciara ended Uncle Brendan's questions with one sentence. Maybe I'm not that good at lying. Certainly not better than her anyway. The last thing we need right now is Uncle Brendan ringing Mum and Dad to check up on me. Aunt Peggy was Dad's sister. Dad took ages getting over her death. Almost as if he took it personally. He ran a marathon to raise money for a cancer charity the year after she died and raised fifty-five thousand pound. That's a huge amount of money. He talks about it all the time — more than he actually talks about Aunt Peggy.

I can feel Harriet stare over at me from the chair she's sitting in. She's so clever. I wouldn't be surprised if she knows we've been lying. I turn to look at her and she nods her head towards the stairs.

'Wanna go up to my room? Three of us can have a girly talk?'

I'm off the sofa before I even say 'yes', Ciara following me.

It's a tiny house is Brendan and Harriet's. Especially compared to our homes. The hallway is barely a hallway. There's only enough room for a tiny table that the house phone sits on. The kitchen doesn't even have room for a table. It's only about the size of our downstairs toilet. That's why I often say to Ciara that poorer people are happier. If you're in my house, you can sometimes hear Mum and Dad argue. If you're in Ciara's, you're almost guaranteed to hear her mum and dad argue. That's if her dad is in. But here — in

Harriet's — it's always quiet, even though the house is tiny. She's much closer with her dad than me and Ciara. It kinda makes me jealous a little bit. Only I don't mean anything bad about being jealous of Harriet. I love her too much to have any bad feelings for her. She's always been a cool cousin. The only cool cousin I have. She's five years older than me, but she has always spoken to me as if I am the same as her. Nobody else in my life does that. Cept for Ciara.

'What's up with you two?' Harriet asks as she holds the door to her bedroom open for us to walk into under her arm.

It's a super cool bedroom she has. She's into the coolest old bands. Bands I've barely even heard of. There's a picture of two crazy lookin' fellas with crazy hair cuts from a band called Oasis over her bed. And another one of a weird looking blond fella called Kurt Cobain.

'Eh... nothing much. Same stuff,' I say.

She looks at me with a funny face then shuts the door.

'Don't give me that. You can't lie to me, Ingrid. I can see right through you. It's this boy, isn't it? What-his-name again, funny name he had?'

I look at Ciara, then rub at my nose.

'Stitch,' I say.

'That's it! Stitch. Because he had one stitch in his lip one day in school that was hanging out, right? What did he do on you?'

I look at Ciara again. I'm not sure what to say. Or really, I'm not sure how much to say.

I can see Ciara tapping her shoes off the carpet. She's nervous too. Maybe coming to say goodbye to Harriet wasn't the best idea. She might get everything out of us. She's too bloody clever.

'G'wan,' Ciara says sighing, 'tell her what happened with Stitch last night.'

21:10

Ciara

SHIT. MAYBE THIS WASN'T A GOOD IDEA. HARRIET IS TOO intelligent. She might make Ingrid cave in and tell her everything.

I can feel Ingrid staring at me; trying to get a hint from me about how she should answer Harriet's question. So I look back at her and before I can even stop myself, the words come out of my mouth.

'G'wan, tell her what happened with Stitch last night,' I say.

Bleedin' hell. I hope she doesn't tell her everything. Because Harriet will talk her down; will make her feel better. Ingrid will refuse to do this... refuse to kill herself with me. And we need to do it. We need to do it tonight. We can't let anyone change our minds.

'We were at a party last night. He made fun of me in front of everybody in our school year,' Ingrid says.

'The little bollix,' Harriet says. I laugh. Then hold my hand up in apology to Ingrid. It's the way Harriet says things sometimes.

Ingrid sits herself on the edge of Harriet's bed. 'Me and

127

him, we were… we were supposed to go to the party together to let people know we were… y'know…'

'Boyfriend and girlfriend?' Harriet says.

As Ingrid nods her answer, I sit beside her.

My head is talking to me as I sit. In fact, not just talking to me. It's screaming at me. It's telling me I should interrupt Ingrid. She might say too much. I know what Stitch said last night isn't the only reason she wants to kill herself. But it is the reason she finally agreed to do it. So talking about it — giving Harriet the chance to mend her broken heart — might make Ingrid change her mind about ending it all. Only I don't know what I can say to stop her.

'He wouldn't even look at me the whole night. He was too busy mucking around with all those eejits he hangs out with.' I look up at Harriet and notice she is pulling one of those faces. Like a sympathy face; her lips closed tight, her eyes squinting. 'And when I tried to talk to him, he just sort of hushed me away. He was like… I don't know… he's a different person when it's just me and him.'

'Boys,' Harriet says. 'They're all like that. It's not just when you're thirteen. Boys are different around their mates than they are their girlfriends their whole lives. All my fellas have been like that. Boys are dopes.'

'How many boyfriends you had, Harriet?' I ask. I already know the answer. She's on her fourth. She told us that before. But maybe asking this will help change the conversation.

'Four,' she says. 'Just finished with Conor there a couple weeks ago.'

'Finished?' I ask.

'Same thing. Too immature. Was always changing plans when we were to meet up and stuff. Did me head in in the end. He started crying like a baby when I dumped him. Told him it was all his own fault.' She turns to Ingrid and rubs at her knee. 'This won't be your first heartbreak, honey, trust me. Specially someone who looks like you.'

I look down at my lap. It's always awkward for me when people mention looks. I know I'm not the prettiest. Never will be. But sometimes I think the better looking you are, the more attention you get from the boys. And who would ever want that?

'Boys don't notice me,' Ingrid says.

Harriet tips her head back and laughs.

'Yeah right? Ciara, do all the boys fancy her or wha'?'

I shoot my head up and twist my neck to look at Ingrid. Then I laugh a little and nod my head.

'Course they do,' I say. But I'm lying. The boys don't fancy Ingrid. I don't know why. She's probably the prettiest in the class. Either her or Tiffany Byrne. But the boys never seem to mention Ingrid. Or notice her at all. I think it's cause she hangs out with me. We're seen as the two little quiet weirdos.

'No they don't,' Ingrid says, making a funny face at me. I just shrug my shoulder. I wasn't really sure what to say. The truth? That my fat cheeks puts all the boys off her too?

'So where were yis last night?' Harriet asks.

'A guy in our year had a free house; his mum and dad were away for the weekend,' Ingrid says. 'Mum took a lot of persuading to let us go, but she did in the end. Told her it was a normal birthday party and that his parents would be there. About fifty people from our year turned up. We weren't really invited. Stitch and his mates were, so I asked Stitch if it was cool if we went too, so me and him could kind of...'

'Come out?' Harriet says.

Ingrid nods her head.

'But it just ended up with me and Ciara standing in the corner all night, eating bloody Cheesy Puffs.'

'I love Cheesy Puffs,' I say, before I realise what I've said. Harriet looks at me and laughs a little through her nose.

'So, what happened... did you confront him?' Harriet asks, turning back to Ingrid.

'It was when the slow music came on, wasn't it?' I say.

Ingrid nods.

'Yeah, the fella whose gaff it was, he had music playing all night. Then it switched to slow songs, so that the boyfriends and girlfriends could get up and dance together. I didn't know what to do. I was really nervous. And the room was so quiet because the music was so low. I just... I just walked up to him and tried to hold his hand.' I can feel Ingrid's insides cry, she almost bends herself over in two while sitting on the edge of the bed. 'He just looked at me as if he hated me. "What the fuck are ye doing?" he said. "Get your bleedin' hands off me you... ye fuckin smell like fish fingers".'

I look up at Harriet and notice her face go all funny.

'*Fishfingers?*' she says.

'There's always been this thing,' I say, 'that Ingrid smells of fish fingers because she's half Swedish. It's been going on for years... from when we started Primary School.'

'*Fishfingers?*' Harriet says again, this time really high-pitched.

'We don't get it either. It doesn't even make any sense.'

Ingrid sniffs some wet snot back up her nose.

'And then everybody just laughed. Really loudly,' she sobs.

'Ohhh... Ingrid.'

Harriet walks over to her, kneels down and gives her a big hug.

I hope she doesn't make Ingrid feel better. Well... better enough to not want to do what we plan to do. We better not have said too much already.

Charlie has to almost jog to keep up with the wide-open strides of Helen.

'Jaysus, I hope he knows this kid,' he says, bounding up behind her.

'If the kid is from this area, then he'll definitely know him. We just needed to find the right Headteacher is all. We had the wrong area earlier on. But now we've got it. I'm sure of it.'

They cut through a narrow side entry — squeezing up a gap between an overgrown bush and a semi-detached home — and on towards the laneway the neighbour had pointed them to.

Then Helen stops, bends over slightly and holds her hands to her knees.

'Sorry, Charlie, I'm moving too fast for a woman of my age.' She looks up at him, still bent in her own unique way, and then sucks a large breath in through her nostrils. 'How old you reckon I am?'

Charlie's eyes widen a little. He pivots on his heel, swaying one way, then the other.

'Jee, I don't know...' he says before blowing out his cheeks. 'Fifty-odd, mid fifties?'

'Ha,' Helen shouts out, almost too loudly. 'Nope. Sixty-three. Can you believe that?'

Charlie can believe it. He politely aimed low with his estimation. Her face looks every inch the face of somebody in their sixties, perhaps even in their late sixties. There are heavy lines around her mouth, two rows of bags under each eye.

'Really? Wow. You don't look it. And your... eh... movement, sure, Jaysus, I have to run to keep up with ye,' he says.

'Well, you don't have to run now, do you? I've stopped. Gimme a second to grab my breath.'

Charlie swallows, then pivots again on his heels as he waits on Helen to stand back up.

'I won't move so fast this time,' she says, holding out a hand to Charlie. He grabs it, allows his weight to help Helen to straighten up.

'People always say I look younger. I think it's the hair.'

Charlie swallows again, then stares at the back of her hair as she walks on. He still hasn't worked out what colour it's supposed to be.

'Yeah... it's cool,' he says. 'Bet you're a really cool grandmother.'

Helen balks a little, but keeps walking.

'Never got a chance to be a grandmother,' she says.

A cringe runs down Charlie's spine. He slaps himself in the forehead, then sets off after Helen, trotting again to keep up with her.

'I'm so sorry,' he says. 'I eh... I want you to know. I am just as determined as you are to find these two girls before they do the wrong thing. We'll save their lives, okay? We'll save their lives in Scott's memory.'

Helen stops walking to glance back at Charlie.

'Thank you,' she says. Then she paces again, forgetting that she said she'd slow down.

'Never in a million years would I have thought he'd do it. I mean suicide… Scott? And every parent I've talked to since, who has had a child who has done the same thing, they say exactly that. Not in a million years could they have even guessed their child would end it all. I bet… I bet you any money that the parents of these two girls haven't one darn clue what's going on tonight.'

Charlie stretches out his arm and gently pats Helen between her shoulder blades as he catches right up to her.

'You never get over it, y'know? Well, I didn't anyway,' she says.

Then she stops walking again and pinches the top of her nose.

Charlie pivots on his heels, then winces a little before wrapping his two arms around her.

Neither of them say anything as he hugs her in the middle of the dark laneway. Then Helen swipes her nose with the sleeve of her leather coat, pushes Charlie gently away and walks on.

'C'mon, let's get to this Headteacher. What time's it now?'

Charlie reaches for his phone and stabs at the screen so the light comes on.

'Just gone quarter-past nine,' he says.

'Fuck sake. Not that long to go. Right….' Helen says, blinking her eyes as she continues to walk. 'If we can get a name for this boy from this Headteacher, we'll be fine. We can get to him, get the names of the girls out of him, track them down. If he knows they are gonna kill themselves, then he'll likely know where they're planning on doing it. We're going to stop them from doing what they want to do.'

Charlie nods his head, though his instinct is telling him

Helen's plan doesn't sound particularly genius. There are no guarantees to any part of what she's just said. He squelches up his face, then decides to talk.

'But, Helen, why didn't he leave all that information... the girls' names and everything else... why didn't he share everything he knew when he made the calls?'

Helen twists her head to face Charlie, still striding forward, then shrugs her shoulder.

'It's happened thousands of times before, people ringing in to the station and offering up tiny bits of information.'

She notices Charlie's face contort.

'It does, Charlie. Happens all the time. I don't know whether these guys just like to get their kicks from it... or... I don't know. He's a young kid. He's probably frightened. Maybe he's the reason they're planning on killing themselves... there might be a lot of guilt on his part, that's why he rang it in. And perhaps he's too frightened that it'll all come back on him.' She stops walking and holds a hand out towards Charlie. 'Listen; the psychologist will have a field day with this boy after we bring him in. But we're not the psychologists are we? Our job is to investigate and act. And that's what we'll do.'

Charlie swallows again, then nods his head. And they both walk on, past the last of the bush that squeezed them into the laneway and out into an open road.

'Where the fuck is this pub?' Helen says, spinning around, her palms face up.

Charlie takes a few steps forward and peers around the bush.

'Here it is,' he says.

The pub looks like a large cottage house, topped off with a hay-brush rooftop.

'Jaysus, never knew there was a pub around this neck of

the woods,' Helen says before swiping some of the bush away and forcing her way through a gap.

She puffs out her cheeks as they cross the small car park and towards a lit open porch.

'Bar or lounge?' Charlie asks.

'Locals always drink in the bar,' Helen says, pulling at the door to their left. She steps aside, allowing Charlie to enter first.

The murmuring of chatter she heard as she opened the door immediately stops.

'We are looking to talk to Brother Fitzpatrick,' she says to the dozen people sitting at low tables.

Heads pivot around the room.

'He was here a minute ago, hardly did a bleedin' runner did he?' an elderly man says.

A mumble of laughter sounds out before the man behind the bar, drying a pint glass with a stained tea towel, cocks his head at Helen.

'He's in the Gents, Guards. Be out in a minute.'

Helen and Charlie take one step backwards and then both clasp their hands in front of themselves in unison as they stand still. Nobody's eyes divert from them and only the hum of a distant hand dryer creates any sound at all.

'Can I get yis a drink?' the barman, still drying the same pint glass, asks.

Helen waves a 'no' at him, almost managing a smile in the process.

The sound of a door creaking turns everybody's heads in the opposite direction. Then the door with 'Gents' written on it swings open and a bearded man limps into the bar; suddenly stopping upon noticing all faces staring at him. Then he spots the two strangers — one in a Garda uniform — and he staggers backwards, resting his shoulder blades against the wall.

'You're in trouble, Brother,' one man calls out. Most of the other patrons laugh. But their laughter sounds cautious, non-committal.

'Brother Fitzpatrick, I assume?' Helen asks, taking a stride forward towards him, staring at the clerical collar that she can see behind thin strands of his beard.

'Oh sweet Jesus, Mary and Joseph,' Fitzpatrick says, blessing himself.

Helen squints her eyes when she gets closer to him, can tell by his glazed look that he's had a few too many already.

'We eh... we need to speak with you as a matter of urgency.'

Helen points her hand towards the door behind her.

Fitzpatrick doesn't move.

'Unless you would eh... like us to talk to you here in front of everybody, Brother?'

'Hold on, hold on,' he says, raising a palm to the air. 'Gimme a second.'

He steadies his feet, sucks in a stuttering breath, then exhales slowly before leaning off the wall and walking, one foot in front of the other, as slowly as he can — past Helen, then past Charlie and finally out the door.

He's leaning against the porch wall when Helen and Charlie get outside.

'I'm so sorry,' he says. 'I eh... it's all really innocent... it's...' he shrugs his shoulders.

'What are you sorry for?' Helen says, folding her arms.

Fitzpatrick stares at her, then eyeballs Charlie before repeatedly blinking.

'Huh?' he says. Helen looks back at Charlie and whispers a 'fuck sake'.

'What are you saying sorry for?' Charlie asks.

'I.... I... need to speak with a what's-it-called? A eh... someone who eh... a legal thing?'

'A lawyer?' Charlie steps forward so that he's shoulder-to-shoulder with Helen.

Fitzpatrick nods his head, burping quietly as he does so, then re-steadies himself against the porch wall in an effort to rid himself of the swaying motion that's going on inside his head.

'How much you had to drink?' Helen asks.

'Eh… few pints. Just a few. I'm not driving. I just live down… see that lane way over there?' he says, almost tripping over his own feet as he turns to point.

'We know where you live, Brother Fitzpatrick. We've just called by. A neighbour said we'd find you here.' Fitzpatrick turns back slowly. 'Now before we tell you why we're here, mind telling us why you feel you need a lawyer… why you are apologising to us?'

Fitzpatrick tries to focus on both faces by repeatedly blinking again.

'I think I need a lawyer,' he says.

Helen holds her fingers to her forehead and stares down at her red Converse trainers.

'We don't have time for a lawyer,' she says, 'and we don't have time to deal with, well… whatever it is you are sorry about. We believe two of your students are in grave danger tonight and we need to track them down as quickly as possible.'

She looks up to see Fitzpatrick readjust his standing position, a hint of relief causing his brow to straighten.

'Oh,' he says. 'Students? Which students?'

'That's what we need to find out,' Charlie says.

'Brother, we need you to look at this image and tell us if you know who this boy is,' Helen clicks her fingers as she's finishing her sentence. But when she looks at Charlie, she notices he has missed his cue again. He fumbles into his pocket, grabs his phone and thumbs through the screen until he comes to the fuzzy CCTV image.

Helen takes the phone from him and stretches it towards Fitzpatrick's face.

Fitzpatrick squints, then blinks, before moving even closer to the phone and blinking again.

'Shurr what am I looking at here? I just see black and white,' he says, his glazed eyes narrowing.

Helen peers around at the phone, then points her finger at the screen.

'This, here... this boy... can you make out the face? Do you know who he is?'

Fitzpatrick blinks some more, then falters his step backwards, so that he's leaning against the wall again.

Helen puffs out a sigh and hands the phone back to Charlie.

'Back in a sec,' she says. She opens the door to the bar and holds up her hand.

'Pint of tap water, please. Cold... lots of ice.'

The barman grabs at a glass, then turns to the tap.

'Actually, make it two glasses,' Helen says.

'Brother Fitzpatrick okay?' the barman asks.

'He will be in a minute.'

The barman shovels ice cubes into both glasses, then hands them over to Helen who mutters a 'thanks' before storming back outside.

'Brother Fitzpatrick?' she says approaching him quickly. When he looks up at her, she flings her wrist, drenching his face.

'Sweet Jesus, Mary and—'

'Joseph,' Helen says, finishing his blessing for him. 'Here's another glass, Brother Fitzpatrick; drink it up, sober up and take another look at this image. Two of your students are in grave danger and the clock is ticking. There's no time for messing about.'

Fitzpatrick swipes at his face, removing as much water as he can. Then he holds out his hand, takes the full pint glass from Helen and swigs on it, slowly at first, then gulping until the ice rattles back into the glass.

'Now let's try again, Brother,' Helen says, clicking her fingers. Charlie reads her cue this time. 'I need you to look closely at this image and tell me if you know the boy in it.'

Charlie stretches the phone towards Fitzpatrick who wipes at his eyebrows before inching his nose closer. Then he begins to nod his head very slowly.

'Yeah. I know him. He's one of ours,' he says. 'Tommy Smith. He has some funny nickname they all call him... can't quite remember it. All the boys have weird nicknames. But yeah... that's definitely him. Little Tommy Smith. He lives in one of those bungalows up at the Harold's Cross Bridge.'

21:20

Ingrid

I PUSH MY FINGER INTO THE CORNER OF MY EYE TO TRY TO stop a tear from falling out.

Harriet kneels down, wraps her arms around me and I lean my ear on the top of her head, looking up at Ciara. She widens her eyes. I know she's feeling scared; scared that I will say too much and let Harriet change my mind.

'Boys are feckin' eejits,' Harriet says into my chest. She pulls away from me and looks into my eyes. 'Honestly, don't let this little fecker bring you down. You're better than that.'

She's right. I am better than that. I know I am. It's just... nobody else does; certainly nobody at school. And nobody at home. They all treat me as if I'm a bother to them. Or I certainly feel as if I am a bother to them. The only people who have ever treated me as I should be treated are in this little bedroom right now. These two and Miss Moriarty... that's it. One friend. One cousin. One old teacher. I realised this morning as I was lying on my bed just how sad that is.

'Y'know what I've been thinking about lately?' Harriet says, getting to her feet before she plonks down on to the bed, pushing herself back so she's lying, her legs hanging off the edge. 'Girls don't need boys; women don't need men. They just don't understand us. Never will. Besides, what the hell do boys offer the world anyway? We're the ones who do everything. We do all the housework, all the cooking, all the... we give birth. A man can't give birth, can he? All he can do is offer sperm and sure d'ye know what I read in a book once? There's loads of sperm stored in hospitals and stuff, so much so that men are useless to women. The world doesn't need 'em anymore.'

She twists the back of her neck, so that she can look up at us. I don't like the word sperm. It sounds horrible.

'Lie down, girls, let me tell yis something.'

I push out my bum, then lay my back down so that I'm lying in between Harriet and Ciara; all of us gripping our hands behind our heads and staring up at the cool posters on Harriet's ceiling. *Moseley Shoals* the one I'm staring at reads. Whatever the hell that means. I just know that it's cool. It must be if Harriet likes it.

'With me and Conor, even though it was me who dumped him, it still hurts me a lot. I'm not really sleeping that well at night; find meself thinking about him all the time. But I'll get over it. I know I will. Because the books I read... they tell me that I don't need a boy to make me happy. Here...' she says, stretching her arm towards her windowsill. She grabs one of the books and then lays it on my stomach. '*Backlash* it's called,' she says. 'Give it a good read. S'all about how women are going to take over the world. Feminism... ye know what that means?'

She lies back down after asking this, back in to the same position she was in seconds ago; her legs dangling, her fingers gripped behind her head.

'About female-something?' Ciara says, leaning up on her elbows.

'Yep,' Harriet replies. 'All about how women are better

than men and that, y'know, we don't need them. Feminism…
the movement for women to become king.'

'Cool,' I say, before turning my face to look at Ciara. She
raises an eyebrow, then shrugs her shoulder. I turn my face,
so I'm staring at the posters again. 'You're into the coolest
stuff, Harriet,' I say. 'Wish I could be more like you.'

Harriet laughs out through her nose.

'No you don't. Jaysus, I wish I was like *you*. Any idea how
much the boys are gonna be swarming over you when you're
older? You're gonna be a model, just like yer mam.'

Ciara sits up.

'But sure, what's the advantage of being pretty and getting
all the men if we don't need men?' she says.

That's actually a good question.

Harriet tilts her neck so she can stretch her eyes to meet
ours.

'Exactly,' she says.

Ciara stares down at me, her eyebrow raised again. I don't
think she's getting what Harriet is trying to say. I'm not sure
I get it either.

'Ah, you're too intelligent for us two, Harriet,' I say.

'You'll understand when you're older. Read these kinda
books. They'll open your eyes.' She pats the book that's lying
on my stomach.

So I pull myself up to a seating position and look at the
front cover.

'*Backlash: The Undeclared War Against American Women*…
hmmm,' I say and then I begin to flick through it. It's a long
book. Very long. And the writing is really small in it. I can't
imagine I'd ever read a book like this.

'The first chapter is called 'Blame it on Feminism,' I say.
'What's that mean…? I thought you said feminism was a good
thing?'

'Huh?' Harriet says, sitting up. She takes the book from

me and begins to read through the chapter. 'Ah… it's just some women think the feminism movement goes too far.' Then she hands me the book again and lies back down. 'It's a warzone out there,' she says. 'But the truth is, we have to be strong. Everyone has to be strong. Especially women, though. Men have ruled the world for far too long and all they want from us is food and sex.'

I turn my face to look at Ciara again. She squidges up her nose. And so do I. I always feel uneasy when the word sex comes up.

'Sorry,' Harriet says. 'Some of the subject might be a little… what's-the-word… mature for your age. But the sooner you learn all about this stuff, the stronger you'll become. Do ye think you need that… *strength?*' she asks.

I look over at her. She's just staring up at the ceiling, waiting on my answer.

'I'd love more strength,' I say. I feel Ciara nudging me in the back but I ignore it. 'How do I get more strength?' I ask.

Harriet stretches her neck again to look up at me.

'Read that book… and all these kinda books,' she says nodding her head towards her windowsill. 'They'll help you understand what life is all about. And how you'll find that the small things such as some little tosser calling you Fishfingers is so insignificant.'

I sit up straighter and run my finger down the front cover of the book. That's interesting. If reading this book means it won't hurt me anymore when somebody calls me Fishfingers surely I should just try to read it.

'Do you wanna take that one home with you?' Harriet asks.

I sniff through my nose, then find myself nodding my head.

'Yeah… yes. I'd love to. Thanks, Harriet.'

21:25

Harriet

I stare up at my crappy posters, my hands creating a little pillow for the back of my head.

'You're into the coolest stuff, Harriet,' Ingrid says. *Jaysus. Cool? Me? If only.* 'Wish I could be more like you.'

I laugh.

'No you don't. Jaysus, I wish I was like *you*,' I say. 'Any idea how much the boys are gonna be swarming over you when you're older? You're gonna be a model, just like yer ma.'

Ingrid isn't gorgeous yet. She's pretty, definitely. But it's so obvious that she *will* be stunning when she grows up. When she grows into her nose, when she develops her body shape, when her eyebrows thicken. Every bloke in school will regret the day they didn't find her attractive. Whoever this Stitch guy is; he's gonna be pulling the mickey off himself thinking about Ingrid in a few years' time. And he won't be able to touch her. She'll be way out of his league by then.

'But sure, what's the advantage of being pretty and getting all the men if we don't need men?' Ciara asks me.

I look back her.

'Exactly,' I say. My answer doesn't mean anything. But I

hope it's enough to shut her up. I don't need her testing me on my beliefs. Because I don't even know what my beliefs are. I'm a bullshitter. Always have been. If I'm good at anything — and I'm not good at much — it's pretending I'm somebody I'm not. I constantly bluff. Constantly make up who I am. What I stand for. I try to be cool. But there's absolutely feck all cool about me. These books... these posters... my nose ring... my clothes... my CD collection.... it's all bollocks. I've never even listened to a full Oasis album in my life. I don't even know who Kurt Cobain is. Give me a Take That record any day of the week. But Jesus, I wouldn't let anyone know that's the kinda stuff I'm into. These posters, this whole room. It's just for show. It's just all about a person I want to be seen to be. It's not me.

'Ah — you're too intelligent for us two, Harriet,' Ingrid says.

'You'll understand when you're older. Read these kinda books. They'll open your eyes,' I lie, patting at the book I placed on her stomach. I've no idea what's inside that book. Never read it. Never read any of em.

She sits up and begins to run her finger down the front cover. It'll be fine if she asks me questions. Bullshitting to my little cousin is easy. It's the bullshitting to my mates that's difficult. I'm always paranoid that they'll see right through me; that they know I don't really know what feminism means, that they'll know I couldn't tell the difference between Liam Gallagher and Noel Gallagher if they were stood right in front of me.

'The first chapter is called 'Blame it on Feminism,' Ingrid says. 'What's that mean...? I thought you said feminism was a good thing?'

'Huh?' I say before swallowing hard. I sit up and stare at her eyes. It's always best to hold somebody's eyes when you are bluffing. I take the book from her. 'Ah... it's just that some women think the feminism movement goes too far,' I lie, then hand her the book back. 'It's a warzone out there. But the truth is, we have to be strong. Everyone has to be strong. Especially women, though. Men have ruled the world for far too long and all they want from us is food and sex.'

Shit. Maybe mentioning sex to my thirteen-year-old cousin wasn't cool. Jaysus, Aunt Greta would kill me if she knew I was talking about sex with her precious little Ingrid.

'Sorry,' I say. 'Some of the subject might be a little... what's-the-word... mature for your age. But the sooner you learn all about this stuff, the stronger you'll become. Do ye think you need that... *strength*?' I ask. It's a genuine question. Jees, I'd kill somebody for more strength. I'm so weak. Bizarrely weak. Always have been. People think I'm strong because I took over all of the women duties in the house after my mam died. All of our family and the neighbours kept telling me how strong I was. They'd no idea I was crying my little heart out every night. Still do sometimes. Have been for the past couple weeks since Conor dumped me. Fucker was seeing somebody else behind my back. I miss him like crazy.

'I'd love more strength,' Ingrid says. 'How do I get more strength?'

Jesus, Ingrid, I wish I knew.

'Read that book... and all these kinda books,' I say tilting my head towards my windowsill. 'They'll help you understand what life is all about. And how you'll find that the small things in life such as some little tosser calling you Fishfingers is so insignificant.'

That's actually not bad advice. Jaysus, if only I could listen to my own advice.

Ingrid sits up. I think she's intrigued by the book. I must be selling it well; even though I don't even understand what the title of that one means exactly.

'Do you wanna take that home with you?' I ask her.

'Yeah… yes. I'd love to. Thanks, Harriet.'

'No bother,' I say. And then I continue to stare up at these old posters on my ceiling. I get them out of *Rolling Stone* magazine. Seven quid every month that bastarding magazine costs me — just so I can continue to lie to everybody that that's the sort of shit I'm into. I don't know why I plaster my walls and ceiling in these posters, nobody really comes up to my room anymore anyway.

'Have you decided if you're going to college?' Ingrid asks.

Yep. I have decided. And no I'm not going. Can't afford to.

'Yeah… thinking about doing a course in music in Ballyfermot College. Supposed to be a really cool course there.'

I don't know why I've lied about that. She'll find out soon enough that I'm not going to college; that I've taken a shitty shelf-stacking job in the local supermarket for the summer. I just need to keep up the pretence that I'm cool; to Ingrid more than anyone. She looks up to me. It's nice to have somebody look up to you.

I'd love to go to college. But we need money coming into the house. Dad hasn't worked for years… over a decade. Not since mam died. He's on benefits. It's all we have to live on. Which is why paying seven quid on *Rolling* fucking *Stone* magazine every month makes absolutely no sense whatsoever. I'm a fuckin loser. Always have been.

'Yeah — you should totally study music,' Ingrid says. 'That'd be so cool. Everything you do is cool.'

CHARLIE HAS THE ENGINE REVVING, THE BLUE LIGHTS FLASHING and his finger resting on the switch to start the siren's wail by the time Helen has hobbled into the car. She started sprinting, as soon as she got the name of the boy from Brother Fitzpatrick but waned before she had even reached the laneway. From there, she slowed down — into a jog, then a trot — before she finally huffed and puffed herself into Charlie's passenger seat.

She twirls her hand in the air as soon as she's settled, signalling that Charlie should get going.

'Jesus; I'm wrecked,' Helen says, leaning her head back on the rest.

Charlie smiles on one side of his face then nudges the car into gear and speeds off.

'You're doing great, Detective,' he says. 'You were so right in thinking we should go to the local Headteacher first. That was genius investigating. Course the Headteacher would know all of the teenagers in the area.'

Helen nods.

'Wonder if the others have found out the name yet?' she says.

Charlie stares over at her as he nudges the stick into fifth gear, the car now speeding.

'Huh?'

'The others; the other dicks... Detectives. I wonder if they've managed to get the name yet... Tommy Smith.'

'Oh... yeah, lemme ring that in, in case we're ahead of them,' Charlie says.

He reaches for his car's radio but before he can lift the receiver, Helen's hand is on top of his.

'Let's look after our investigation first,' she says. 'We'll pass on all of our information once we've caught up with this fella.'

Charlie's eyes narrow, the nub of his nose so pronounced that it forms into a perfect square.

'Really?'

'Yeah... if they get to him before us, we'll never get a chance to speak to him. They'll be questioning him all about Keating. They'll take the wrong path. We need to get to him first and find out the name of these two girls without playing games with him. We'll pass the other dicks on any information we get after we've caught up with Smith first.'

She turns her face, to gauge Charlie's reaction. But he remains motionless and expressionless, his foot heavy on the pedal.

'Trust me,' she says, touching his shoulder.

'They might be ahead of us already, Helen,' Charlie says.

'Hopefully not.'

They both stretch their necks when they pull into the bungalows, on the lookout for any other blue flashing lights ahead.

'Nothing,' Charlie says, pulling the car over. 'Okay... where'll we start?'

Helen already has one foot out of the car by the time he's finished his question. She paces straight up to the nearest door and rattles her knuckles against it.

A middle-aged woman answers, holding a spoon in one hand and a cup-o-soup in the other.

'Jaysus, what's wrong?' she says, her eyes widening at the site of the police car in front of her home.

'Nothing, ma'am,' Helen says just as Charlie catches up with her. 'We are looking for the house Tommy Smith lives in… he's about fourteen or fifteen years old. You know that name?'

The woman tilts her chin upwards.

'Ah… not surprised you're looking for one of them,' she says. She looks up and down the street, then steps out of the house and whispers. 'They live in that one over there, the red door.' She nods her head across the narrow street.

'Thank you, ma'am,' Helen says turning back to see the woman closing her hall door without any further comment.

Charlie and Helen trot across the street, Charlie getting to the red door first. He holds the bell down and then stands back.

The door opens slowly after the person behind it has wrestled with an inordinate number of locks.

'Wha' d'yous want?' a rotund man with a strange neck tattoo asks.

'We need to speak with Tommy as soon as possible,' Helen barks.

'He's not 'ere.'

'Sir, we have reason to believe a couple of Tommy's friends are in grave danger—'

'I don't know anythin' about his friends.'

The man attempts to edge the door closed, Helen holding the palm of her hand against it to stop him.

'Sir… Mr Smith is it? Are you Tommy's father?'

The man puffs a sigh out of his nostrils.

'He's not here. What do yis want me to say?'

Charlie looks to Helen.

'Tommy! Tommy!' she roars, twisting her head so she can see beyond the man's round frame and into his home.

The man steps out.

'Will ye shut the fuck up, woman. Jesus. He's not here, I told ye. Stop causing a scene.'

Helen sighs.

'Where would he be, Sir? Two young girls' lives depend on it.'

The man squints a little.

'Wha' d'ye mean?'

'Two girls from Tommy's school are planning to die by suicide tonight. Tommy might hold the answer to where we can find them. We believe he knows them well.'

The man smiles a wide grin at Helen, then shifts his gaze to Charlie, the grin widening.

'That's a good un,' he says. 'Never had a cop use that kinda tactic before.'

'We're not making it up, Sir. We believe Tommy rang in calls to two Garda stations a couple hours ago suggesting two girls from his school were planning on killing themselves at midnight tonight. We have to find them.'

'Will ye get the fuck outta here... think I'm buyin' that shite?' The man laughs.

'Sir, we're not lying,' Charlie says as calmly as he possibly can. 'Where can we find Tommy?'

'Tommy doesn't hang around with girls... Jesus.'

'Sir, we need to find out where your son is.'

The man takes a step back, inching the door closed again. Helen holds her palm to it, but the man is unforgiving this time, forcing his body weight behind the door until it shuts tight. Helen balks back, shaking the strain from her hand.

'Fat fuck,' she whispers to Charlie. 'I knew as soon as he took an age opening all those locks that they were a dodgy family. Ye never get answers from a dodgy family. Ever.'

Helen sucks her lips, places her hands back in the pockets of her leather coat and then turns around.

'Over here,' she says.

Charlie follows her across the street, straight towards the door they had knocked on earlier.

'Jaysus, not letting me enjoy me supper this evening are yis, coppers?' the woman says, twirling her spoon in her cup-o-soup.

'You eh… you mentioned you weren't surprised when we told you we were looking for one of the Smiths. How come?' Helen asks.

The woman raises an eyebrow, then takes half a step outside her home and peers up and down the street again.

'Bunch o' weirdos,' she says. 'The oul fella's been in and out of prison I don't know how many times. The son's gonna be worse. Little scumbag he is.'

'Tommy.'

'Yeah… that's him. Comes and goes from that house at all times of the night and morning. I've heard him coming home, shouting and screaming, pissed as a fart at like four-five a.m. His parents don't give a shit.'

Helen inches closer to the woman.

'Ever seen Tommy palling around with girls?' she asks.

The woman sticks her bottom lip out, then slowly shakes her head.

'Nah… he hangs around with a load o' blokes his age. There's a big gang of em. About a dozen of em. They all hang around under the Harold's Cross bridge, swigging flagons of cider.'

Helen looks at Charlie.

'Do ye think that's where he'd be now?' she asks, turning back to the woman.

The woman sticks her bottom lip out again.

'It'd be my best guess.'

'Thank you, ma'am. You can eh… you can finish your soup now. Sorry to be a bother.'

Helen twists her neck sharply as a siren grows in the distance. Then she looks up at Charlie before pacing past him, into the middle of the road to stare up as much of it as possible. She makes out the familiar sound of the siren twirping to a stop.

'Guess we just about got here before them,' she says, turning back to Charlie. 'Now let's get to the bridge before them. We gotta talk to Tommy, we can't let them take control.'

'Really?' Charlie asks. 'Isn't it just a case of finding Tommy. Does it matter who gets there first?'

'Yes! Yes it does, c'mon?' Helen moans, pulling at the locked passenger car door. 'Charlie!'

Charlie doesn't answer her, he just stares at the cop car coming their way.

He bends down slightly as it passes; makes out a familiar figure in the driver's seat.

'A sergeant from my station. Louis Kavanagh. Know him?' he asks Helen.

Helen shakes her head.

'C'mon, Charlie. Honestly. We need to act fast.'

Charlie holds his hand up at Helen as he trots past her, towards the cop car that has pulled in.

'Charlie, how ye getting on?' Louis says, lifting his stocky frame out of the car and sticking his Garda hat over his ginger hair. All of the hair on Louis' head is ginger; his eyebrows, his eye lashes, even the loose strands that hang from his nostrils.

'Grand... grand... You here for Tommy Smith?' Charlie asks.

'Yeah... you too? You chasing down the caller?'

'Yep,' Charlie says, a touch of pride in his answer.

'How d'ye get here before me?'

'Myself and Detective Brennan over there — from Rathmines station — tracked him down. Soon as we saw the CCTV footage, we paid a visit to the local school's Headteacher.'

Louis nods his head.

'Good thinking.'

'He's not in. The father answered, wasn't willing to give us much, but a neighbour here behind us, she—'

'Evening, Sergeant,' Helen calls out, creeping up behind Charlie.

Louis stretches out a hand.

'Nice to meet you Detective Brennan,' he says. 'Good work so far. No sign of Smith at home, no?'

'We haven't laid eyes on him yet, but that's his house there. Red door. Maybe you can have more impact on the father than we've had. Best of luck. Let's go, Charlie.'

Charlie only moves after Helen has tugged at his elbow. He follows her to the car and, as they reach it, they both notice more blue lights flashing in the distance.

'Jaysus, they're all getting here now,' Helen says as they climb into their seats.

Charlie turns the key in the ignition and, as they pull off, Helen scoots down in her seat, her eyeballs soaking in each of the figures in the two Garda cars that pass. In the second car she notices Eddie, and scoots down even further, pulling the collars of her coat over her cheeks.

'Right... come on, Charlie, let's go visit that bridge. It's not far from here.'

Charlie flicks on the lights, and edges his way out of the narrow estate.

'What's with you, Helen?' he asks.

'Whatcha mean?'

'Why are you being all secretive with the other cops? What's going on?'

Helen sits more upright, flattening down the collar of her coat.

'It's just… well, it's two separate investigations. We need clarity and full focus on our investigation, don't we? We can't get derailed by theories that the phone call was made as a hoax distraction.'

Charlie flicks his eyes to the rear-view mirror.

'It must be a hoax distraction, though,' he says, taking his hand from the gear stick so he can point his thumb backwards. 'Sure the whole bloody force is out chasing Tommy Smith because they think he has links to Alan Keating. It's only me and you that seem to think his phone calls were a suicide warning.'

Helen coughs into her clenched fist.

'Exactly,' she says. 'That's why we have to conduct our investigation separately. Let them conduct theirs and we'll keep focused on ours.'

Charlie pivots his neck from side to side, producing tiny bone cracks.

'Suppose you're right,' he says. 'It's cool though isn't it? All of them; only two of us. Yet we're always one step ahead. You'll turn me into a Detective by the end of the night, Helen.'

Helen laughs, only because she is relieved that she's managed to pull Charlie back around to her way of thinking.

'Well… it'll only be a success if we save these girls,' she says. 'Remember; focus, Charlie. I enjoyed the thrill of the chase when I first started investigating too. But you'll come to learn you are focusing your energy in the wrong places when you let the thrill get the better of you.'

Charlie turns to Helen.

'Thank you. You've been great to learn from this evening. Think you eh... think you could let me take you out for a coffee sometime. Just so I can pick your brain about how I can become a Detective? I'm bloody sick of sitting in the station filling out paperwork.'

Helen snuffs out another laugh. Not many would understand Charlie's frustration with administrative work more than her. Her career's gone in the opposite direction. From top Detective back down to envelope stuffer. She lost the run of her mind after Scott died by suicide. Could never get her head back on the job. Eddie had stronger mentality. Still does. He managed to get himself back to the station a month after Scott and his mates ended their lives. Five years later, after he became the station's superintendent — and after much nagging from his wife — he made sure she got a job as administrative assistant. Mainly because he could keep an eye on her. Helen always said it was for the short-term. Even suggested that she'd open her own private investigator practice one day; Eddie knocking her back insisting those guys don't make any money. It caused quite an awkward argument between them earlier this year when one PI managed to secure himself a million euro house for five hours work in Dublin. Still, Eddie knew she'd never carry through her threat. He knows Helen wouldn't have the know-how to run her own business.

'Course, no problem. We can do coffee anytime you want,' Helen says.

Charlie is smiling to himself when he's pulling the car over on the double yellow lines that run parallel to the canal.

They both get out as quickly as they can, trotting their way to the steps that lead to the under path of the bridge.

By the time they're at the bottom step, they can hear the giddy laughter of teenagers.

Charlie reaches for his torch, flicks it on and shines it towards the narrow pathway in front of Helen. They can both see the butts of joints being tossed into the canal as they approach.

'What the fuck do you pigs want?' one teenage boy calls out.

21:35

Ciara

ME AND HARRIET ARE STILL LYING BACK ON THE BED, OUR hands behind our heads, staring up at posters of bands and movies I've never even heard of.

But Ingrid is sitting up now, flicking through the book Harriet handed to her a couple minutes ago. She just said she'd love to take it home with her. Bleedin' hell! She better not be serious. I knew coming to Harriet's wasn't a good idea. I'll go mad if Ingrid decides to put our pact on hold just so she can read that stupid book. It's all nonsense anyway. As if women will ever rule the world. I like Harriet and all, but sometimes the things she says don't make any sense to me at all. I think she thinks she's cleverer than she really is.

I sit up and stretch my hand towards Ingrid.

'Gis a look,' I say.

I take the book from her and flick through it myself, pretending that I'm interested. Jaysus... Ingrid won't read this. It's way too long.

'What time's it?' I ask.

'Coming up to twenty to ten,' Harriet says. 'Jee... it's almost my bedtime. I normally turn in about ten. How come you guys are out so late? Don't ye have school in the morning?'

I stay silent to see if Ingrid will answer. But she just continues to stare at the ceiling.

'Eh... yeah,' I say. 'Yeah we do. I actually didn't realise it was that late. We better get going. Ingrid just wanted to drop by... to let you know about Stitch.'

Harriet tuts.

'Fuck Stitch,' she says, sitting up to join us. She smiles at Ingrid. 'I know Aunt Greta would go mental if she knew I was cursing to ya. But I mean it. Fuck him. He's gonna be way beneath you in a couple years time.' She places her hand on Ingrid's shoulder and rubs it. 'You sure you're okay, cuz?'

Ingrid turns her head slowly towards me.

'She's fine,' I say quickly. 'She'll be okay in the morning.'

'I don't wanna go to school,' Ingrid says, holding her hands to her face.

I reach out and rub her back.

'Everything will be okay, Ingrid,' I say.

'Course it will. Listen to Ciara. What she's saying is right,' Harriet says. I smile a tiny smile over Ingrid's shoulder at Harriet. 'You walk into that school tomorrow with your head held high and a 'fuck you Stitch' attitude, you hear me? That's what I've had to do since me and Conor finished. You just have to get on with it. You've a long life to live.'

I cough to distract the conversation. I don't like where it's going again. I don't trust Ingrid to not break down and open up to Harriet about not wanting to live any more. I nudge at her back and keep doing it until she's got to her feet.

'I guess we better go,' she says, staring at the ground.

'Here, don't forget the book,' Harriet says, stretching over to where I'd almost hidden it under her pillow. She hands it to Ingrid who grabs it into her chest. 'If you have any questions on it, let me know... won't you?'

Ingrid sniffs up her nose and then nods. I can tell she's almost in tears. This is her hardest goodbye of them all. She loves Harriet. But as I said to her last night, Harriet is not enough reason for Ingrid to stay alive. Harriet will move on soon; to college, to a job, to a husband with kids. She's not going to have time for Ingrid forever. Barely has time for her now. They used to be in each other's lives a lot more when they were younger. Now they only see each other if Ingrid ever bothers to call out here.

'You sure you're okay, cuz, you look like you're about to cry again?' Harriet says.

Then she stands up and rests both of her hands either side of Ingrid's waist. I've already inched my way towards Harriet's bedroom door. We really need to leave.

I watch as Ingrid nods her head before she nestles it onto Harriet's shoulder. Harriet looks over at me, her bottom lip turned outwards.

'I'm telling ya,' she says, 'in a couple months' time you won't care who this Stitch bloke is. It'll only hurt for a little while. It's a little bit of heartbreak... that's all. The heart mends.'

Ingrid wipes the sleeve of her tracksuit top across her face.

'It's... it's.... it's not just that,' she sobs. 'It's not just Stitch.'

Oh bleedin' hell!

'Huh?' Harriet says, removing Ingrid's arm from her face. 'Tell me... you can say anything to me... what's wrong?'

A creak sounds from outside, then a huff and a puff. It's Brendan, making his way up the stairs. He enters the room next to us, the latch on the door locking.

'Tell me, cuz, what's wrong?'

'It's nothing,' I say, walking towards them both. 'It's the whole school thing... how everybody will be calling her

Fishfingers in the morning. But don't worry, Harriet... I'll look after her. I promise.'

Harriet offers me a sad smile, then she turns to face Ingrid again.

'You sure, Ingrid? Is there anything else you want to say to me?'

Ingrid opens her mouth.

Then we hear an almighty fart. As if thunder is rolling over our heads.

21:40

Ingrid

THIS IS THE HARDEST GOODBYE YET. I CAN'T STOP THE TEARS from pouring out of my eyes. And out of my nose. I didn't think it would be this hard.

Harriet hugs me and tells me everything will be alright. Again.

'I'm telling ya,' she says, 'in a couple months' time you won't care who this Stitch bloke is. It'll only hurt for a little while. It's a tiny bit of heartbreak... that's all. The heart mends.'

I wipe my face clear of the tears and snot and then nod my head.

'It's... it's…... it's not just that,' I say. 'It's not just Stitch.'

Maybe I shouldn't be saying this. Ciara will be hopping mad behind me. I know she will. I still want to do it... commit suicide. I think I do anyway. But I really wouldn't mind talking to Harriet, just to get a different opinion. She's so intelligent, so cool. She might understand why I hate the thought of being called Fishfingers for the next six years. She might understand that I feel like I'm bothering Mum and Dad if I tell them I feel sad.

'Huh?' Harriet says, taking my hand away from my face. 'Tell me... you can say anything to me... what's wrong?' I hold my eyes closed and nod my head, as if I'm telling myself I shouldn't say what I want to say.

'It's nothing,' Ciara interrupts. I knew she would. 'It's the whole school thing... how everybody will be calling her Fishfingers in the morning. But don't worry, Harriet... I'll look after her. I promise.'

I swallow hard. I'm not sure if I'm grateful for the interruption or not. My mind is too... too full; full of horrible thoughts; full of sadness; full of disappointment; full of fear. But that's why I want to die, isn't it? I want my mind to stop feeling all these bad things all the time.

'You sure, Ingrid? Is there anything else you want to say to me?' Harriet says.

I suck up a sob, and as I'm doing so, I decide I'll tell her; tell her that I'd rather die than feel the way I do. Then, just as I'm about to open my mouth, I hear a huge fart — like one of those crackling fireworks. It goes on and on.

I laugh, and as I do, my tears spray onto Harriet's face.

She falls back onto the bed, her hand over her mouth, doing her best to not laugh too loudly. I look behind, through my tears, and notice Ciara has slidden down the wall. She has her knees up beside her ears, her face buried behind them, her shoulders shaking. Squeals of laughter are squeaking out of all three of us. Then another fart comes; not so loud this time, more a splat. And suddenly I'm on my knees, holding my lips closed as tightly as I can so no more squeals of laughter can sneak out.

Then Uncle Brendan lets out a gasp and I am certain I am about to wet my knickers. Ciara can't hold it in anymore either. Her laughter gets loud. Harriet rises from the bed, her face purple, her eyes tightly closed, tears glistening on the edges of them and she begins to wave her hand at Ciara —

trying to get her to shut up. But she can't. Ciara is flat on the floor now, on her stomach, laughter roaring from her. Then my dam bursts too; my lips ripping open and laughter pouring out. I fall flat onto my belly and begin banging my fists on the carpet.

'Bleedin' hell!' Ciara says, in between gasps.

I manage to suck in some air and fill my cheeks, to try to stop the laughter and return to normal. I look up at Harriet and see her drying her eyes with her poncho.

'He always does that!' she whispers to me. 'He doesn't know how loud he is.'

My lips blow out more laughter. I'm getting scared now, as if I'm gonna suffocate and die right here, right now. Jesus. Wouldn't that be a lovely way to go? Ciara has researched suicide for so long now that she came up with the quickest and least painful way for us to do it, but I bet she never thought about dying of laughter.

I manage to slow down my breathing and finally sit up, resting my back against the bed. Ciara does the same, then grips my elbow and when I turn to her she winks at me.

'Jesus, Harriet, why did you choose the bedroom closest to the toilet?' Ciara asks, a ripple of laughter still squeezing out of her mouth.

Harriet dabs at her eyes again.

'The house is tiny, all of the bedrooms are close to the toilet,' she answers as she steadies herself to stand. 'I'm so sorry, girls. That's so embarrassing.'

'Jesus, don't be silly,' Ciara says. 'All men are the same. I wonder if it talks about men's pooing habits in your books?'

The three of us laugh again, but a normal laugh this time; one we are certain we can recover from.

'Well there ye go,' Harriet says. 'There's your recipe for getting over Stitch, huh? Your uncle having a noisy shit.

You've gone from crying to laughing in a split second. Told ye pain doesn't last long.'

I reach out and hug her again. She grips me tight.

'Here, take this,' she says, handing me the book. 'Read it and get back to me. If you ever need an ear, phone me. Or drop by. Anytime. Both of you.'

I shake my head, nuzzle it onto her shoulder and breathe in her hair.

'Love you, cuz,' I say.

She leans off me and stares into my eyes.

'Not like you to say "I love you",' she smiles. 'But I love you too. Always have, Ingrid. I'll see you soon, yeah?'

I nod my head; not sure whether I'm lying to her or not. Then I hold her book close to my chest and watch as she hugs Ciara.

'Actually, tell you what... Dad! Dad!' Harriet shouts over Ciara's shoulder.

'Gimme a sec!' he calls out from the toilet.

To stop myself from laughing again, I stroll around the room, pull at a little drawer below Harriet's CD player and flick through her CDs. She strolls over towards me and pushes it closed.

'Dad!' she shouts again.

'Jesus. I'm trying to wipe me arse!' he says. The three of us laugh again. Out loud. Not minding that he hears us this time.

'I'm just wondering if you can drop the girls home? It's late. Ten to ten. Do you mind?'

'No, no... Jesus no,' Ciara butts in.

'It's no problem. Any excuse to get him out of the house. Sure, it's only a ten minute drive... he'll be fine.'

Uncle Brendan sighs.

'Go on then,' he says. Then the toilet flushes and the bathroom door opens. 'Let me get me shoes on.'

'Uncle Brendan,' I call out, opening the door of Harriet's bedroom. He's stopped at the top of the stars, is staring over his shoulder at me. I pause before saying anything — not because I don't know what to say, but because the stench from the toilet has just reached my nose.

'Doesn't matter... Uncle Brendan. Thank you. We'd appreciate the lift. We'll be down in a second.' I say all that in one breath, then close Harriet's bedroom door.

'Oh my God, the stink,' I whisper.

Harriet and Ciara laugh. I don't. It's hard to laugh when you're pinching your nostrils and holding your lips tight together.

Eventually I let go and puff out a breath.

'Okay — I guess we better go now,' I say. I hug Harriet again and thank her for the book.

As me and Ciara are walking down the stairs, she begins to strike up some sort of argument without saying anything. She's speaking with her hands, her face all creased up in that angry way she gets sometimes. I'm not sure if she's giving out about me for taking the book or whether she's angry that Uncle Brendan is going to give us a lift. Maybe it's both. Or maybe she feels I've changed my mind — that I'm not going to follow through on our pact.

I just hug the book a little tighter to my chest and ignore her.

HELEN STRIDES IN HER OWN UNIQUE WAY — POKER STRAIGHT, arms in pockets — towards the group of teenagers as Charlie, close behind, shines his torch over her shoulder.

'Which one of you is Tommy Smith?' she asks.

She notices their heads spin and murmurs spark amongst them, echoing off the dome wall under the bridge.

'Which one of you is Tommy Smith?' she asks again, this time more direct.

'We don't talk to pigs,' a boy with bad acne says. He's a lot taller than the others around him, though Helen notes he can't be much older than them. They all look to be in their mid-teens, maybe even a year or two younger.

Helen sniffs her nose and then takes a large stride forward, so that she's only inches from the group. She isn't afraid of much. Except for water. Would go into a full blown panic if this confrontation got heated and she somehow found herself in that canal.

She takes in each face in front of her; eight boys, three girls.

'We have reason to believe two of your friends may be in

grave danger. We're not looking to cause any trouble; we're only here to help save lives. You can keep drinking your cider, keep smoking that cheap weed. All I want is to speak to Tommy. Now... which one of you is Tommy?'

'He's not here,' the smallest of the girls says.

'Shurrup, Audrey,' the boy with the acne says. 'We don't talk to pigs.'

Audrey takes a step behind her friend to try to stifle her embarrassment by hiding her face.

Helen looks back at Charlie, then turns to the group again.

'Thank you, Audrey. Listen, guys, we're not here to disturb your evening. We have good reason to believe two girls, of about your age, will die tonight if we can't get to them first. Tommy knows who they are, and where they are. We need to speak with him as soon as possible.'

The boy with the acne takes a step closer to Helen, then sniffs his nose as loudly as he can before folding his arms and standing more upright.

'I get it,' Helen says, 'you don't speak to pigs.' She strains her neck, so she can peer past him. 'What about the rest of you?'

'We don't believe you,' another boy shouts.

Helen takes her hands out of her pockets and holds her palms up.

'I am not lying. I swear to you. To each of you. We just need to speak to Tommy for two minutes, then we'll be on our way.'

The boy with the acne sniffs his nose loudly again. No noise comes from the gang behind him.

Helen fidgets with her fingers, then sucks on her lips.

'Okay... let me ask you this. Do any of you know of any girls from the area or from your school who you feel might be tempted to commit suicide? It's imperative you tell us. We need to save their lives.'

The boy with the acne looks behind him. Then he turns back to Helen and sniffs his nose again.

Helen runs a hand through the back of her orange hair, scrunching it up in frustration.

'You're a funny looking pig aren'tcha?' the boy with the acne says. 'And you... you with the torch, ye look like a bleedin' rat. All that's missing is the whiskers.'

An echo of laughter sounds around them. Helen eyeballs as much of the group as she can, noticing that the cowering Audrey is the only one not finding acne boy particularly funny.

'How old are you, Audrey?' Helen asks.

Audrey's eyes go wide at the mention of her name, then she stares down at her Nike trainers.

'Well, if you're not gonna tell me, maybe I should guess,' Helen says. 'Thirteen? Fourteen? Well, the two girls who we believe are going to harm themselves tonight are your age. I don't suppose one of em is you, is it?'

Audrey looks up, then shakes her head rapidly.

'Shurrup, Audrey,' the boy with the acne says. 'Don't tell these pigs nuttin.'

Helen looks back to Charlie again and sighs. He takes a step forward, shining the torch in the boy's acne-ridden face.

'You're hardly one for judging people's looks, young man,' he says. 'Now, the rest of you listen up. Two girls' lives are in the balance here. We are not looking for any information other than where we can find Tommy Smith so he can give us the name of these girls. Which one of you is Tommy Smith?'

'He's not here,' a boy from the back calls out. 'He don't hang round here no more. Hasn't hung with us in months. He fucked off with another bunch of mates.'

Charlie nods.

'Thank you. Now, can you tell me where I *can* find him? Where does he hang out with these new mates?'

The group fall silent again. Charlie pivots his wrist, so he can shine the torch in to each of their faces. Every time a face lights up, its eyes look down. They don't want to talk.

'You're only thirteen, right?' Helen says stepping in front of Charlie and staring at Audrey.

Audrey shakes her head.

'Fourteen?'

Audrey nods.

'Okay then… you are under arrest for underage drinking, you are coming with us.'

'Hold the fuck on,' the boy with the acne says, holding his hand in front of Helen.

Helen eyeballs him, the two of them having a staring competition in front of the group of teenagers, torchlight shining between them.

'You wanna be done too for assaulting a police officer?' Helen asks after the staring match has carried on for way too long.

The boy removes his hand and Helen holds hers out to Audrey.

'C'mon, Audrey, you're coming with us.'

'Why y'only pickin' on her… we're all drinking, we're all smoking joints?' one of the boys asks.

Helen coughs into her hand.

'Audrey here confirmed her age for me. You all wanna do the same? You all wanna come to the station with us?'

She looks around at the gang, hoping they all stay silent. Things would get a hell of a lot more complicated for Helen if they all admitted to being under age. If they all wanted to go to the station as a protest to support Audrey, Helen's plan would fall apart. She nods at the silence. Relieved.

'Good,' she says. 'We only need to formally address Audrey. We'll have her back with you in a few minutes.'

Helen stretches her hand further. Audrey creeps out slowly from behind her friend and then walks towards the torchlight and out from under the bridge; Charlie in front of her, Helen behind her.

'Fuckin pigs,' one of the gang shouts out.

Charlie leads both Audrey and Helen up the steps and towards his Garda car. He holds the top of Audrey's head as she bends into the back seat and then Helen walks to the other side of the car, gets into the back seat too.

'You can go back under the bridge,' she says, 'back swigging your cheap cider in a couple minutes, Audrey. I just have a couple of important questions I need to ask you.'

Audrey nods her head, and then eyeballs Helen before staring over at Charlie who has just got himself into the driver's seat. Her knees are shaking.

'Two girls' lives are in danger, so I need you to be totally honest with me. I don't care if you are drinking cider and smoking weed, I don't care if Tommy Smith is from a family of scumbags who have been in and out of prison. Honestly, whatever you or any of your mates have done in the past, I couldn't give two shits about it. All I want to do tonight is save these girls' lives.'

Audrey nods her head and swallows at the same time.

'Do you know of any girls who might want to harm themselves tonight?'

Audrey's shoulders hunch up, then down.

'No,' she says. Helen squelches her face up in disappointment. 'I'm being honest. No. I don't know any girls who would commit suicide.'

'Okay. Where can we find Tommy Smith? He holds the key to us tracking these two girls down. We need to find him.'

Audrey allows a light sigh seep its way out of her nostrils.

'Ye can't tell him I told yis where he hangs out,' she says.

Helen shakes her head.

'We won't.'

'He eh... he's started to hang around with some older blokes. I don't know who they are. But I think they mostly hang around the snooker hall in Terenure, ye know it?'

Helen looks at Charlie.

'Yeah, I know it,' Charlie says. 'It's called Cue, right?'

Audrey nods her head. She looks disappointed in herself; as if she's revealing some dark secret she swore she'd never tell.

'It's all okay, Audrey. We aren't looking to arrest Tommy for anything. Our only concern is saving the two girls,' Helen reminds her.

'Really? Yis aren't messing with me? This is really about two girls committing suicide?'

Helen places a curled finger under Audrey's chin and lifts it so that she can stare into her eyes.

'I promise,' she says. 'Now do you think Tommy will be in Cue right now?'

Audrey raises an eyebrow, then shakes her shoulder towards Helen.

'I assume so... it's where he normally is. But as I said, I don't really hang around with him anymore. He stopped hanging around with us months ago.'

'Do you go to the same school as Tommy?'

Audrey laughs through her nose.

'He doesn't go to school, are ye mad? Don't know when's the last time I saw him at school.'

'But you do go to St Joseph's School; Brother Fitzpatrick is your Headteacher, right?'

Audrey's eyes widen.

'Are the two girls from my school? Who are they?'

Helen removes her finger from underneath Audrey's chin.

'That's what we need to find out. Audrey... tell us, do you know of any girls from your school who you feel would put their lives in danger?'

Audrey holds her lips tight together, then begins to shake her head slowly.

'I'm sorry. I'd tell yis if I did. I want to help. I hope yis find these two girls, but I... I can't help ye. I can only tell ye where I think Tommy might be. Hopefully he can help yis.'

Helen squelches her face up again, then she takes out her phone to check the time. 21:56. Time is running out.

'D'you have Tommy's phone number?' she asks Audrey.

Audrey shifts her bum cheek off the seat and reaches into her back pocket. She scrolls through her screen, then turns it to face Helen. Helen reaches her finger towards it and presses at Tommy's name.

'Ah Jaysus, don't ring him from my phone,' Audrey says, 'he'll think I'm checking up on him.'

'Shush, shush,' Helen says, taking the phone and holding it to her ear. The ring tone dials, and dials... then cuts out. She sighs, then takes out her own phone and types in Tommy's number.

'He never bloody answers his phone anyway,' Audrey says.

'What do you think, Charlie?' Helen asks, placing her hand on his shoulder.

'If you've got his number and we have a location, let's get there,' he says.

Helen offers Audrey a thin smile.

'You're good to go.'

21:55

Ciara

'WHAT THE HELL IS GOING ON HERE?' I TRY TO SAY THROUGH my teeth — without moving my lips — as we get into the back of Brendan's car.

Ingrid just looks at me and then shakes her head.

Bleedin' hell. This is crazy! We're supposed to be going to Miss Moriarty's house to say our final goodbye. Not getting a bloody lift home from Brendan. Ingrid better not be changing her mind. I swear to God that if we don't go through with this tonight, I'll never be her friend again. She can't write a pact with me and then not follow through on it.

'Y'okay, girls?' Brendan says, turning to us in the back. 'What yis mumbling about?'

'Nothing, Uncle Brendan,' Ingrid answers, gripping that stupid book to her chest.

I eyeball her, but she doesn't turn to look at me.

'When you gonna have time to read that?' I whisper.

She shrugs her shoulder.

'Ingrid!'

She pulls a bizarre funny face at me, then nods her head towards Brendan.

'Shhh,' she says.

This is really frustrating. We can't even talk now. We gotta get out of this car. We gotta talk this out. I knew we shouldn't have gone to Harriet's. I knew she would say things that'd make Ingrid change her mind. That bleedin' book is doing my head in; she's hugging it as if it's just saved her life.

I reach for it, take it from her and then sigh as I open the first page.

'Load of shite,' I whisper to her.

She looks over at me for the first time since we got into the car and offers me that tiny half-smile she likes to do every now and then. I'm not sure what she means by it.

'Ingrid,' I whisper without moving my lips. 'You're not planning on reading this bleedin' thing, are you?'

She gives me that funny face again, then pushes her lips together to shush me.

I twist my neck to look out the back window.

'We're going in the wrong direction, we're supposed to be going to Miss Moriarty's,' I grind through my teeth.

'Jaysus, you two like whispering, don't yis?' Brendan says, twisting at his rear-view mirror. 'What yis talkin' about?'

'Don't worry, Uncle Brendan… it's just girlie talk,' Ingrid says.

'Talking about me, are yis? Let me guess. Yis heard me in the bathroom. I forgot yis were in Harriet's room.'

I laugh. As loudly as I can. So does Ingrid.

'I bloody knew it!' Brendan says. 'Listen, a man's gotta do what a man's gotta do.'

When I stop laughing I place my hand on Ingrid's knee. Then she places her hand on top of mine.

'We all do it,' I say to Brendan. And suddenly I feel a little bit more relaxed, even though we're heading in the wrong direction.

I stare out the side window and recognise where we are. The canal road.

'Brendan… if you don't mind, can you stop at the garage here at the next bridge, I need to pick up something before we go home?'

He sighs a little, then smiles back at me through the rear-view mirror.

'Go on… don't be long,' he says, clicking his indicator. He turns into the garage and parks up in one of the small spaces around the back.

I cock my head at Ingrid, telling her to follow me and we both get out and walk slowly towards the garage's shop entrance.

'What the hell is going on?' I say when we're out of sight of Brendan's car.

'What d'ye mean?'

'I know it's part of the pact that we can't ask each other if we're changing our minds or not… but you just better not be!'

Ingrid shrugs her shoulder again… then shakes her head.

'No… no, course not,' she says.

'Well what about this bloody thing?' I say, holding up the book.

Ingrid swipes the book from my hand, then stares at the front cover.

'Ingrid!' I shout.

She widens her eyes, shakes her head again.

'No, course I'm not gonna read it. I was just being nice to Harriet. She handed it to me… what was I supposed to do?'

I breathe out a happy breath. She *hasn't* changed her mind. We're still gonna do this. I think.

'It's just… I got the feeling you were changing your mind. You were all upset and then suddenly we're all rolling around Harriet's bedroom laughing our heads off. It frightened me a little. I thought just because your uncle had a shite that suddenly your life got better. I got worried when you took the book and when you accepted a lift from Brendan.'

She reaches out and rubs her hand up and down my arm.

'It's not like that, Ciara,' she says. 'I just wanted to be polite, y'know. I didn't want to tell my uncle I wasn't accepting his lift. And I didn't want to tell my cousin I didn't want to read her book. I was just being nice. Just being me.'

I breathe a happy breath again. I'm so happy; happy that Ingrid hasn't changed her mind; happy that our lives are nearly over.

'Okay... what we gonna do now?' I ask.

Ingrid squelches up her mouth, then shrugs her shoulders again. She's always been like this; crap at making decisions. I'm pretty sure I've made most of the decisions in her life for her.

'We gotta tell Brendan we don't want a lift home from him; tell him we'll be okay from here. Then we can catch a bus back towards Miss Moriarty's house. Here... leave the book in the car with him.'

Ingrid sucks air through her teeth, then breathes out slowly through her nose.

'Okay,' she says, 'I have an idea.'

22:05

Ingrid

IT WASN'T THE LAUGHING AT UNCLE BRENDAN HAVING A POO that was changing my mind. It was before that. It was Harriet talking to me, telling me we don't need men; telling me that I'd be stupid to allow Stitch to control all of my feelings; telling me that if I read her book then I might not feel stupid every time somebody calls me Fishfingers at school.

The pooing didn't change anything. All that did was make me laugh — really, really hard. Harder than I have laughed in ages.

Then, when the laughing stopped, I still had that pain in my belly; still had the dark thoughts going round and round in my head. That's the worst of it. When I return to the pain and to the dark feelings after they've gone away for a little while, that pain and those feelings always seem to be worse... deeper... heavier. It's like when I get high from laughing or something, the downer after that is so hard to take. It makes me think that I should never get high; that I should never laugh, never try to enjoy life. Because when I do, I know that coming down from that is painful. I could feel it as I was getting into Uncle Brendan's car. I was returning to sadness and heartache after laughing non-stop for two minutes. And it hurt. It hurt really bad.

That's why I agreed to commit suicide, I think. I can't even enjoy laughing for crying out loud. Why would I want to be alive?

'C'mon,' I say, dragging at Ciara's elbow. We both run into the tiny garage shop. 'Excuse me, do you have a pen I could borrow?' I ask the man behind the counter.

He stares at us, then points towards the Lotto stand at the end of the shop counter.

'Thank you,' I say. I turn to the tiny desk at the Lotto stand and open the book on top of it before snatching at a cheap pen that's attached to a small chain.

Ciara squints her eyes as I write.

I love you Harriet,

Ingrid. x

'Okay,' I say, slapping the book closed. 'Come on.'

We race each other out to the car.

'Here, Uncle Brendan, give this back to Harriet,' I say after I snatch the passenger door open. 'Tell her I'm sorry. We're eh… we're going to make our own way home from here, okay.'

'What… what are you talkin' about, girl?' he says.

'I'm sorry, Uncle Brendan; for getting you out of the house. And thank you for the lift this far. But… we're gonna go, okay?' I slam the door shut, then grip on to Ciara's hand and we leg it out of the garage courtyard as fast as we can.

'Ingrid! Ingrid!'

I hear Brendan roar after us but I just wave my hand in the air and keep running.

It's crazy that I feel happy. I've been at my happiest all day when I am certain I want to do it. And the great thing about feeling happy now — just before I kill myself — is that this time I know there's not going to be a come down. Because I'll be dead. I know that I am doing the right thing; that *we're* doing the right thing. All of this nonsense; the ups and downs, the stresses of school, the bullying, the heartache, the headaches... they'll all be gone soon. Gone forever.

'MIND IF I ASK YOU A QUESTION?' CHARLIE SHOUTS OVER THE siren.

Helen removes the tip of her thumb from her mouth.

'Of course.'

'You're a little bit nuts, aren't ye?' he says, his smile wide. He's starting to relax in Helen's company. Is really beginning to feel as if she's the one taking *him* for the ride... even though they're in his car. He believes she will foster him through to Detective status; help drag him from the dregs of administrative work.

Helen lifts her head, slowly — taking in what was just said to her — and then eyeballs Charlie, her stare a little hostile.

'Sorry. I mean. What I'm trying to ask is,' Charlie says, as he shifts awkwardly in his seat, 'Detectives... they have to be erratic, don't they? You have to go beyond the line in order to investigate properly, right?'

Helen squints at Charlie. He turns his face to her, then straight back out the windscreen. He's desperate to engage her in conversation, but is also juggling his concentration levels with speeding seventy miles per hour down the canal straight.

'Ye know…,' he says. 'The way you see on TV all these Detectives who go over the line to get what they want. You eh…' he takes his hand from the gearstick, scratches at his hair. 'You eh… you know the way you have kinda gone over the line; throwing the drink in Brother Fitzpatrick's face… being off duty and being a bit sneaky with your role in this investigation… and when you said to little Audrey back there that she was being arrested for underage drinking when she wasn't.'

Helen takes her eyes from Charlie and stares down at her lap.

'You gotta do what you gotta do in this job,' she says.

'So it is kinda like on TV? Like in *The Wire* or things like that; Detectives have to bend the rules?'

Helen sniffs.

'*The Wire*? Calm down, Charlie,' she says, her voice loud. 'All I did was splash a bit of water on a drunk man's face to sober him up.'

Charlie stiffens his grip on the steering wheel and holds a blink closed.

'Fuck sake, Charlie,' Helen roars.

Charlie swings the car away from a cyclist.

'Shit. Sorry. Sorry,' he says to Helen.

'Concentrate will you?' she barks.

Charlie puffs out his cheeks, then wipes at his brow, using the back of his hand.

'I was just… I was just trying to learn, that's all. I just really want to be a Detective.'

Helen wiggles her bum on the car seat into a more comfortable position and then flattens down the seatbelt over her shoulder.

'No harm asking questions, Charlie,' she says. 'You didn't

need to call me nuts is all.' Charlie turns to her, his mouth ajar. 'Just concentrate on the road for now,' she says, waving his face away.

They're almost there. At Cue. Helen had been thinking about how to play it with Tommy Smith before Charlie started shouting stupid questions at her over the blare of the siren. Tommy's family and friends didn't seem like the most welcoming bunch. It's unlikely he's going to be any different. The apple very rarely falls far from the tree. She'd been wondering if he'll want to talk to them at all; she's still coming to terms with somebody ringing in a suicide warning without giving any names. She was stewing — before Charlie asked if she was a "bit nuts" — the realisation that Tommy is more likely involved with gangland crime than he is some kind of good Samaritan concerned by the welfare of two girls from his school. Still, she isn't taking any chances. She knows this is the greatest opportunity she'll ever have of ensuring Scott didn't take his life in vain. Helen's awareness of suicide — and how those who commit suicide think — is what gave her the gut instinct to follow the phone calls up as legitimate. If she's right, and the rest of the Garda force is wrong, she'll be a hero in a multitude of ways. Her face would probably be splashed all over the newspapers. Might be invited on to *The Late Late Show* for an interview. Might even be offered her old role as a Detective back until Eddie finally decides to retire and whisk her away for her dream life in Canada.

'Here we are,' Charlie says, slowing down the car.

Helen looks out her passenger side window at graffitied shutters. Then she allows her eyes to flitter towards a red neon light above them.

'Cue', it reads, the 'e' flashing.

'Looks like a lovely place,' she says over the top of the car after they both get out. 'Kinda place I used to hang out in when I was a kid.'

Charlie puffs a laugh out.

'Told you you were nuts,' he says, before holding his hands up in mock apology.

Helen stops walking and stares at the back of Charlie's head. She's still wondering how to react to his quip when he spins to her again, his palms back up, his laugh loud.

'Cheeky bugger,' she says, mock swiping at his face. 'Jesus, you've grown in confidence over the past couple hours, huh? I couldn't get a word out of you earlier.'

Charlie's still laughing when he pushes at a door that provides entry to a narrow, steep staircase. The only light inside is coming from the top of the steps; an eerie bright red bulb that suggests there may be more than a game of snooker on offer upstairs.

'Creepy,' Charlie whispers as they take the first step. Each of the thirty-one steps creaks under their feet as they climb. When they reach the top, Helen bends down again, her hands on her knees.

'Nobody can say playing snooker isn't a work out if you're playing snooker in this kip,' she says, while trying to catch her breath.

Charlie laughs again; is really beginning to think this is the best shift of his career so far. He'll be glad of the experience, regardless of what the outcome is by midnight.

'This way,' he says to Helen when she stands back upright.

Charlie pushes at another door and the sound of nineties Brit Pop begins to crackle out of cheap speakers. He pauses at an empty bar, then rattles his knuckles against it.

'Hello?' he calls out.

Helen steps to the side, takes in the entire snooker hall. It's the first time she's been in one since she was a teenager. She does a quick calculation; two banks of eight tables.

Sixteen in all. Yet only two are in use right now. Two middle-aged men playing at the one closest to them. And a group of guys in the back corner. She thinks a couple of them are only teens. But they're too far away for her to be certain. So she squints up at the black and white monitor over the bar, at live CCTV footage of them, but that gives no clarity on whether a couple of them are young enough to be Tommy Smith or not.

'The guy running the place is down there,' one of the middle-aged men says to her.

Helen tilts her chin upwards, acknowledging the heads up. Then she begins to walk, in her own unique way, between the two banks of tables and towards the group.

'This way, Charlie.'

'Oi, oi,' a man sweeping his hand up and down a snooker cue says as he watches them approach. 'How can we help you, officers?'

'I'm Detective Brennan. This here is Officer Guilfoyle. We're looking for a boy we believe hangs out around here.'

The man takes a step towards them, resting the butt of his cue into the carpet.

'Who?' he asks.

'Tommy Smith.'

The man looks back over his shoulder at the group who are all perched on a bench that runs around the back corner of the hall. When he turns back, his bottom lip is sticking out, his head shaking.

'Never heard of him,' he says.

'Sir, we believe two young girls' lives are in grave danger. Tommy Smith can lead us to them. We need to speak with him as a matter of urgency.'

The man's cheeks rise high as he produces a fake grin.

'I'm serious, Sir. I don't want to speak to Tommy about anything other than the fact that he made calls to two Garda stations a few hours ago saying two of his friends are planning on dying by suicide tonight.'

The man's eyes narrow. Then he looks back over his shoulder again. Charlie tries to track his line of vision, to see who or what he's looking at exactly. There are only two in this gang who could possibly be Tommy Smith; only two of them look to be in the appropriate age range.

'Are either of you Tommy Smith?' he asks, stepping forward.

The two boys look at each other, then back at Charlie.

'Never heard of him,' they both say, almost in unison.

The man with the cue bends over the table, misses a red to the far corner pocket.

'Bollix,' he says, standing back up. 'Yis are putting me off my game. Do yis wanna have a game of snooker? Or...' he rolls his shoulders.

Charlie swallows, then looks over to Helen for support. He notices that she probably didn't hear what was said, is too busy sticking her nose into her phone. Then she holds the phone to her ear.

A ringing sounds out; an annoying tone that sounds more like a crackling vibration than an actual ringtone. It's coming from one of the teenage boy's jeans pocket.

Helen presses at her screen, hanging up the call, then takes a stride forward.

'Tommy, we need to speak with you right now!' she says.

Tommy pounces to his feet, races past Helen and through the two rows of snooker tables before reaching the top of the stairs.

22:25

Ciara

I SPIN THE BUS STOP TIMETABLE ROUND AND ROUND THE POLE after I've caught my breath back.

'It says there's one due at half ten, but ye can never really go by these things, can you?' I say to Ingrid.

She's got her arms folded and is leaning her back against the glass of the bus shelter.

'Nah… they just get here when they get here… normally two or three at the same time,' she says.

I stare down the road, waiting to see the light of a bus number coming towards us. Nothing.

It's starting to get cold, so I turn around and hug my best friend; for a bit of warmth more than anything. Ingrid rests her chin on my shoulder while I stare at a fuzzy reflection of myself in the glass of the shelter, neither of us saying a word.

It's mad that we're getting close to the last hour of our lives. I know it's sad that we feel we have to do this. But I feel happy because I *know* we're going to do it. Being alive might be good for some people, but it's never been for me. I was born into sadness… can't remember either of my parents laughing in our home. Not in each other's company anyway. No wonder I'm bleedin' miserable.

The only person I ever remember laughing in our house was Debbie. And now I know why. She was probably out of her face on cocaine. I can't believe it. She was the only adult who I ever felt really liked me, really. I'd no idea she was so stupid that she would take drugs. Doesn't matter anyway. Whether I saw cocaine or not in her house tonight, we were still going to do this; still going to end it all. I just never thought I'd end it all while not loving Debbie anymore. I guess you never really know people — even the ones you love the most. Makes me wonder if Miss Moriarty has any dark secrets.

'You think Miss will be happy to see us?' I ask, still staring at my reflection.

'She'll be wondering what the hell we're doing knocking to her house on a Sunday night but... yeah... she'll be happy to see us. She loved us.'

I nod my head.

'Our very last goodbye, huh?' I say. And then I feel Ingrid nodding her head on my shoulder.

Her nose sniffles. I bet she's crying. Her mind better not be bleedin' changing again. Wouldn't surprise me. The two of us were giggling our little heads off as we ran to the bus stop. It wouldn't be unusual for me to be crying straight after I've been laughing. I think depression works that way. Does for me anyway.

I lean off her, place my hands either side of her face.

'You okay, Ingrid?'

She smiles her eyes.

'Fine,' she says.

'You sure?'

She looks downwards, at our feet, and then nods her head again.

I put my hand under her chin and lift her face towards me.

'Ingrid.'

'Yeah — I'm fine,' she says, shrugging her shoulders.

'Just over an hour left. Quick visit to Miss Moriarty's, then a bus ride back to Rathmines…' I arch an eyebrow.

She nods again.

I grab her in for another hug; this time to feel her love as much as the warmth.

It was almost twelve hours ago that we came up with this plan. Around eleven o'clock last night. I'd never seen Ingrid so upset; had never seen anyone so upset. I couldn't stop her sobbing, no matter how hard I held her close to me. Her chest, her shoulders, her head — everything was shaking quicker than I ever thought body parts could shake. It took ages for them to stop.

'Here we go,' she muffles into my ear.

I turn around and see a bus coming towards us.

'I'm gonna ask you one more time, Ingrid. You sure you are okay?'

Ingrid looks at me, then looks towards the bus.

'Ingrid!'

She releases her grip on me, strolls slowly towards the curb and places her hand in her pockets. When she steps on to the bus, she reaches a fistful of change towards the driver.

'Two fares to Crumlin,' she says.

The driver stares at both us of us, then taps away at his tiny little machine before scooping the coins out of Ingrid's hand.

'There y'are, girls,' he says, passing Ingrid two paper tickets, 'hope yis are havin' a good night.'

We both nod a thank you to him and head up the aisle, towards the back of the bus.

'Ingrid?' I say again as we sit down.

'Yes!' she says. She sounds a little bit annoyed. 'You don't have to keep asking me, Ciara. *Yes*. I'm fine.'

I hold her knee, squeeze it a little and then we both sit in silence as we stare out of opposite windows at nothing because the night is too dark.

'It's just,' I say turning back towards her, 'I don't want you doing this just for me.'

She turns her head to face me, then tilts it sideways. But she doesn't say anything. I hold my eyes closed and try to think everything through as the bus rattles its way down the canal road. I'm one hundred per cent certain I want to do this. And I'm one hundred per cent certain I want to do it this way; me and Ingrid doing it together. But I'm not one hundred per cent certain she wants to do it. I know she's really sad now. Last night broke her little heart. But she might be okay in a couple weeks time; just like Harriet said. Whereas I know I won't be. I'm depressed. And I'll be depressed forever... until I kill that depression by killing myself.

But I don't want to keep on asking her if she's okay and I certainly don't want to break the pact by asking her if she still wants to go ahead with it. So I bite my tongue. Literally. I hold it between my teeth and try to not say anything more about it.

The bus heaves over the speed bumps and our bums are lifted up and down on the seats but we keep our faces straight and our mouths closed. I try to look out the window again... see if I can make anything out in the dark. But all I can see is my own reflection staring at back at me. And I can almost hear my mind screaming at the reflection.

You have to ask her, Ciara. Go on. Ask her!

I bite my tongue, hard this time; until I can taste a bit of blood. Then my teeth unclench, my head spins around and my hands reach for Ingrid's pretty little pale face.

'Ingrid Murphy, I love you very much.'

She squints her eyes, then reaches her hands either side of my face, cupping my cheeks.

'I love you too,' she says, her eyes heavy.

'I need to ask you — I'm sorry to break the pact.' She holds her eyes closed and I swallow. 'Do you want to do this? Do you want us both to commit suicide as soon as we've finished saying goodbye to Miss Moriarty? I need to know you're ready.'

22:35

Ingrid

WE SIT IN SILENCE, EXCEPT FOR THE ROARING OF THE BUS engine every now and then when it struggles over the speed bumps.

Then Ciara turns to me and places a hand to each side of my face.

I know she's going to ask me if I still want to go ahead with this. I know she's going to break the first rule of our pact. And I get it; she knows me too well. She knows my mind was changing when we were in Harriet's bedroom.

'Ingrid Murphy,' she says, 'I love you very much.'

I give her one of those half smiles, then hold my hands either side of her face too; just to let her know that it's okay to ask the question she's desperate to ask.

'I need to ask you — I'm sorry to break the pact. Do you want to do this? Do you want us both to commit suicide as soon as we've finished saying goodbye to Miss Moriarty? I need to know you're ready.'

'Yes,' I say, without hesitating; without allowing any silence between her asking the question and me answering it.

Then I open my eyes to see her nodding at me, her lips smiling. She brings herself closer to me, so our foreheads touch and we just hold each other. Until the bus juddering over another speed bump makes my chin slap against Ciara's. Her teeth crack closed. She laughs at the strange sound it makes and so do I; the two of us bent over at the back of the bus, laughing on the outside, in pain on the inside. And all my mind is doing is wondering whether laughing at the noise of somebody's teeth closing actually makes life pretty shit... or whether or not finding the likes of that funny is what makes life pretty good. I've never quite understood what parts of life I'm supposed to enjoy.

I answered her question really quickly. Maybe because I knew the question was coming; I was prepared. Or maybe I answered her that quickly because I'm absolutely certain I want to do this. My mind keeps changing. I've just told her ten seconds ago that I'm ready to this. And now I'm not sure I am.

Suicide seems to make the most amount of sense to me, though. The only way I can get rid of the pain is to end that pain. One thing that's making me slightly nervy about doing it now is that I think the goodbyes we made to our favourite people have been pretty cold. It was my idea; the goodbyes. It was something I wanted to be part of the pact.

Ciara found me standing behind a bush at the entrance to that tiny park near Balfey's house. He was the one who had the free gaff last night. I kept playing what Stitch said to me over and over in my head as I stood behind that bush; tears pouring down my face. It wasn't really his words that were hurting me. It was the laughter from everybody else that followed his words. It made my stomach turn, my whole body shake. I wanted to throw up. But all I could do was cry. And cry.

'Oh, Ingrid,' she said when she found me. She hugged me tight and as she did I whispered into her ear.

'I want to commit suicide.'

She pulled away and stared into my face. She'd been threatening that she would kill herself for years. She said I was the only one keeping her alive. She brought the idea of us both doing it together up a few times before; when I used to agree with her that life was shit and that my parents were just as bad as hers. I'm not sure how much of that I really agree with. I think I was just trying to be supportive; felt I was being the best friend I could possibly be to her if I could relate. But that laughter last night — after Stitch said what he said — it just made me realise I can't go on. I can't go to school tomorrow. I can't do a whole six years in secondary school being known as Fishfingers.

We spoke for two hours about our pact, on that cold bench just inside the park. Ciara was all up for doing it last night. I said we should wait to do it tonight so that we could have a chance to say goodbye to our families and those closest to us. I wanted to say goodbye to Mum and Dad. And Sven. And I really wanted to say goodbye to Harriet. But I'm not sure I really did that well enough tonight. I'm not quite sure what I expected it to be like, though. How are you supposed to say goodbye to somebody for the last time when you don't want them to know it's the last time? I could barely look at Mum and Dad when I was leaving the house; in case they could see right through me. I rubbed Sven's hair. That's it. It's all I did to say goodbye to my little brother. And I hugged Harriet and told her I'd definitely read the book she gave me. I promised I'd catch up with her soon so we could talk. Then I just left in the back seat of Uncle Brendan's car as she waved at me from the doorway. At least she'll get the book with my note in it. That's nice, I guess.

'Maybe we should write suicide notes after all,' I say, as the bus jumps over another speed bump.

Ciara wrinkles her face up a bit.

'Really?'

I shrug my shoulder. I don't know. We both decided last night that writing suicide notes would be too difficult; not just difficult because of how emotional it would be, but difficult because we're both not great at writing. Our parents would have that note forever. And I just don't think we could have written something good enough. That's why we agreed to spend the day at home with our families to say our last goodbyes, and why we decided to visit the people we truly loved before we ended it all. We felt a last goodbye to all our loved ones would have more impact than a note. Now I'm not so sure.

'Oh... maybe not, I don't know,' I say. 'I think writing that small note in Harriet's book is making me think it would be nice to leave a little message for Mum and Dad and Sven.'

Ciara squelches her face even more. She was dead against suicide notes last night. More so than me. She doesn't seem to have changed her mind.

'Don't you think... don't you think our goodbyes were a little... cold?' I ask.

She makes a funny face again.

'They were natural weren't they?' she says. 'My goodbye to my mam was like any goodbye I've ever given her. Seems about right to me.'

'What about your goodbye to Debbie... I mean you slapped her in the face?'

Ciara sniffs a small laugh out of her nose.

'What... you want me to leave her a suicide note now?'

'No, no...' I say, sitting back in my seat and slapping my hands against my knees. 'I don't know.' I realise I must be sounding as confused as I feel. I'm probably doing Ciara's head in.

'Listen,' Ciara says, placing her hands either side of my face again. 'Do you want to go home and say another goodbye to your mum? If you do, we can delay this a little bit...'

I breathe in deep. To give myself time to think. Then I find myself shaking my head before I've thought anything through.

'Nah,' I say. 'Let's just say goodbye to Miss Moriarty. Then we can just get this over with.'

CHARLIE AND TOMMY ARE WELL OUT OF SIGHT BY THE TIME Helen pushes at the door and steps outside. She had tried to run fast, tried to keep up, but she needed both hands to hold on to the bannisters either side of her as she trotted down the stairs, allowing them to race way ahead of her.

'Fuck me,' she says to no one when she gets outside. She looks right, then left. No sign of either of them. No sounds either. She reaches for her phone, scrolls through the screen and dials Tommy's number again; then cocks her ear out for any inkling of that annoying ringtone.

Nothing.

She assumes Tommy would have gone left when he got outside. It would have been stupid of him to have run towards the police car. So she walks — in her own unique way — past the row of closed shops and towards a housing estate that looks like a maze of terraced-lined streets.

'Little bollix could be anywhere.'

She contemplates calling out Charlie's name, but bites her tongue. He'll come back to the car soon enough; hopefully holding Tommy Smith by the scruff of the neck.

She's wondering why the little fucker ran; is starting to lose hope that her instinct was right all along about the two girls. She shakes her head in an effort to reduce the growing logic from her mind. But nothing she can think of to support her gut — that the calls Tommy made earlier were legitimate suicide concerns — seems to be adding up. They *must* have been distraction calls; he *must* be working for Alan Keating.

She turns back and stares at the flashing sign for Cue. Maybe all of them up there are working for Keating. That's why the CCTV is gazing down at them. It's planned that way. Bastards will have a proven alibi all night.

Helen stops walking, lets out a sigh and then washes the palm of her hand over her face.

'Your instinct was wrong, Helen,' she muffles into her fingers. 'There aren't two girls out there about to commit suicide. Scott's death hasn't led you to this moment. Scott died. Get fuckin' over it already. It's been twenty-two—'

'Fuckin' hell.'

An approaching voice halts Helen's whispered monologue. She squints into the darkness, sees Charlie approaching her, his hand to his face. He's on his own.

'Fuck ye, Charlie,' she mumbles to herself before walking towards him. They meet under a street lamp.

'Little bollix punched me in the nose,' Charlie says taking his hand away to show Helen the damage.

She stares at his face, notices a fine trickle of blood making its way to his top lip, then shakes her head.

'What the fuck happened?' she asks.

Charlie grunts the stinging pain away before answering.

'Fucker's quick, I'll give him that. I managed to catch up with him, grabbed a handful of his tracksuit top… but he just turned around, knocked me one. I went flying backwards. Stings like hell. By the time I got to my feet he was out of sight.'

Helen clenches her jaw.

'Christ sake, Charlie!' she grinds through her teeth.

'What? What did you want me to do? I was assaulted.'

'You're a bloody police officer; you are supposed to control these situations!'

Helen turns her back on Charlie, her hands on her hips.

He looks at the back of her, his arms outstretched in bewilderment at her lack of empathy.

'We'll get that little fucker for assaulting a police officer. We know where he lives!' Charlie says.

'I couldn't give a shit about arresting him for assaulting a police officer!' Helen barks as she spins back around. 'I'm only concerned about these two girls. Whoever they are. Wherever they are.'

Charlie holds his hand to his nose again, then winces in pain before squelching his entire face at Helen.

'If all this little fucker has is information on two girls planning to die by suicide, why did he run away from us? Helen... we've got to admit we're wrong. The rest of the force are out there looking to stop Alan Keating from carrying out something big tonight. This little prick running away from us proves they're right. He didn't call two Garda stations because he's worried about girls he goes to school with. He rang in a distraction call.' Helen holds her eyes closed, her hands still on her hips. 'C'mon, Helen, you've got to admit that—'

'Shut up, Charlie,' she snaps.

'What d'you mean *shut up*? You know—'

Helen takes a step towards Charlie, grabs him — with both hands — by the collar of his Garda jacket and pins him up against a shop shutter, causing a clang to echo the entire length of the street.

'You listen to me, and you listen to me very carefully,' she spits into his face.

Up this close, Helen can see more of the damage to Charlie's nose; a blue T-shaped bruise already starting to form, spreading itself under both eyes.

'We have to believe we are right. We need to chase down these two girls. If… *if* the rest of the force are right, and Alan Keating is planning something big tonight, so fuckin what? Another theft, another heist. Who gives a shit? It's nothing. Money, material things… it's all fuckin pointless. *But*… if the rest of the force are wrong, and we're right? Is anything pointless? Is saving two girls' lives pointless?'

Charlie narrows his eyes, slows his breathing down and then shakes his head.

'Exactly,' Helen says. 'We have been given an important job to do and we will do it whether we think they were distraction calls or not, ye hear me?' Charlie nods. And Helen releases her grip on him, before flattening down his collar. 'Our task is a hell of a lot more important than theirs. We have to be super thorough. Whether we are right or wrong!'

Charlie reaches his hand back up to his nose.

'I s'pose you're right,' he says as his jacket pocket begins to vibrate. He reaches inside for his phone, then looks up at Helen after he's noticed the screen.

'It's Newell — my SI.'

'Put him on speaker,' Helen demands.

Charlie swipes at his screen to answer the call, then presses at the speaker button holding the phone outwards.

'Guilfoyle, what the hell are you up to?' a voice barks down the line. 'Louis Kavanagh told me you were at Tommy Smith's house half an hour ago… what are you playing at, son?'

Helen shakes her head, pinching her forefinger and thumb together and running them across her closed lips.

'We eh… I eh… I got information from the local school Headteacher using the image of Smith from the CCTV footage. He was able to give me information on the boy; told me his name, gave me his address.'

A scoff is heard down the line.

'Listen, Guilfoyle, I appreciate you are doing your job as well as you can. But leave this to us, okay? You can get your ass back to the station and finish your shift out. Don't go chasing Smith. We're on top of it. You eh... haven't come across him yet, have you?'

Helen shakes her head, pinches her forefinger and thumb across her lips again, her eyes widening.

'Guilfoyle?' Newell barks, having been met with silence.

'No, Sir.'

Charlie holds his eyes closed in disappointment, his chin tucked into his neck with shame.

'Good. We don't want him getting away from us. Listen,' Newell says, 'Louis told me you were operating with some Detective from Rathmines. Who are ye with, son?'

Helen's eyes go wide again, her head beginning to shake rapidly. She has her finger pointed right in Charlie's face.

Charlie swallows.

'Eh... Detective Helen Brennan,' he says slowly, before mouthing a 'sorry' at Helen.

She grinds her teeth in his face, then spins around, her hands on top of her head as if she's just missed an open goal in the last minute of a cup final.

'Brennan? Never heard of her. Well... you tell her we have everything under control. Leave Tommy Smith to us — that is an order.'

'I hear you, Sir. All understood.'

As soon as the line goes dead, Helen spins back around.

'Ye little rat bastard,' she says, her finger pointing again.

'I had to... he bloody knew I was with somebody. What did you want me to say?'

Helen shakes her head while producing an overly loud grunt.

'I'm gonna get fuckin fired now,' she says.

'I think we both might,' Charlie replies, bringing his hand to his nose again. 'Fuck this, Helen... I have to ring him back. I have to tell him we confronted Tommy Smith. They need to know.'

'Then you *will* get fired,' Helen says. She kicks the shop shutter behind Charlie, causing the clattering sound to echo down the street again.

'Ah Jesus, I've fucked up my career haven't I?' Charlie says, almost sobbing.

Helen doesn't answer. She just stands under the streetlamp, her hands on her hips, her mind racing.

Then she notices them. Across the street. In the window next to the Cue sign. The gang of men staring down at them.

'Fuckers are laughing at us,' she says. 'Let's get back to the car and get our thinking caps on.'

Charlie paces after Helen, still holding his hand to his nose as if it's gonna make the stinging pain go away. When they're inside the car, they sit in silence; Helen staring out the passenger side window, the tip of her thumb in her mouth; Charlie gripping the steering wheel, trying to ease the pain away by sucking air in through his teeth.

'I have to ring Newell back, I *have* to,' he eventually says.

Helen looks at him, then sighs a deep grunt that is filled with disappointment.

'What's that going to achieve?' she asks.

'They are looking for Tommy Smith; the whole bloody force is. I know what direction he ran in... I need to tell them. Fuck it! I'm telling them.'

He reaches into his jacket pocket. By the time he's taken the phone out, Helen's fingers are wrapped around his wrist.

'Charlie; don't be a fuckin idiot,' she says.

'I've been a fuckin idiot all evening,' he replies, wrestling his arm away.

'I'm sorry to let you down, Helen. I'm sorry for... for everything you've been through, but...' he shrugs his shoulder. 'I have to do my duty. I have to ring it in.'

He pulls at the handle, pushes his car door open and holds his phone to his ear.

When he closes the door, Helen slaps both of her hands against the top of the dashboard.

'Mother fucker!' she screams. Then she holds both hands over her face, her breathing becoming long and slow. When she removes her hands, she fidgets at the rear-view mirror, sees Charlie walking slowly away from the car, one hand holding the phone to his ear, the other rubbing the back of his head. She winds down her window, her attempt to hear anything. But there's only silence — he's travelled too far from her.

She grunts again; still struggling to let logic overrule her thinking. She wants to believe there are two girls out there about to end their lives. She needs to believe it. Her life is worthless without Scott having some sort of inspiration on it.

'Help me out, Scott,' she says. 'Gimme a sign. Just something small.'

She widens her eyes, inches her face closer to the windscreen.

Nothing. Just a dark blue sky and — in her periphery — that flashing sign for Cue. Then she flicks her head.

'That's literally a sign,' she says. 'Cue. Cue. Cue. What are you trying to tell me, Scott?'

She stares at it, her eyes moistening. Then a tear escapes and runs down her left cheek. She's not crying because of grief. She's crying because of the realisation of her delusion. She hates herself when she talks to Scott. Hates herself even more when she asks him to send her a sign. It never makes her feel better. It only emphasises his loss more.

Helen's not stupid. She knows she'll never see her son again. They bloody cremated his body twenty-two years ago. Scott's gone. He's ash in a tiny urn that's buried six feet under the ground in a tiny plot at Mount Jerome cemetery. How the fuck could he send her a sign?

She slaps the top of the dashboard again with both hands, then wipes away the tear.

'You're a fuckin idiot, Helen,' she says.

She's sniffling up her nose, wiping all of the moistness from under it when the car door snatches open.

Charlie slouches into the driver's seat; his phone in his hand.

'Well...' Helen says. 'How did your SI take the news?'

'He eh... well, he's not happy. They're on their way here now to try and catch up with him. I've to get back to the station. Back to my desk. I'll be dealt with in the morning.'

'But sure, you were just doing your job. They gave you the job of looking into the calls as if they were legit—'

'Helen!' Charlie snaps, his voice filled with frustration.

Helen shuts up, folds her arms, the leather of her coat squeaking as she does so.

'I'm never gonna be a Detective, am I?' Charlie says.

'Course you will. They'll keep you on. Just tell them this was all my fault. My husband is the SI in Rathmines Station. I'll see to it that you're looked aft—'

'No, Helen,' he says, turning to her. 'I mean... I don't have the bloody skills to be a Detective, do I? I don't have the instincts, don't have the—'

'You do... you do,' Helen says, reaching a hand towards his shoulder.

Charlie laughs out of the side of his mouth.

'I don't though, do I? You walked right up to my desk

about three hours ago, told me you were helping me out with this investigation, brought me to the tram station, to view CCTV footage at the Red Cow, to question two bloody Headteachers...'

'Yeah — you've done a good job with me.'

'Listen,' Charlie snaps. 'All that chasing around with you and y'know what? I never even asked you the first question I should have asked you when I first met you.'

Helen narrows her eyes, then shakes her head at Charlie.

'What question?' she asks.

'I should have asked you to show me your Detective badge, shouldn't I?'

Helen laughs.

'I'm serious, Helen — if that even is your name. Show me your badge.'

22:45

Ciara

BLEEDIN' HELL. INGRID WANTS TO GO BACK AND SAY GOODBYE to her mam and dad all over again. Jaysus. Last night she was all talk about staying at home to say a final goodbye to our families. Now she wants to go back to do it all again. Maybe she doesn't want to go through with this. Maybe she's not ready.

I place my hands either side of her face again and stare into her eyes. I want to sound gentle.

'Listen,' I say. 'Do you want to go home and say another goodbye to your mum? If you do, we can delay this a little bit...'

She sucks in a breath, then shakes her head.

'Nah. Let's just say goodbye to Miss Moriarty, then we can just get this over with.'

I nod my head slowly and wrap my arms around her; squeezing her in for another hug.

'You're doing the right thing,' I whisper to her. 'If you keep changing your mind and going back and forth about all this, you'll just end up sad for years like me. The sadness never stops. It just keeps coming and going and coming and going. And every time it comes back, it feels worse. We're nearly there, okay? A quick goodbye to Miss, then we'll stop this pain forever.'

She squeezes me even tighter and when we finally release I can see the sadness has gone out of her eyes. That sort of half smile is back on her lips. Same sort of look she gave me last night when we wrote this pact.

I squint through the darkness of the side window, to try to make out where we are. Can't see anything. So I stand up, walk slowly up the aisle and look out the front windscreen.

'Almost at our stop, Ingrid,' I say, strolling back to her. 'I don't know the door number, but I'll know the house when I see it. It's only a couple minutes' walk from the stop.'

'Can't wait to see her face when she answers the door,' Ingrid says.

'Me neither.'

We've both been back to our primary school twice since we graduated last June. Miss Moriarty was delighted when we visited. I'm not sure how she'll feel about us knocking at her house late on a Sunday night though. But I'm pretty sure she won't mind. We agreed last night that we'd just tell her we were in the area and thought it'd be rude to walk by her home without calling in to say hello. She'll have no idea we're actually calling in to say goodbye.

She was our teacher for two years in primary school. We had her when we were in fourth class and then again in sixth — our last year in primary. She really cared about us; about our learning, about our lives. I remember her telling me once that me and Ingrid were really lucky to have each other. She's not wrong there. The teachers we have now in secondary school wouldn't even know me and Ingrid are best mates. That's the difference. They don't look up from their desks. They're only interested in doing their lessons; they're not interested in knowing the students. I'm not sure any of them will actually be upset one little bit when they hear the news in the morning. I'd bet any money that the most asked question in the staff room will be 'which two are they?' But Miss Moriarty, well… she will be sad. She loved us; cared about us. I wish, so much, that she was a teacher in our secondary school. That'd probably save our lives.

'C'mon,' Ingrid says, getting up from her seat. She stabs her finger at the small bell on the back of the seat and I follow her as she stumbles her way towards the driver.

'Thank you,' she says to him when he pulls over.

'You get home safe now, girls,' he says. Then he pushes at a button that closes his doors and leaves us standing on the pavement. It's starting to get really cold now.

'This way,' I say, wrapping my arm around Ingrid's shoulders.

I lead her around a corner just off the main Crumlin Road, and towards Miss Moriarty's little cul de sac.

Miss had told us she lived in Crumlin when she was our teacher. I managed to find the exact address when I was flicking through some paperwork in the Headteacher's office sometime last year. I visited the street and stood outside her house for ages one day. I didn't knock or anything. I just thought it was cool that I knew where my teacher lived. Her house isn't as big as ours. Which is a bit weird. Surely teachers should be paid a lot more than anyone else? My dad runs a company that sells boring insurance. And he's loaded. All Ingrid's dad does is talk on the radio for three hours every morning. How the hell are they rich and Miss Moriarty isn't?

'It's this one here,' I say, pointing towards Miss' front door.

We walk towards the garden gate and then stop outside it.

'Okay,' Ingrid says to me. 'We just say we were in the area

visiting a friend and that we felt it was rude to walk by Miss Moriarty's house without knocking in to say hello, right?'

I nod my head.

'Yup. You first,' I say, pushing the gate open.

Ingrid takes two steps into her garden and then lifts and drops her crooked letterbox a few times. Within seconds the door is opened.

'Yes?' a man says.

'Oh,' Ingrid says turning to me. 'We eh… we thought our old teacher Miss Moriarty lived here.'

The man scratches at his head, then turns over his wrist so he can look at his watch.

'Brigid,' he calls out over his shoulder. 'There are two young girls here to see you.'

22:55

Ingrid

I CAN SEE MISS WALKING DOWN THE STAIRS. SHE'S WEARING A bathrobe and her hair is all wet.

'Hey, you two,' she says, smiling, 'what are you doing here?'

I laugh a bit awkwardly, then stand aside, leaving Ciara to do the lying.

'We eh... we were visiting a friend around the corner and thought it would be rude to walk by our favourite teacher's house without knocking in to say hello... so eh... hello.' Ciara waves. And I laugh. Awkwardly again.

Miss Moriarty looks a little lost for words. She doesn't say anything; she just stands there, combing her fingers through her wet hair.

'I'm sorry, Miss. Have we come at a bad time?' I ask.

'Not at all. I'm just out of the shower... was going to dry myself off and get into bed. It's eh... it's late... what time is it?'

'Almost eleven,' a voice from inside the house calls out. It must be the man who answered the door to us. I wonder who he is. She's not married. Her name is *Miss* Moriarty. Not *Missus* Moriarty.

'Eh… well, come in,' she says standing aside and pulling the door a little wider for us.

We step into a square hallway that's no bigger than the welcome mat we have in ours. 'How did you girls know where I lived?'

'We eh… we've always known. Somebody pointed it out to us once,' Ciara says. She lies so quickly. I'd be still scratching my head if it was up to me to answer that question.

'We won't keep you long, Miss,' I say and then I lean into her and hug her. I miss Miss Moriarty so much.

'Oh, Ingrid,' she says, hugging me back. Then she reaches one hand towards Ciara and drags her in to our little huddle. This is what teachers should do; hug their students, care for them. The teachers we have now barely even know our names.

'Let me get the two of you a quick drink. Squash?'

Me and Ciara look at each other, then both nod at the same time.

'Thanks, Miss,' Ciara says.

'Hey, you don't have to call me Miss… it's Brigid, now that you're no longer students of mine.'

She waves her hand to make sure we follow her into the kitchen and then she begins to pour us both a raspberry Ribena.

'So, how you getting on in secondary school?' she asks.

Me and Ciara look at each other again.

'Not great,' I say.

Miss squints her eyes at me as she hands us our drinks.

'What do you mean "not great"?'

'Well… well…' I stumble, fidgeting with my fingers.

'The teachers barely know who we are,' Ciara says. 'It's

not like primary school where you're with the same teacher all day. We change classrooms every forty minutes and... I don't know. It's just hard.'

'Oh... everybody says that about secondary school when they start,' Miss Moriarty says. 'You'll get used to it. It's only been... what's-it?'

'Eight months and two weeks,' Ciara says.

Miss Moriarty smiles.

'Exactly,' she says. 'It's nothing. By next year you'll be used to it. Don't worry. It'll get better.'

Ciara looks at me. I decide to just drink from my glass while staring up at the ceiling.

'Wouldn't you like to be a secondary school teacher?' Ciara asks, looking back at Miss Moriarty. 'You'd be great at it — and you could join our school. Be our teacher forever.'

Miss smiles again.

'Oh you're so sweet, you two.'

She runs her hand through her wet hair again. I don't think she likes us being here. We called at a bad time. Her conversations are very short. She's definitely not her usual self.

'Who... eh...' Ciara says, looking back over her shoulder. 'Who was the man who opened the door for us?'

'Ciara!' I say. She can be so rude sometimes.

'It's fine, Ingrid,' Miss says, 'that's Jamie. He's my partner. My boyfriend.'

'Didn't know you had a boyfriend, Miss,' I say.

She smiles again. I miss that smile so much.

'I don't tell my students *everything*,' she says, patting the top of my head. 'C'mon, come with me.'

She leads us out of her tiny kitchen, into another room.

'Jamie, these are two of my former students: Ingrid Murphy and Ciara Joyce.' Jamie stands up and reaches up his palm for us to high five. 'Ingrid is Terry Murphy's daughter.'

'Ah yes,' Jamie says, 'Brigid told me she had taught Terry Murphy's daughter before. How is your old man?'

I shrug my shoulder.

'Fine… I think,' I say and then everyone laughs a little. 'He eh… works a lot, I don't think I get to see as much of him as most people get to see their dads.'

Jamie and Miss look at each other and then Miss turns to us.

'Take a seat,' she says. All four of us sit in their small sitting room, the tele turned off, just a lamp in the far corner on. The chat goes silent; nobody quite sure what to say.

Then Ciara taps me on the hip. I look at her and see that her eyes have gone really wide. She's trying to mouth something to me. I've no idea what she wants to say. So I shake my head and squint my eyes at her.

'What?' I whisper.

She locks her fingers together, holds them out in front of her and tries to mumble something between her teeth.

What the hell is she trying to tell me?

CHARLIE'S HANDS ARE GRIPPED TO THE TOP OF THE STEERING wheel, his head hanging between his elbows.

'There's no need to be that upset with yourself,' Helen says. 'I *used* to be a Detective. I was a Detective for five years before... before...' she swallows. 'Before my life got turned upside down. After Scott's suicide I just... I couldn't continue working. I was in and out of therapy, in and out of hospital...' She looks over at Charlie. He still hasn't lifted his head. 'I do work at Rathmines Garda station. As I said, my husband runs the shop. He saw to it that I was taken back on in some capacity.'

She hears a puff, the first noise Charlie has made since Helen admitted she wasn't who or what he believed she was.

'In what capacity?' he asks, peeling his back up vertebrae by vertebrae until he's sitting upright.

Helen sucks air in through the gaps of her teeth.

'I do admin work.'

Charlie puffs a darting laugh out of his nostrils as Helen reels backwards in embarrassment.

'Listen, just… just drop me back at your station,' she says, her face reddening. 'My car's there. Please.'

Charlie looks at her, then back out through his front windscreen before he turns the key in the ignition.

'Admin work,' he whispers to himself, shaking his head.

He drives in silence, Helen now the one hanging her head; her fingers forming a diamond shape on her lap.

'I'll take the blame for everything. My husband will understand. I'll be able to talk him around,' she says.

Charlie makes a clicking sound with his mouth.

'I'm sorry you lost your son,' he says. 'And I get it… why you… why you were trying to track down these two girls. Suicide. It can't be… it can't be easy to deal with.'

Helen purses her lips at him.

'It never leaves you,' she says as she stares back out the window at nothing in particular. 'I didn't have one darn clue. Not one clue he was gonna do it. Him and his friends. I guess they were just depressed. But I didn't see one sign of depression in Scott. Not one bloody sign of it. I know he wasn't the best kid in the world. His teachers used to say he could get distracted at school. But at home he was just… just normal. A normal teenager. It's one hell of a body blow to lose your son. But to lose him to suicide… well… the worst thing is I still don't know *why* they did it. What I wouldn't give to know what happened that night. You know what my husband says to me all the time… he says "you *never* will know". Imagine having to deal with that your whole life?'

She holds her hand to her face, her shoulders shaking. Charlie reaches a hand over to her, gives her shoulder a light squeeze. She'd already informed him how her husband has dealt with the reality of Scott's suicide compared to her. It was just as gut wrenching for Charlie to hear the second time around.

'Don't cry, Helen,' he says.

She waves him away. But he keeps his hand on her shoulder, only taking it off every now and then to change gear as he navigates all the way back to the station; not a further word passed between them.

It's always eaten at Helen that she will never know what happened to her son and his two friends the night they decided to end it all. She's tried her best to get to the bottom of it. She discussed it with the other two sets of parents. None of them could come up with answers. One of them blamed Scott... argued that he must have orchestrated it all. The frustration of never knowing what happened has always prolonged Helen's grief. She believes — and has done for a long time — that only a new life in Canada will ever ease her depression.

When Charlie kills the engine outside Terenure Garda station, he waits on Helen to lift her head, but she doesn't move.

'Well I guess it was an adventure at least, huh?' Charlie says, allowing a little laugh to sniff its way out of his mouth. But his joke hasn't hit its audience.

'Helen,' he says. 'We're here.'

She wipes her hand over her face, then leans her head back on to the rest.

'I need to take a leak,' she says. 'Where are the toilets in there?'

Charlie cocks his head while taking the keys from the ignition.

'C'mon, I'll show you.'

They stroll solemnly across the tiny car park and then into the front desk of the station.

'Charlie,' the man at the desk nods, 'Detective.'

Charlie looks back at Helen then twists his face into an awkward smile.

'Through here,' he says to Helen, pushing at a door. 'The Ladies is in the corner.'

Helen smiles with her eyes at Charlie, then holds her arms out.

'You're right, Charlie. It *has* been an adventure. It was… it was good to investigate with you. You're gonna make a helluva Detective one day. I'm sure of it.'

Charlie raises his eyebrow as he leans in to accept Helen's hug.

'I'll see ye around, Helen.'

He releases and then turns away, swirling his key ring around his finger as he makes his way back to the desk Helen first met him at three hours ago. She stares at the items on his desk; it feels like a hell of a lot more than three hours since she picked each of them up and inspected them for no real reason at all.

She strolls to the corner Charlie had pointed her towards and pushes at a door that leads into a pokey toilet with two cubicles.

'Still better than my station,' she says to no one, before rushing towards the sink. She turns on the cold tap, holds her hands out to form a cup and then fills it, before splashing at her face.

'What are you fuckin playing at, Helen?' she says to herself in the mirror as water drops from her brow. Then she enters one of the cubicles, pulls at the toilet paper until she has a ball of it in her hands and begins to dab at her face. As she's leaving the cubicle, she throws the ball of paper over her shoulder, missing the bowl by quite a distance.

She pulls tentatively at the door that leads back into the station, inching it open slowly so she can stare at Charlie. He's scratching at his spikey hair; looks really disappointed in himself as if he's cringing inside.

'Breathe, Helen,' she whispers to herself. 'Calm down.'

'Sorry?' a woman calls out appearing at the toilet door.

'Oh... no, *I'm* sorry,' Helen says, offering a fake smile. 'Bloody talking to myself, aren't I? First sign of madness, huh?'

The woman smiles back, then pushes past Helen and into one of the cubicles. Helen steps out, into the station, and then tiptoes herself towards Charlie.

'Didn't wanna leave without another hug,' she says perching her ass onto his desk. Charlie laughs a little, then reaches his arm around her and takes her closer to him.

'Our little adventure, huh?' he says into her ear.

'Our little adventure,' she whispers back.

'If you ever need someone to talk to, to have coffee with, you know where I am,' Charlie says.

Helen pats him on the shoulder, then stands up.

She walks away, back out through the office floor towards the door and out past reception without paying the man at the front desk any further attention. As soon as she's outside, she swings the key ring around her finger, and heads straight to Charlie's car.

She clicks the button, releasing the locks, and pulls at the driver's door. As soon as she's inside she eyeballs herself in the rear-view mirror, then looks away quickly; her eyes focusing on the road ahead as the car inches forward.

She knows where she's going; made her mind up when she was holding her face as Charlie drove back to the station. She also realised then that she needed the police car. It was the only means in which she could justifiably pass as a Detective — it's a tough lie to carry out if you don't have a badge to flash. She knows. She's tried it before.

'You're doing the right thing,' she says to herself. 'You're doing the right thing.'

She picks up speed, then reaches for the button that sets off the siren before pausing.

'Nah… better not,' she says. She flicks her eyes to look at herself in the rear-view mirror again, then holds them closed.

'What the fuck am I doing?' she whispers. 'What the fuck am I doing?'

She opens her eyes, shifts into fifth gear and speeds down the canal road. She can hear herself breathing, her breaths growing sharper as the digits on the speedometer rise.

'What the fuck am I doing?' She shouts it this time, laughing.

Then her pocket vibrates, causing her to blink as she eases off the gas. She takes out her phone and presses the green button.

'What the fuck are you doing?' Eddie screams down the line.

23:00

Ciara

JAMIE HOLDS HIS HAND UP FOR ME AND INGRID TO HIGH FIVE —
and we do. He looks nice. But sure… of course he's nice. He's
Miss Moriarty's boyfriend. She's way too lovely and clever to
ever have a horrible boyfriend.

'Take a seat,' Miss says.

And we all do; me, Ciara and Miss sitting on the grey
sofa, Jamie on the tiny green armchair across from us.

I watch as Miss struggles sitting down; pulling the belt of
her bathrobe tighter across her belly. Her belly is big; never
knew she was that fat… hold on.

I tap at Ingrid's hip, then try to mumble to her.

'Id ee egnan,' I say through my teeth.

Ingrid looks at me as if I'm mad, then shakes her head a
little. She can't make out what I'm trying to say. I hold my
hands out over my belly, make a bit of a round shape with
them. She's still shaking her head.

'Yes, young girl,' Jamie says. 'We are pregnant.'

'What!' Ingrid says. She reaches her arms towards Miss
and gives her a big hug. So I do the same, joining in.

'Congratulations, Miss. That's the best news, like, ever,' I say.

The three of us stay in a hug for ages.

'Twins,' Jamie says.

I hold my hand to my mouth as I sit back into the sofa.

'Yep,' Miss says. 'They're due the end of August.'

I'm so happy for Miss. This is the happiest I've been in… jee… I don't know how long.

'Ah… two little Moriartys running around the place. I can't wait to—' Ingrid stops herself talking, then sits back in the sofa. I know what she was about to say; that she can't wait to meet them. Until she realised she never will.

'Two Roses, you mean,' Jamie says.

'Huh?'

'Two Roses… my name.'

Ah… Jamie Rose. Makes sense that he'd have such a nice name. I bet he'll make a great dad. Better than mine and Ingrid's anyway. He won't be stuck at work all the time; he won't tut at them when they have their first period.

I had my first one late last year, just before Christmas. I didn't know what to do, had no idea what was going on. I just screamed.

'What the hell is wrong with you?' my dad said, poking his nose into the bathroom. He saw me standing there, staring into the bowl at all of the red that had just poured out of me.

'What *is* wrong with me?' I asked him.

'Ah, here…' he said, shaking head. 'It's eh… a subject your mam will have to talk to you about… or Debbie. Wait till Debbie gets here in the morning.'

'Debbie doesn't mind me anymore, Dad!' I said. Then I began to cry. He left the bathroom. I didn't see him again for a few days.

'You'll both make great parents,' I say to them.

Jamie smiles at me.

'It's two girls,' Miss says, rubbing her belly.

Me and Ingrid squeeze each other and let out little squeals.

23:10

Miss Moriarty

THE TWO OF THEM CLING TO EACH OTHER AND PRODUCE A cute little high-pitched squeal.

I love Ingrid and Ciara; always have. My heart has always gone out to them. They never really palled around with anyone in primary school, apart from with each other. And me. They'd try to include me in their plans for lunch and would spend break time trying to make sure I didn't get any work done. Even though I've a lot going on, I still kinda miss them. It's a shame they're not enjoying secondary school, but I can't get involved. At some stage you just have to let kids grow up. They have to take responsibility for themselves.

'You'll both make great parents. They're going to be lucky girls,' Ingrid says.

How adorable. Ingrid's going to an impressive woman when she grows up. She's intelligent, pretty, comes from good stock. Her mam used to be a model — made quite a big name for herself in Sweden back in the day. And her dad's a bit of a national treasure. He used to be a personality on tele; now has his own radio show. She's a little bit sensitive though; conjures mountains from molehills with way too much ease. But once she grows out of that, she'll be grand. I'm not so sure about Ciara, though. Ciara's parents aren't up to much. I'm sure her mam is too fond of the drink. She used to turn up for parent-teacher meetings a little squiffy. At least she turned up though; not like her husband. I tried to ring him a couple times over the years, just to let him know how Ciara was getting on at school. He always claimed he was too busy to talk. He runs Fullam's insurance and accountancy. I'm sure the business gets more of his attention than his family does. Ciara always seemed to focus on the negatives in life; her glass was always half-empty. I'm not surprised though; if parents show a lack of belief in their kids, then it's inevitable that the kids themselves won't have much belief. No matter how good a teacher is, there is only so much impact we can have. I've often worried about Ciara over the years. But having Ingrid as a best friend is good for her. She'll be fine.

I hold my hand to my mouth and yawn.

'Sorry, girls,' I say. 'I'm so tired.'

I'm not lying to them; not trying to rush them out of my house. It's just ever since I fell pregnant I've been feeling wrecked. And nauseous. Standing at the top of a classroom all day is torturous when you've got two little ones growing inside you. They seem to weigh me down that extra little bit every day. And I've three more months to go before maternity leave. I'm not sure how I'm going to get through it.

'Oh sorry, Miss,' Ingrid says. 'We know it's late. Maybe we should let you go to bed.'

'That'd be great, girls,' Jamie says, walking towards me and placing his hand on my belly. 'Brigid needs as much rest as she can get.'

'Tell you what,' I say, 'when the girls are born, why don't you two call by again? I'd love you to meet them.'

I smile at the girls; knowing how much they'll love that

invite. But they don't smile back. Ingrid stumbles a reply and then shakes her head. That's odd.

'Eh... yes. Okay... okay,' Ciara says, holding a hand to Ingrid's knee.

I squint my eyes at them.

'You two okay?'

Ciara nods, and then Ingrid mirrors her.

They're probably jealous of the babies; because they've seen themselves as my babies for so long. That's cute. I've read an article about that before; students feeling envious when their favourite teacher becomes a parent.

'So how you two getting home then?' I ask.

'Bus,' Ingrid says.

'Bus? At this time of the night?'

'No... no... don't be silly, Ingrid,' Ciara says. 'She's...' Ciara winds her finger around her temple. 'We're getting a lift from Ingrid's dad. He's around the corner in our friend's house.'

I squint again. These two are up to something. I can sense it. Teacher's intuition.

'The friend's house that you say is around the corner... what's the family name?' I stare at Ingrid as I ask this, knowing I can read her better than Ciara. I think Ciara mastered the art of bullshitting from her father. It's probably the only trait she's ever picked up from him.

Ingrid looks at Ciara.

'Sally Sweeney,' Ciara says.

'The Sweeneys? I don't know any Sweeneys that live around here,' I say.

Ciara laughs.

'Ah they do... around two corners actually. They live just off the main Crumlin Road.'

I don't believe her.

'Eh... why don't I ring your parents, Ingrid?' I say.

225

'I'VE JUST GOT OFF A CALL FROM SUPERINTENDENT NEWELL AT Terenure Garda station.'

Helen holds her eyes closed.

'I'm sorry, Eddie,' she whispers.

'Off investigating the suicide angle? Bringing some rookie with you on a wild goose chase?'

'I'm sorry.'

'You told me you were tucked up on the sofa watching TV.'

'I'm sorry, Eddie,' she says, ensuring this time that each word is pronounced clearly and slowly.

'How bloody dare you? I don't know whether I'm more angry at you dipping your nose in further than you ever have before, or more angry because you lied to me.'

Helen stays silent. There's only so many times she can say the word 'sorry' — especially if it's making zero impact.

She's still cringing, outwardly anyway; her right shoulder slumped lower than her left, her head tilted, her teeth clenched tight. But inside she's feeling somewhat relieved. Eddie isn't aware she's stolen a police car. He only knows that Helen was out with Charlie, sticking her nose in where it doesn't belong.

'Christ, what were you thinking? You bloody chased away the most significant witness we have.'

'It wasn't me who chased him away, Eddie. It was the naivety of the young officer I was with—'

'You shouldn't be anywhere *near* a young officer. Nowhere near one!' Eddie's voice is getting sterner now; Helen wincing at the obvious fury in his tone. He's been so patient with Helen for so many years that she feels really guilty when she irritates him. Yet sometimes — especially when it comes to work — she just can't help herself. Though she's never gone this far; had never taken another officer on a wild goose chase, pretending to be a Detective. 'I'm mortified… imagine being told my administrative assistant is out leading an investigation, posing as a bloody Detective.'

Helen hangs her head when she stops at a red light, allowing another silence to settle between them.

'Where are you now?' Eddie says, trying to regain control of his tone.

Helen shifts her head slightly forward, so she can look upwards through the windscreen at the buildings surrounding her. She can make out the old Victorian houses of the Highfield Road to her right; the Rathmines Clock Tower standing tall in the distance.

'I'm on my way home,' she says.

Helen hears Eddie mumbling to himself. It's undecipherable, but the fact that he's even doing this is quite telling. Eddie doesn't normally talk to himself; not like Helen does.

'I hope to hell you are,' he grunts.

Helen says nothing; then shifts into first gear and takes off slowly across the junction.

'I'll speak with you first thing in the morning. Forget

going out for breakfast; you and I need to have a serious conversation. We need to re-evaluate what you do in our station; whether or not you should be doing anything at all.'

Helen's nostrils stiffen.

'Eddie—'

'I'm serious, Helen. Deadly serious. I blame myself. I shouldn't have said a word to you about these calls. I shudda known as soon as you heard the word suicide that you would go off on one. I just... I can't keep taking the blame and dealing with the guilt every time you fuck up at work.'

'Eddie. Don't... I'll do anything. *Anything*. If I don't have my job... I have nothing.'

'We'll talk in the morning.' Eddie's tone is softening, his volume lowering. 'Just... just answer me this question, will you, Hel?'

Helen holds her eyes closed again.

'Go on.'

'Did you take your pill today?'

She opens her eyes wide and then rolls them backwards, just as she's rolling the car to a slow stop. She stares out the driver's side window and brings the phone a little closer to her lips.

'Yes!' she says.

'Good... good. I hate prying about that, but... y'know. Just felt like I should ask.'

'Good night, Eddie,' Helen says.

She presses at the red button; her eyes still haven't blinked since she started to stare out the window.

She shuffles in the car seat, so she can place her phone back into the pocket of her leather coat, then pushes the door open and steps outside, crunching the gravel beneath her feet as she strolls across the car park.

She takes one large breath when she reaches the small porch way and then pulls at the heavy door.

'Ah… hello again, Detective,' the barman calls out. He's stopped drying glasses; is resting his forearms on the bar, chatting with one of the punters.

Helen nods a hello back at him, then begins to peer around the square room at all of the faces in attendance. She spots him at the back of the room, holding a pint glass to his mouth, his eyes peering at her over the rim of it.

'You need to come with me again,' she says.

He places his glass back down on the table to a tsunami of mumbles floating around the bar, then rises slowly out of his seat, placing both sets of his fingers on the table for balance.

Helen watches as he brushes his feet against the carpet, shuffling his way towards the exit. She spins on her heels, takes in everybody's face, ending with the barman, and then paces out the door after him.

'Brother Fitzpatrick, you need to sober yourself up as quickly as you can,' she says. 'Two of your students' lives are in serious danger. And you and I have less than an hour to save them.'

Fitzpatrick bends over slightly, his hands resting on his knees.

'Course I'll help,' he says, a slight slur in his delivery. 'I'd do anything for my students.'

Helen stares at him, her hands on her hips.

'I bet you would,' she says, before storming towards the Garda car.

'Hey… what does that mean?' Fitzpatrick calls after her. He then burps into his chest while rising to a standing position and shuffles towards Helen. By the time he's climbed into the police car, Helen is staring him down. As if she's the Headteacher and he a student who's just got caught smoking behind the bike shed.

'Where you taking me?' he says, looking up at her.

'Your house.'

'My house? *My house?* For what? I don't want the neighbours seeing—'

'Brother! Two of your students are in grave danger. You need to understand the serious nature of what the hell I'm saying to you.'

Fitzpatrick holds both of his hands aloft.

'Okay... okay,' he says, blinking. 'You're eh... quicker walking to my house, down that lane-way back there.'

'The last time I ran down that lane,' Helen says as she reverses the car from its space, 'I ended up like you were a few seconds ago, Brother... my hands on my knees, struggling for breath. We'll take the car, thank you very much. Won't be long.'

Fitzpatrick lays the back of his head on to the rest and they both sit in silence, save for the odd clicking of indicator lights every so often, before Helen is pulling up the handbrake and removing the keys from the ignition. Fitzpatrick's head pivots to look out any window he can see out of in search of neighbours' curtains twitching.

'Right,' Helen says. 'We're gonna go inside. We're gonna sober you up. And then...' Fitzpatrick stops staring around himself to look at Helen, his eyes glazed over. 'And then I'm going to ask you about something you mentioned to me when I first met you earlier.'

'Huh?' Fitzpatrick says, tilting his head like a puppy dog.

Helen puffs out a small sigh.

'When I first brought you outside that pub an hour or so ago, the first words that came out of your mouth were "I'm sorry".... As soon as you sober up, Brother, you better explain in detail to me just what the fuck it is you were saying sorry for.'

23:20

Ciara

'The friend's house that you say is around the corner... what's the family name?' Miss asks.

Ah bleedin' hell! I think she might be trying to catch us out. She knows we've been lying to her.

'Sally Sweeney,' I say as quickly as I can. Don't know where I pulled that name out of, but I knew I had to answer before Ingrid caved in.

'The Sweeneys? I don't know any Sweeneys that live around here,' Miss says.

I laugh a little, just to come across as if I'm calm. I always do this when I'm lying.

'Ah they do... around two corners actually, they live just off the main Crumlin Road.'

Miss Moriarty stares at Jamie, then back at me and Ingrid.

'Eh... why don't I ring your parents, Ingrid?' she asks.

Oh no. This isn't going to end well.

'No, there's no need,' I say, standing up. 'They're not in anyway. They're around in the Sweeneys' house waiting on us to get back to them. We said we'd pop around to see you for ten minutes and I guess... well, we really shouldn't be taking up too much of your time.'

Miss Moriarty's forehead wrinkles as if she's just become an old woman in the space of two seconds.

'Girls, are you sure?'

'Yeah, yeah, yeah,' I say, tugging at Ingrid's elbow. 'C'mon, Ingrid, it's getting on to midnight. Let's leave Miss and Jamie to it.'

Ingrid stands up but I can tell by her face that she's ready to crack. I need to get her out of here quickly. She throws her arms around Miss again.

'I'm gonna miss you,' she says.

'Miss me? Sure you can call by anytime you want. Don't be silly.'

'She's only getting sentimental because you're pregnant, Miss,' I say, laughing. Jamie laughs too. 'C'mon, Ingrid.' I yank at her elbow again.

When Ingrid finally releases her grip on Miss and turns to face me, I hold my hand up to high five Jamie once more. And then Ingrid does the same.

Miss follows us into the tiny square hallway and, after I've opened the front door, I turn to her and hug her myself.

'You're the best teacher in the world,' I say. Then I turn away from her for the last time ever and step into her small garden.

'Stay safe, you two,' she says, as we open her gate. And suddenly her door is closed and we both know we've finished our last goodbyes. I don't know how we managed it, but we did. I wasn't a big fan of the last goodbye thing; it was Ingrid's idea. But it's kinda cool that we got around to doing it. I'm glad I found out Debbie takes drugs. I can die knowing who she truly is. And I'm glad we found out Miss Moriarty is pregnant. She deserves all the happiness she gets. Maybe her having twin girls come into her life in a few months time will take away the sadness she will feel for us dying. They'll be like our two little replacements in life; our two substitutes.

'Hey, I wonder if Miss' twins will be us being reincarnated,' I say as we walk towards the bus stop.

Ingrid laughs out of her nose.

'Could you imagine Miss Moriarty being your mum? Wow. How perfect would that life be?' she says.

I know Ingrid doesn't believe in any of that nonsense about reincarnation or religion at all. I've always known, but we had a long conversation about it after we came up with the pact last night. We don't believe we're going to come back in other bodies, we don't believe we're going to end up in some Heaven. We just know that once we die, that's it — we're gone. And that's why we're doing it. Because we want to be gone. We want our minds to shut up; to stop going round and round and round in circles. I can't imagine going to Heaven and having to stay with these thoughts for eternity. That wouldn't be Heaven. That would be Hell. Anyway; it's all bullshit. You'd have to be really stupid to believe life goes on and on and on forever.

'I wonder what she'll call the two girls; might call them Ingrid and Ciara, in memory of us,' I say.

Ingrid laughs through her nose again.

'Could do,' she says. 'It's a pity we'll never meet them though, isn't it?'

I stop walking and turn my face to her, just as we're stepping onto the main Crumlin Road.

'You're not changing your mind just so you can see Miss' twins are you?'

Ingrid laughs again.

'No… jeez, course not,' she says, and then she throws her arm around my shoulder and we continue to walk, like Siamese twins, to the bus stop.

'I really thought we were in trouble there,' I say. 'She asked a hell of a lot of questions, didn't she?'

'She just knows us so well,' Ingrid replies. 'I saw the way she was looking at us, she kind of knew something was up. She just couldn't put her finger on it.'

I nod my head.

'Yeah, I really thought she was going to catch us out when she was asking about our made up friend around the corner. And then... jeez, when she asked if she could ring your parents... I didn't know what to do. The last thing we need right now is your mam finding out what's been going on. She'd just want to ring the police straight away, wouldn't she?'

23:25

Harriet

Uuugh. I can't sleep; can't get Conor out of my head. The bastard. I bet he's curled up with her somewhere now, his arms wrapped around her waist, his cock hard against the crack of her ass. I wish he was doing that to me right now. I'm such a fucking idiot. Why do I always fall for the bad boys? I never learn. I hate being a girl. Boys have it so much easier.

I turn over in my bed again, facing my window and stare at all of the books sitting on the windowsill. I make a silent promise to myself that I'll read them… one day. But I've been making that same promise for months… maybe even years at this stage. I really need to grow up.

It's so difficult for me to try to face the reality that I'm an adult now. Eighteen. And supposed to have it all sussed. It's so shitty that people of my age are supposed to know what they want to do for the rest of their lives. I haven't a clue what I want to do next week, never mind thirty years from now.

I'm just going to take that job in the shop, bring in a few quid for the summer and then think about what I want to do with my life. I wouldn't mind travelling; going to Australia for a year or something. But I couldn't leave Dad alone. He'd be lost without me. Not that we do a lot together; he's normally downstairs slouched on the sofa watching TV while I'm up here listening to Take That CDs, thinking about boys.

I face the other way, away from the books and then try to breathe really slowly. I imagine a flock of sheep in a field, taking turns to jump over a bale of hay.

Uuugh. This is bullshit. Whoever said counting sheep will help you fall asleep? I can't get past nine without imagining Conor's perfect teeth when he smiles. I'd love to be kissing that smile right now, my tongue circling his mouth.

I circle my tongue in my own mouth and realise it's dry. I really should bring a glass of water to bed with me every night. I never do. I always seem to catch myself stewing whether or not it's worth it for me to get out from under my warm duvet, walk down the stairs and step onto the cold tiles of the kitchen to fill a glass of water.

Fuck it. I turn over again, stare at the window blind as if that's going to quench my thirst and help me fall asleep.

Then I let out a yelp and whip the duvet away from me. I step out of bed, stretch my arms over my head and decide to brave the coldness of the kitchen tiles.

I can hear the TV blare as I make my way down the stairs. He's watching some cop show; probably an old episode of *Hill Street Blues*. I wish he'd get up off that sofa; go down the pub or something and talk to some people. Perhaps he'd even meet another woman; a step mum that could help me answer the thousand questions I have about being a woman. But I know he never will. He's married to my mam until he dies too. It's kinda cute I guess... but also a little sad. He has lots of years left. And I just know he's going to spend all of them on that sofa.

I hiss as I tip-toe over the cold tiles to get to the sink, then I fill a glass and down it as quickly as I can before filling it back up and strolling towards the stairs again. I notice the time on the microwave clock as I pass it; 11:30.

'Holy fuck!' I say, my body jumping, some of the water leaping from my glass. 'Jesus, Dad, don't sneak up on me like that!'

'Sorry, love,' he says, 'I wasn't sneaking up on you. Was just gonna have meself another cup of tea.'

I let out a disappointed sigh; not because I got a fright, not because I have to soak up the spillage, but because I've snapped at Dad. Again. I hate snapping at him. He never deserves it. He just seems to get in the way of my shitty life every now and then.

'No, *I'm* sorry,' I say.

He grabs at a tea towel and begins to mop up my mess for me.

'Ye can't sleep, huh?' he asks looking up from his crouched position. I shake my head. 'You haven't been able to sleep right these past couple weeks... everything okay?'

'Course it is, Dad,' I say. 'I'm just stressing a little about the Leaving Cert exams.' That's a lie. I genuinely couldn't give a shit about them; not now that I've decided I'm not going to go to college.

'You'll be fine, love,' he says, standing back up to nudge his knuckles against my cheek.

'Thanks, Dad,' I say, taking a sip. 'You eh... get the girls home okay?'

'No,' he says, folding the tea towel in half. 'The two of them legged it on me. They got me to stop off at the garage on the canal road and then just said "thanks" and ran off.'

I squint my eyes

'Really? I thought they were acting a little bit odd when they were here. Wonder what the hell they're up to?'

Dad shrugs his shoulders.

'It's the age they're at now, isn't it? They want to be independent. Oh…' he says, 'Ingrid gave you your book back. It's on the sofa. She said to say "thank you".'

I cock my head, try to remember what it was specifically that felt so odd about Ingrid and Ciara when they called by about an hour ago.

'Hmmm,' I say. Then I spin on my heels and stroll into the living room. Dad follows me and watches as I pick up my book and flick through it.

I love you Harriet,

Ingrid. x

My mouth opens wide.

'Look… why would she write that?' I ask Dad. 'They were acting really strange when they were here.'

'It's just their age, isn't it?'

I shake my head.

'Nah… something's up. I'm worried about them. We've gotta ring Auntie Greta.'

I slap the book closed then walk to the phone in the hallway, pick up the receiver and begin to dial.

HELEN PACES INTO THE KITCHEN, RUNS THE TAP AND THEN grabs at the kettle. She fills it, places it back on its base and clicks the switch. Whilst it's bubbling towards a boil, she roots around in the cupboards until she finds where Fitzpatrick keeps his glasses. She fills two of them with tap water, then places one aside and gulps from the other.

She lets out a heavy gasp before filling the empty glass again and carrying both back into the living room.

Fitzpatrick is sitting upright on the sofa, fidgeting with his fingers. She flicks her wrist, flinging water into his aged face again.

He sucks in a long breath, then wipes at his eyes before staring up at Helen.

'How did ye not see that coming?' she says to him, handing him the second glass. 'Here… drink up, sober up. And let's get down to business.'

She watches as Fitzpatrick sips from his glass.

'Get it into ye,' she says. She takes a step towards him, holds the bottom of the glass up, helping the water pour.

He lets out a sigh, spitting and spluttering some of the drink back into the glass.

'Ye trying to kill me?' he says.

'Me? I'm the one giving you water... y'know, that liquid we all need to stay alive. You're the one poisoning yourself with alcohol.'

Fitzpatrick puffs his cheeks out, swirls the glass in front of his eyes and then tries to down it again; this time almost finishing the job. He holds the glass towards Helen who takes it from him, just as the kettle confirms it has boiled by producing a click sound.

'Where d'ye leave your tea bags?' she says as she makes her way back into the kitchen.

'Eh... in the press under the kettle,' Fitzpatrick slurs while wiping at his mouth.

Helen grabs a cup that had been left to dry on the drain, tosses a tea bag into it and pours the kettle. She whistles as she turns to the fridge, then pinches at her nose.

'Sweet fuck,' she says, balking backwards. 'The bleedin' stench of your fridge. You keep dead rats in here or something?'

After swiping the air away from her nose, she turns around, sees Fitzpatrick staring at her, leaning against the kitchen door.

'Rarely use it,' he says. 'I eat in the school, or down the pub at night.'

Helen spins back around.

'Have ye no milk?'

Fitzpatrick burps into his chest.

'Nope,' he says.

Helen rolls her eyes, then grabs at the cup and hands it to him.

'Here, drink this without milk. It's tea. The only hangover cure I ever found that worked when I used to drink.'

Fitzpatrick lifts the cup to his lips, then takes a step back, his eyes tearing up.

'Jesus, sweet Mary and Joseph,' he says, 'that's bloody boiling.'

'Well... looks like it's woken you up.'

Helen walks by him, back into the living room.

'Brother Fitzpatrick, time to start talking. These girls don't have the time to wait on you to fully get your shit together.'

She hears him shuffle his feet back into the room after her.

'Whatcha ye need to know?' he asks.

'You need to tell me what the hell you were apologising for earlier?'

Fitzpatrick brushes his feet off the cheap wooden floorboards of his modest terraced home and then sits back into the sofa.

'It's nothing,' he says, shaking his head.

'It's not *nothing* now, Brother, is it? You were worried about something when me and Officer Guilfoyle spoke to you earlier. It's vital you tell me what that was all about.'

Fitzpatrick has both sets of fingers wrapped around his cup, the heat offering him the only comfort he could possibly feel right now. He coughs, blinks his eyes and then shakes his head.

'It is nothing. Nothing to do with whatever you are here for. If you were here for that, you wouldn't need me to explain it now would ye?'

Helen squints her eyes.

'You've sobered up quite quickly, Brother. Used to it, are we? Sobering up after a heavy night on the sauce? It's what you have to do all the time, isn't it? Drink all night, run a school during the day.'

Fitzpatrick lifts one hand from the cup, only so he can pinch at his temple.

'You tell me why you're here,' he says, 'what's this about; two of my students being in danger?'

Helen stands tall, her hands stuffed into her coat pockets.

'Are they in danger because of you, Brother Fitzpatrick? Is that what you're apologising for? Do you abuse your students? Have you pushed two in particular too far?'

Fitzpatrick reels his head backwards.

'What are you talking about, Detective?'

Helen puffs out a tiny laugh; she's trying to act menacingly nonchalant, just as she used to when she first became a Detective all those years ago. She adopted her nonchalant persona from the best of the best; Colombo. The Peter Falk series was all the rage in the early eighties, just as Helen and Eddie were being promoted to Detective status — Helen being one of the first females in the entire country to ever hold such a rank. She was such a promising young Detective. It's a shame she never got to fill her potential.

Helen sits, keeping her hands in her pockets.

'Tell me what you were apologising for…'

Fitzpatrick shakes his head.

'I need to speak to a lawyer,' he says.

Helen shakes her head this time.

'Impossible. We don't have time for that. Two of your students have just over half an hour to live and you need to tell me who they are.'

Fitzpatrick holds his eyes closed.

'Hold on, Detective,' he says, 'why are you here? Are you genuinely here to find two of my students who you think are in danger — or are you here to find out about… about—'

'About what?' Helen says.

'I want a lawyer.'

242

Helen holds both of her hands in front of her face and grunts her annoyance into them.

'Are you telling me that whatever it is you wanted to apologise for earlier has nothing to do with two young female students at your school?'

'No... no, course not,' Fitzpatrick says, his eyes still closed.

Helen sucks on her lips, as she usually does when she has a quick decision to make.

'Okay... listen to me, Brother. Whatever it is that you need to apologise for, I'm gonna come back to that, you hear me? Whatever dark shit you've got going on... it won't be forgotten about. Unless.... unless you can help me. I believe two of your students are going to kill themselves at midnight. We need to find them before it's too late. Do you know of any girls from your school who are so depressed that they might want to take their own lives?'

Fitzpatrick blinks his eyes open, refocusing them on the strange face in front of him. Then he shakes his head; slowly at first, then more aggressively.

'Bollocks,' Helen says.

'Hold on... are you serious? Two of my girls are going to commit *suicide? Tonight?*'

Helen rolls her eyes.

'I've been bloody saying this to you since I first took you out of the pub you stupid f—' she stops herself.

'I thought this was all about something else,' Fitzpatrick says. He stands, holds both hands clasped behind his head. Then he blesses himself, mumbling a thank you to a God he doesn't even believe in.

'You need to talk to Abigail Jensen. She's the welfare officer at the school. She knows all there is to know about all of the students. If anyone can help you identify them, she can.'

Helen bows her head. She's no further along in her investigation than she had been four hours ago; hearing from a Headteacher that she should ring his welfare officer. Last time she did this she ended up with a list of one hundred and sixty-four names. She sighs as she stretches her hand towards Fitzpatrick, opening and closing her fingers.

'What?' Fitzpatrick asks.

'Your phone... with Abigail's number ringing.'

Fitzpatrick pats at his chino pockets.

'Oh, I don't carry my mobile phone. Hate the bloody thing,' he says. Helen's eyes roll. 'I eh... I eh....' Fitzpatrick stutters. 'I have a Filofax up in my bedroom. Her number is in that. I'll go get it.'

Helen stares around the Brother's living room as he stumbles up the steps, noticing the array of framed photos hanging on his wall; most of them of Fitzpatrick with his arm draped around celebrities. Fitzpatrick with Eamonn Holmes. Fitzpatrick with Brian O'Driscoll. Fitzpatrick with the Pope.

'Fuckin weirdo,' she whispers. 'Bet this guy's into some dark shit. Probably a kiddie fiddler. Aren't they all? Those bloody church fellas. Hiding behind the dog collar.'

She walks into the hallway as she hears him trudging back down the stairs, her right hand gripped to her phone.

'Here,' he says, stretching a piece of paper towards her. 'That's her mobile number.'

Helen takes the paper from him, then punches the number into her phone. Both her and Fitzpatrick stand in the cold hallway, the ring tone bouncing off the walls.

'Hello.'

'Hello, Abigail, this is Detective Brennan. I'm with Brother Fitzpatrick.'

'Oh no... is he in trouble?'

Helen lifts her gaze from the phone, to look at Fitzpatrick. He just holds his arms out wide.

'He's not, no,' Helen says. 'But two of the students who attend your school are.'

Helen hears a gasp on the other end of the line.

'Which two?' Abigail asks.

'Well… that's an answer I was hoping to get from you. We had an anonymous phone call made to our station from one of your students a few hours ago. Tommy Smith. You know him well?'

'Yeah… Tommy. Of course. Is he okay?'

'Oh yeah — that little fella is more than okay… wherever he is. But he told us two of his friends — both girls — were planning on killing themselves tonight. He didn't give us names… I'm hoping you can.'

'*What?*' Abigail says, all high pitched. 'Suicide?'

'Abigail. I know this may be shocking news to you right now, but I really don't have the time for you to absorb it all. I just need you to get your thinking cap on. Are there two girls who know Tommy who you think could be depressed enough to want to end their lives?'

Helen holds the phone away from her ear as Abigail blows a puff of her cheeks down the line.

'Jee… well… the truth is, we have quite a number of girls who have come to me this year describing symptoms of depression. I don't know what it is about the modern age; online bullying I think more than anything, but girls and boys are developing depression now more than any time I've worked in education.'

'Sorry, Abigail, I don't need a lesson on the growing rates of depression. I just need to find these two girls before it's too late. *Think.* Think thoroughly. Two girls Tommy Smith knows who suffer from some form of depression or have shown you any signs of it recently…'

Helen stares at Fitzpatrick as the line falls silent, noticing he's leaning against the wall for support. He doesn't look drunk anymore, just tired. As if he could fall asleep standing up.

'Yes,' Abigail says. 'I'm pretty sure I know which two girls you're talking about.'

23:30

Greta

I STARE AT THE CLOCK ABOVE THE MANTELPIECE, THEN stretch my arms above my head and yawn. I normally go to bed around eleven o'clock, but can't seem to shift myself tonight. I've been watching some awful movie called *French Kiss* that I thought might be alright because Meg Ryan was in it but… nah… too cheesy. Although, in fairness to the movie, it didn't have my full attention. I couldn't stop worrying about Ingrid. And Ciara.

Ingrid's going to be in a whole heap of trouble when she finally gets home. I'm going to ground her for two weeks; stop her pocket money for the rest of the month.

How dare she lie to me. I'm not sure I'm going to be able to cope with her being a teenager. I've too much on my plate looking after Sven.

I stretch and yawn again, then decide to click through the channels, even though I know I'm not going to watch anything. The phone ringing makes me cock my head and I hop off the couch to catch it as quickly as I can; not just because I'm hoping it's Ingrid and she's going to tell me she's okay, but more so because Terry will fume if it wakes him.

'Hello,' I say, snatching at the receiver.

'Auntie Greta… it's me… Harriet.'

'Oh hey, Harriet, please tell me Ingrid is with you.'

There's a pause. A pause that makes my stomach flip itself over.

'Eh… she's not with me right now. But she was here. She left about an hour ago and well… well… I don't know how to say this, but her and her friend Ciara, they seemed a bit… eh… they were acting a bit weird. As if they're up to something.'

I hold fingers to my forehead and close my eyes.

'Oh Jesus.'

'She eh… left a note in a book I had given her a loan of — she wrote that she loved me in it. She never does that. And Dad was giving them a lift home and half-way there they asked him to pull over at a garage and then they ran from him.'

'Oh Jesus,' I say again. 'She eh…' I hold my hand flat out in front of my eyes and watch it tremble, 'she eh… she seemed a bit distant when she left here earlier. They said they were going to spend the night at Ciara's house, but when I rang Ciara's mum a couple hours ago, she told me they'd said the opposite to her.'

I suck in a breath. 'Harriet, what did they say to you when they were at yours?'

Harriet clicks her tongue.

'Ingrid told me that she had been embarrassed by a boy in front of everybody at a party last night.'

'A boy. *I knew it!*' I say, covering my mouth after I've said it. 'Who is this boy, Harriet?'

'I don't know… he has a weird nickname. Stitch they call him, I think… something like that.'

'I had a feeling they were hanging around with boys. I said it to Terry. Terry wasn't having any of it.'

'Listen, Greta,' Brendan says joining in the call. 'They're just young girls. Whatever it is they're up to, I bet it's not as serious as you think. They'll be home soon.'

I hold my hand to my forehead again and try to slow my breathing. Maybe I shouldn't be overreacting. They both lied to their parents to say they were staying in each other's houses when they've probably called back over the see this boy. Is that such a big deal?

'If they call by again — or if you hear from them, Harriet — you make sure to ring me straight away, okay?'

'Course I will, Auntie Greta. I told Ingrid I'd bring her out soon and we can sit down and have a good chat.'

I put the phone down without saying goodbye, my mind racing. Then I stare up the stairs and before I even realise it I'm climbing them... slowly. When I reach our bedroom, I push the door open as gently as I can and watch his breaths heaving the duvet up... then down. He's almost on the verge of snoring. He'll go crazy if I wake him. I know he will. If he didn't have the big interview with the transport minister in the morning, I might be tempted. I close my eyes, to try to engage with the thoughts racing through my head, then decide to quietly pull the door closed and walk back down the stairs.

I shuffle my feet into my trainers, reach for my coat that's hung on the bottom bannister and then snatch at my keys. My hands are still shaking. I make sure I open the hall door quickly, so that it doesn't creak and, before I realise what I'm doing exactly, I'm out in the darkness, walking down our drive and turning right.

They only live four doors down. I say 'they'. I mean 'she'. He's never really there. I've sometimes wondered if they have an open marriage or something like that. It's certainly not conventional anyway.

I whisper an apology to nobody as I hold my finger

against their doorbell. I must be going mad; talking to myself. Then I hear the latch turn in the door and suddenly I am not talking to myself anymore.

'I'm so sorry, Vivian, but I'm getting ever so worried about the girls. I don't suppose they came back here, did they?'

Vivian blinks her eyes. She looks jaded. Or drunk.

'No... no... they didn't come back here. What time is it now?' she asks.

'It must be gone half eleven, something like that,' I say. 'It's just... my niece rang; said the two girls called over to her about an hour ago and they were acting suspiciously. Do you mind if I come in?'

Vivian takes a step back, giving me room to enter. This is actually the first time I've ever been in their house. It's lovely. They've much more light in their hallway than we have and their walls have been more recently painted than ours. It's easier to maintain a home if you only have one child, I suppose. Certainly easier if you have cleaners like these guys do.

'My brother-in-law offered to give them a lift home, but he only got half-way with them before they got out of the car and ran off. There's definitely something going on. Do you know much about the party they were at last night?'

I rest both of my hands on my hips and stare at Vivian as she shakes her head, folding her bottom lip out.

'No, sorry,' she says. Then she walks by me, into her living room. 'C'min.'

I follow her; across their massive TV screen, over the expensive rug and past their Chesterfield sofa until we're in the kitchen.

'Cup of tea... anything like that?' she asks as she grabs at the stem of a wine glass and swigs from it. 'Or,' she gasps after she's swallowed, 'this is an expensive Merlot. My favourite. Fancy a glass?'

I blow out an unsteady breath and then find myself squinting at Vivian, trying to work out just how many glasses of that expensive Merlot she must have had tonight. There's a certain unsteadiness to how she's standing in front of me; her eyes almost narrowed.

'No,' I answer in what I know is an irritated tone. 'We need to find out where our daughters are. Vivian... we need to ring the police.'

23:35

Ciara

THE TWO OF US ARE FACING EACH OTHER, HOLDING EACH other's hands, staring into each other's faces while we wait on the bus to come and pick us up to take us to our last stop.

'Whatcha think our parents are doing now?' I ask.

Ingrid rolls her eyes up to the stars.

'Probably be in bed. Dad will be anyway. He goes to bed around eight o'clock.'

'Eight o'clock,' I giggle. 'Does he stay up later than Sven?'

Ingrid smiles back at me.

'He's got to get up at five a.m. to do his show, doesn't he?'

I nod my head.

'Of course. And your mum?'

'She'll probably be going to bed about now. I think she stays up until around eleven-ish, watches movies and stuff. What about your parents?'

'Well… I'm pretty sure my dad is out somewhere, probably still working. Or that's what he'll be telling my mam he's doing anyway. I never know where he is up to be honest. My mam… well… we both know where she'll be right?'

'Sitting at the kitchen island drinking a glass of wine.'

'A *bottle*, Ingrid!'

Ingrid closes her eyes and shows me her teeth.

'Sorry. Of course, a bottle. I always get that wrong.'

'I'm not sure what time either of them go to bed at,' I say. 'They don't have a routine. It's not like your house.'

Ingrid grips my hands even tighter and the two of us leave the talk of our parents there.

I'm not going to blame my parents for my death. I only blame them for my life. I never asked to be born. Nobody does.

I think having kids is the most selfish thing anybody could ever do. It's one of the main reasons I don't want to become an adult. Adults tend to do so many selfish things. They never think of others. I've often lay down on my bed and thought about it; there actually can't be anything more selfish in this world than deciding to have children. How can anybody be so bloody selfish to do that! Look at Ingrid's little brother. Poor Sven is going to be a vegetable his whole life. He can barely talk. He never asked for his life. But you don't even have to have a sickness to wish you were never born. I've never been ill, aside from the odd cold here and there, and I certainly wish I was never born. Unless you count depression as a sickness. Though nobody has ever offered me a pill for it. I did wonder once whether or not I should go see a doctor and ask him about my feelings. But I just wouldn't know what to say. I rang a Childline number once as well, but hung up as soon as the questions got a bit tough for me. Suicide is the only way out. It makes total sense.

'How long's the bus ride back to Rathmines from here?' Ingrid asks.

'Bout fifteen minutes this time of night. There'll be no traffic. You all set?' I squeeze her fingers tighter in mine as I ask my question.

She looks down, nodding her head.

'Ready as I'll ever be,' she says. 'Mad to think we only have about fifteen minutes left though, isn't it?'

I squeeze her fingers again.

'Suppose it is. But that's a good thing, right? Only fifteen minutes left of being depressed, fifteen minutes left with the bad thoughts going round and round our heads.'

She looks up and smiles at me with her eyes. Then nods her head slowly again.

'I can't wait for it to be over,' she sighs out of her mouth. And then, over her shoulder, I see our bus coming.

'Isn't it mad to think nobody has any darn clue what we're up to? Just me and you, buddy; that's all. Everybody will be totally shocked in the morning, won't they? I don't think one person we know will say they saw it coming. I read about that once y'know,' I say.

'Read about what?'

I stop talking as the bus pulls in and its doors flap open.

'Two fares to Rathmines,' Ingrid says to the driver. He doesn't say anything; he just fiddles with his little machine until our tickets come out and then he holds his hand out for Ingrid to pour her coins into.

There are four people sitting downstairs, so we decide to head to the top deck. We sit at the front, right against the window and when we sit down I finally answer Ingrid's question.

'I read about suicide. It was in one of my mam's old magazines. It said loved ones never see it coming. And that it's usually the people who act happiest that end up doing it.'

'Not sure people would call us the happiest, would you?' she says to me.

I puff out a small laugh.

'Suppose so. But they'll all be surprised won't they?'

'Definitely,' she says.

23:35

Vivian

I curse. But only inside my head. This is the last thing I need. They'll be fine for fuck sake. They're teenagers.

'C'min,' I say, leading her through the living room and out into the kitchen. I don't mind her seeing me drink; it's not as if it's eleven o'clock on a Tuesday morning; it's a weekend night. Nothing wrong with that.

'Cup of tea... anything like that?' I ask as I grab at my glass. 'Or... this is an expensive Merlot. My favourite. Fancy a glass?'

She looks me up and down.

'No,' she says abruptly; as if she's angry with me. I knew she'd be a bitch. You can't be as attractive as she is without being a bit of a cunt in some way. 'We need to find out where our daughters are, Vivian... we need to ring the police.'

I place my glass back down on the kitchen island and walk towards her.

'Aren't you overreacting a bit? They're just teenagers having some fun on a weekend night.'

'They've school in the morning, Vivian. Besides, they lied to us. They told me they'd be here, they told you they'd be at my house. This is…' she turns around, holding her hand to her forehead as if she's some God-awful Hollywood actress, 'serious. Something is definitely going on between them.'

I don't know how to handle this level of drama. This is why I like to drink alone.

I find myself turning around, pulling at my cabinet and reaching for another glass. I half fill it with Merlot and then hand it to her.

'Here, calm down and let's talk,' I say.

She eyeballs me and lets an awkward silence settle between us before she accepts the glass, nodding her head as she does so.

'Thanks.'

I take her by the elbow and lead her to the kitchen island.

'Greta, the police won't be able to do anything. The girls have been missing for what… a few hours? Don't they have to be missing for, like, twenty-four hours at least before the police will get involved?'

She sits, takes her first sip of my Merlot, her hand a little shaky, and then nods her head.

'Suppose you're right. I'm being a bit over-dramatic, aren't I? That's not like me.'

Yeah right that's not like you.

I just smile back at her.

'Nice house you have. You used your kitchen space really well. I keep saying to Terry that we should put a skylight in ours… you can't beat a bit of natural light.'

I look up through our skylight, into the black sky.

'I didn't even ask Michael for permission,' I say. 'I just got it done, gave the builder Michael's bank account details.'

Greta pushes out a small laugh. She seems to have relaxed. Wine works wonders.

'Where is Michael?' she asks, looking around herself.

I push out a huff.

'In work, probably.'

'On a Sunday night?'

I sip from my glass.

'He never stops. He's in that office more than he is here.'

She takes a fistful of that beautiful golden hair she has and tugs it over her shoulder, then rings her fingers through it.

'I think we might share ambitious husbands as well as troublesome thirteen-year-old daughters,' she says.

As I stare at her playing with her hair, I remember the amount of times Ciara came home to say that the Murphys would like to invite us to their house for dinner.

'Yeah… we've probably loads in common. We should — for the sake of our girls — get to know each other a bit more,' I say.

'That'd be nice.'

The kitchen falls silent. Seems as if we've run out of things to say already. I lick at my teeth, a habit I have when I drink red wine because I hate the thought of my teeth staining, and then refill my glass. I don't bother offering more to Greta; she's barely touched what I've given her already.

'Sorry,' she says, shaking her head. 'I hate to bring it back up, but I just can't understand why they'd run away from Brendan if he was giving them a lift home. It keeps coming into my head. I can't relax.'

She stands up. And so do I.

'There's not much we can do; let's just wait here until they come home.'

'We could go out and look for them,' she says.

I look down at my slippers.

'Let's think it through. Who else might know where they are? Do you know of any boys they hang around with at school?' I ask.

Greta puffs out her cheeks, then shakes her head again.

'No… jee. I thought they didn't have any other friends, never mind boyfriends. I thought Ciara and Ingrid were just two peas in a pod.' She looks up at me, her eyes widening. 'Do you know if they have any other friends?'

I scoff. Then tug at my ear. Jesus. I don't know anything about Ciara really. It's just… it's just so boring, parenting, isn't it? I haven't enjoyed any stage of it. I'm not quite sure what I would get out of questioning my daughter. It holds no interest to me. Not that I'd ever say that out loud.

'No, sorry. Same as you. I thought they were just two peas in a pod myself. Ingrid is the only friend Ciara's ever had. Well… apart from Debbie.'

Greta's head cocks up again.

'Debbie. The girl who minded Ciara for years right?'

'Uh-huh,' I say before taking another sip.

'Think they might have called out to her house tonight?'

I shake my head as I swallow.

'Course not, why would they do that?'

'Well,' Greta says, standing a little taller, 'I'm wondering why they called out to Ingrid's cousin. I know it's late… but maybe you should ring Debbie. See if she's heard anything from the girls.'

I sigh and hold my eyes closed for a couple seconds longer than I probably should.

'Really?' I say when I reopen them.

'Please.' Her hands are clasped, her eyes sad. I feel sorry for her.

So I place my wine back on to the island and shuffle my way to the phone.

Fitzpatrick has slumped back into a seating position on the stairs — his head in his hands — by the time Helen has hung up the call. She drops the piece of paper he had handed to her minutes ago with Abigail's number on it and then spins on her heels to head out the door. But she stops, turns again, takes two steps towards Fitzpatrick and leans over him.

'You better hope I catch up with these two girls before it's too late, Brother.' She breathes heavily at him, giving herself a moment to think of what to say next. 'Bloody drinking so much when you have such an important job to look after young people. How dare you. I bet... I wouldn't be surprised if you're somehow responsible for these girls suffering with depression. I know you've got dark secrets — and I'm going to find out what they are. I'll be back, Brother Fitzpatrick... and I'll find out just what exactly it is you wanted to apologise for.'

Fitzpatrick takes his hands from his face and sits into a more upright position just as Helen is pulling at his front door.

'It's not that bad!' he shouts after her as she storms down his narrow pathway, towards the Garda car she stole half-an-hour ago. 'It was only a few quid I stole from the school funds. I'll pay it back. I swear.'

Helen doesn't bother to look back at him. She's fully focused on saving these two girls. She got names, got addresses — all from Abigail — and is intent on being their hero; the hero she failed to be for Scott.

She speeds off from outside Brother Fitzpatrick's house, noticing curtains twitching in a couple neighbours' windows as she does so. By the time she's at the end of the road, she switches the sirens on, the sound blaring, the lights flashing.

'C'mon, c'mon, c'mon,' she instructs the car, tapping her palms against the steering wheel.

She dips her head slightly, to see the digital clock on the dashboard. 23:36. Then she smiles.

'You're gonna do this, Helen. You're gonna catch them. You're gonna save them. You're gonna save yourself. By the time the morning comes around, nobody will be bothered that you stuck your nose in, nobody will be bothered that you stole a police car. They'll be lauding you, offering you your old job back. Eddie might even ask you to help him run the station. Just as you and he planned when you first joined the force and fell in love.'

She eyeballs herself in the rear-view mirror, the grin widening across her face.

Two girls. Both thirteen. Both being bullied at school. Both have parents who don't give a shit. The information Abigail gave her over the phone wasn't surprising — not to Helen. She'd been researching teen suicides for over twenty years. Is obsessed with the subject. Boys are more likely to commit suicide, though not until they're in their twenties. That's when they realise they haven't met the expectations society has placed on them. They become disillusioned, begin to compare themselves to their peers — believing everyone else's bullshit — then they top themselves because they're confused and too proud to speak out about how they feel. Girls on the other hand are much more mature than boys from an early age. They realise as early as their teens that they might not be meeting expectations placed on them. They look to their peers, especially the popular ones, and feel mightily inadequate. Whereas males are most likely to end their own lives in their mid-twenties, females are more likely to want to do it in their mid teens. Though, fortunately, they're less brave than the opposite sex; less likely to carry out a suicide attempt to full fruition.

But it seems — to Helen — that these two girls are beyond that. They're not looking for attention. They *want* to do this. They're going to end their lives tonight. They've made a pact; just like Scott and his friends did twenty-two years ago. And they're not going to change their minds.

Helen knows all of this information from studying statistics released by the National Suicide Research Foundation every year; has noted the rapid increase in numbers across both genders with every report that gets published. Each year she tuts as she reads the latest figures, and on each occasion she thinks to herself 'if only I could have talked to one of them before they did it, it might make up for me losing Scott.' That's why her adrenaline is rising now; she is certain that tonight is the night — is adamant she's finally gonna save, not one, but two teenagers from doing exactly what Scott and his friends did.

She screeches the car on to the canal road, swerving around those who have pulled in to let her pass; her heart racing as quickly as the speedometer, her mind flashing forward to tomorrow when she will receive plaudits of heroism from all around her.

Then her eyes blink back to the present. But it's too late.

Her car comes to a sudden stop, crashing into the back of the Land Rover in front of her. She jerks forward, then back in her seat.

'Ah for fuck sake!' she yells, yanking at her door handle. She gets out, at the same time a middle-aged man gets out of the Land Rover.

'Jesus, did you not hear my siren?' she says.

The man holds both of his palms up towards her.

'I did, officer, I was trying to pull over, you just came too fast... way too fast.'

They meet where their cars met, and both bend down to survey the damage.

'It's not too bad, the man says... your car took the brunt of it. These things,' he says patting at the wheel arch of his Land Rover, 'can take a bashing.'

'You really need to be more careful when you hear emergency services on the roads,' Helen scoffs. The man stands back up straight, stares at her, his eyes squinting.

'You okay?' he says. 'You didn't hit your head, did you?'

Helen tuts.

'I'd feel better if you moved your bloody car so I can get on with my job.'

The man swivels his head, taking in the two pedestrians who have ran towards them.

'Don't we need to swap insurance details or whatev—'

'Contact Terenure Garda station tomorrow, we'll sort it out then,' Helen says as she strides away from him

'But eh... what's your name?'

Helen doesn't answer. She hops back into the police car, reverses it, the front bumper hanging off, and then waves her hand at the man as she speeds off again.

The noise of the bumper scraping against the road can be heard over the siren, but Helen doesn't care. She'll deal with the whole mess in the morning. Eddie will look after it. A new bumper will mean nothing in the grand scheme of things. Saving lives is the most important thing a copper can do; isn't that what the police force is for: serving and protecting the public? She's going to protect two members of the public in the most heroic way imaginable.

'I'm coming, girls,' she screams to herself. 'Hold on. Don't do anything yet. Helen's on her way.'

She turns the car, its wheels screeching, its bumper scraping and its siren blaring, onto the road Abigail said the two girls lived on and then slows down so she can make out the numbers on the doors of the large houses. She's not surprised the girls seem to come from good stock. That tends to be the way. It's rare that it's poor girls who attempt suicide. It's more likely those who feel they can't live up to the expectations set on them by their successful parents. She thinks that might have been why Scott did it. He showed no signs of depression. Perhaps he just felt inadequate because of their regarded status as Detectives. Though — having wracked her brain for twenty-two years — Helen really hasn't come to any conclusion. It eats at her that she will never know the answer. That's why she's eager for her and Eddie to move to Canada. The quiet, the calm. She's certain it will dilute the prominence of that question repeating itself over and over in her mind.

When she sees one of the numbers she's searching for, she abandons the car in the middle of the street, strides towards the front door and lifts the knocker before slamming it back down three times as loudly as she possibly can.

A light comes on in the hallway before the door inches open,

'Jesus, why you knocking so hard, everything alright?' a woman says. She notices the police car over Helen's shoulder and then holds a hand to her mouth. 'Oh Jesus.'

'Ma'am, I'm Detective Brennan from Rathmines Garda

station… I need to speak with your daughter as a matter of urgency.'

'Oh my God, what's she done? What's she done?'

The woman takes a step backwards, her eyes widening, her fists forming into a ball.

'We believe your daughter's life is in danger. It's imperative I speak with her as soon as possible.'

The woman holds both balls of fists either side of her face, digging them into her cheeks.

'Mum, Mum. What's wrong?' a girl appearing at the top of the stairs, wearing polka dot pyjamas, calls out.

The woman looks up at her, then swallows.

'Louise, you need to get yourself down here right now! The police are here to talk to you.'

23:40

Terry

'*THAT'S ALL VERY WELL AND GOOD THAT YOU THINK YOU ARE doing the right thing, Minister, but I put it to you that your opinion is wrong. Just give me a second here to read you out some statistics. Four years ago, the number of road deaths in Ireland was one hundred and eighty-eight. The following year one hundred and ninety-three. The year after that, one hundred and sixty-two, then back up to one eighty-six. Yes, the following year there was small drop again, to one-five-seven, but in each of the past two years the number has slightly increased again. I put it to you, that labelling the methods you have introduced over the past six years as 'a fantastic success' is nothing more than a fairy-tale. Isn't that right Minist—*'

'Terry, Terry... wake up.'

My eyes dart open. I can't see a thing, but I can hear her — and smell her.

'What the fuck, Greta?' I say, slapping the mattress.

'Terry, Ingrid is in trouble. Something's definitely up.'

I hold my eyes closed as tightly as I can, then open them wide, just so I can try to focus. I turn to the digital clock on my side table. 23:41.

'What are you talkin' about?'

'Terry — Ingrid and Ciara… they called over to Brendan and Harriet's house earlier, they were also at Ciara's former child minder. We've just been on calls to each of them; they all say the girls were acting really weird. I'm so worried, Terry, I … I…'

I can feel her knees vibrate against the bed, so I hold my hand out to reach her; see if I can calm her down a bit. Then I pull back the duvet and manage to throw my legs out of the side of the bed, yelping out a yawn as I do so.

'Calm down, Greta,' I say, 'there's no need to get all dramatic. Start again. What did you wake me up for?'

She takes a deep breath, then sits down beside me.

'Ingrid and Ciara visited two houses tonight. Two that we know of. And they acted really strangely in both of them. I told you… I told you when they were going out that door tonight that Ingrid couldn't even look me in the eye. Something's up… something major.'

'Like what?' I ask, twisting the balls of my palms into my eye sockets.

I hear her shrug.

'I dunno,' she says.

'Well, then, how am I supposed to know? I've just been asleep, haven't I? How do you suppose I know what the hell our daughter's up to when I've been snoring my head off?'

I hear her gasp a little bit. Maybe that was a bit harsh. But she knows darn well I have a big interview in the morning.

'Terry, your daughter might be in trouble,' she says.

I stand up, click at the switch on the lamp by my bedside and then sit back down, holding the palm of my hand to my wife's lower back.

'How the hell do you get from her visiting her cousin to her being in trouble, Greta? Are you sure you're not being a bit dramatic here? Ingrid and Ciara — they're teenagers now.

This is the sorta stuff teenagers get up to…. Listen,' I say, moving my hand up to grip her shoulder, 'I'll give her an earful tomorrow when she gets back from school. But…. I mean, there's nothing I can do right now, is there? I'm in my bloody boxer shorts, and I have to get up in five hours' time.'

'Terry… Brendan was giving them a lift home when they both got out of his car and ran. They left a book behind; a book Harriet had lent to Ingrid. Ingrid had signed it before she handed it back, writing 'I love you Harriet'. You know that's not like our daughter. I think she might be running away; her and Ciara.'

'Huh?' I say. 'What would they be running away for?'

Greta shrugs again. She's really good at posing questions; is shit at answering them. A bit like the politicians I interview.

'Well… have you checked her wardrobe, did she take any clothes or anything like that?'

Greta stands up, then sprints out of our room. I hear her as she rifles through Ingrid's wardrobe, sweeping hangers aside.

'No… no everything seems to be here', she shouts out to me.

'Shhh… Jesus, be quite will ye. You'll wake Sven.'

I hold both of my hands over my face and then sigh as deeply as I can into them.

'Terry, I'm really frightened. I don't know what's going on, I just know I don't like it,' Greta says, pacing back into our bedroom.

I *hate* that I'm awake right now. Hate that it'll play havoc with my performance tomorrow. But I know I can't really have a go at Greta, especially while she's shaking so much and almost in tears. It's just… I don't know what it is she wants me to do.

'Let me go get you a cup of tea and we can have a little

chat, huh?' I say, standing up, tapping her on the shoulder as I walk by and then scratching my balls as I head down the stairs.

'What the fuck!?' I say, reeling back, cupping my hands over my boxers.

'Sorry,' the woman says. And then I recognise her. It's her from up the road, Ciara's mam. What's-er-name... 'I eh... didn't realise you were going to come down the stairs half naked.'

'Oh sorry, Terry,' Greta says, running across our landing. 'Yeah... Vivian's here. We're both a bit unsure what to do. That's why I decided to wake you.'

I stare up the stairs at my wife, then back down at Vivian.

'Well, first things first...' I say, 'How about I get some clothes on.'

HELEN STARES AT THE BACK OF LOUISE'S POLKA DOT PYJAMAS as she follows her and her mother into their plush kitchen, all the while wondering what the hell Louise is doing dressed for bed when she is supposed to be killing herself in a half an hour.

The light is so bright in the kitchen that it makes the windowed patio doors look as if they've been painted jet-black.

Louise's mother pulls out a chair, motions for Helen to sit it in and then seats herself in the chair next to it, her hands shaking. Louise walks around the opposite side of the table but remains standing, her arms folded.

'There's no need to be shaking,' Helen says, gripping the mother's hands as she sits. 'I'm here now, everything is okay.'

'Wh-what is going on?' the mother stutters.

Helen purses her lips at her, then flicks her eyes towards Louise.

'Louise… whatever it is you are planning to do at midnight, I'm here to save you. I am the mother of somebody who—'

'*What?*' Louise screeches, her face contorting.

Helen grips the mother's hands even tighter.

'Tommy… Tommy Smith, he told us what you and Sinead are planning on doing tonight.'

Louise pulls at the back of a chair, scoots it towards herself, sits in it, then rests both of her elbows on the table and stares at Helen.

'What are you talking about, officer?'

Helen looks back at the mother, then at Louise again.

Silence.

'Officer… please, please tell us what's going on,' the mother says, her voice shaking as much as her hands.

Helen swallows.

'Louise, be honest with me now, be honest with your mother. As I was about to say to you, I am not just a Detective, I am the mother of a son who died by suicide… I have studied suicide for many years. Decades. You need to be honest. Are you and Sinead Longthorn planning on ending your lives at midnight tonight?'

Louise breathes out a laugh. Her mother's eyes go wide, her arms — releasing from Helen's grip — stretch across the table, so she can cling to her daughter's fingers.

'Mam,' Louise says, shaking her head. 'Relax. This is all… this is…' She rolls her shoulders, shakes her head with disbelief.

'It's okay, Louise,' Helen says slowly. 'Open up to us now; I'm here to tell you life is worth—'

'What the hell are you talking about, officer?' Louise says, standing back up. She walks around the table, to her mother, and places her hands atop both of her shoulders. 'I was asleep in bed until you came banging down the door.'

Helen swallows again, then her eyes dart from left to right.

'Officer?' The mother says, squinting.

'I eh... I... where is Sinead Longthorn?' Helen asks.

'The Longthorns, they're in Majorca aren't they, pet?' the mother says, turning to look up at her daughter.

Louise nods her head.

'Yeah, they've been away the past couple weeks during the mid-term, they're due home on Saturday.'

Helen holds her eyes closed, reality washing through her stomach.

'In Majorca,' she whispers. Then she opens her eyes. 'So you two aren't... you eh... you didn't make a pact?'

'What the hell is going on here, Louise? Tell me!' the mother says, standing up and turning to grip her daughter in a bear hug.

'Relax, Mam, I don't know where this officer is getting all of this from.'

Helen stands too, causing her chair to squeak across the kitchen tiles.

'The welfare officer at your school — Abigail — she said you and Sinead have shown signs of depression over the past few months, says you are dealing with a big bullying issue.'

'What!?' the mother says, leaning herself off her daughter so that she can stare into her eyes.

'Yeah... we reported some bullying that's been going on and Ms Jensen — Abigail — gave us some leaflets about depression and teen suicide statistics last week. But it was... it was nothing. Me and Sinead looked at the leaflets and wondered if Jensen was going crazy. It was way over the top. We're getting bullied at school... and a bit online... but it's... I mean, we're not going to kill ourselves. We never would. We were just reporting the bullying.'

'Oh sweet Jesus,' the mother says, grabbing Louise in for another hug. 'Why didn't you tell me... sweet Lord.'

'Relax, Mam... it's all okay. It's nothing.'

Helen stares at Louise and her mother holding each other

in the middle of their kitchen, before her eyes flick to the microwave clock. 11:45. Fifteen minutes left to save… whoever it is she is supposed to save. And here she is, standing in the wrong fucking kitchen.

'Louise,' she says tentatively. 'Is there any reason Tommy Smith would ring in to two police stations to tell us two girls are planning on committing suicide?'

Louise releases the grip her mother has on her, then sticks her bottom lip out and shakes her head.

'I don't think anybody believes anything Tommy Smith says. I mean… somebody told me he's hanging around with a gang of older fellas now.'

Helen holds a hand to her face, covering her eyes so she can squeeze them shut in an attempt to defuse the migraine that is threatening to flare up.

'Are there any girls, that you know of from your school, who you think might be planning on ending their lives?' she asks, her hand still covering her face.

Louise puffs out her cheeks.

'No,' she says.

'No girls who might be depressed?' Helen asks.

Louise puffs again, this time almost laughing.

'Who isn't depressed these days?' she says. 'All of the girls talk to Ms Jensen about some problem or other. I think she just diagnoses anyone who has a small problem as being depressed. She's just ticking boxes, isn't she? Isn't that what working in a school is all about? That's what me and Sinead have noticed since we started going to secondary school. All the teachers are just following protocol. They're just protecting themselves in case anything happens. They aren't interested in the students, not really. They're only interested in themselves.'

'Louise, please. Think. I have good reason to believe two

girls from your school are going to kill themselves tonight. If it's not you and Sinead... who is it?'

Helen removes the hand from her face, takes one large stride towards Louise and grips her shoulders. Louise is tiny, the top of her head just about reaching to Helen's chest.

'I'm sorry. I don't think there's anyone at my school who is suicidal. Of course I don't. If I believed that, I'd have reported it, wouldn't I?'

Helen's eyes glaze over as she stares down at Louise, then she lightly pats her on both shoulders and spins on her heels.

'I'm so sorry to bother you two,' she says as she walks out of the kitchen and down the long, narrow hallway before reaching the front door.

'Is that it?' the mother yells after her. 'Officer... officer, is that it? You're just gonna leave us with that bombshell?'

Helen doesn't answer. She pulls at the door and steps out into the garden, then sucks in some fresh air through the gaps in her teeth. It's more of a cringe than a breath.

She wobbles down the garden path, her head racing. Then she sees it. The police car with the bumper hanging off and the front light smashed.

'Oh for fuck sake, Helen,' she whispers to herself.

23:45

Ingrid

Neither of us have said a word to each other since we sat upstairs on the bus. We were holding hands for a few minutes, then Ciara let go and leaned in to me. I have my arm wrapped around her; her head snuggled into my chest.

The bus seems to be moving in slow motion, swaying us a little as it makes its way out of Crumlin. We'll probably arrive in about ten minutes or so. Our last stop. Ever. At least I think it is. I'm pretty sure we're actually going to go through with this.

There's not much time to back out now anyway. There was a tiny part of me that had always felt Ciara was too frightened to commit suicide, no matter how many times she spoke to me about it. But last night, as we were coming up with our pact, I could see in her eyes how excited she was that she was finally going to do it. The fact that I was on board obviously made a huge difference to her. She told me I was the reason she had stopped herself doing it before. But if I wanted to die, then so the hell did she.

I stroke her hair and as I do, she places one of her hands on my knee. We're both just staring out the front window

274

of the bus, at nothing because it's too dark to make anything out. The pictures in my mind are more clear than the picture in front of us. I've been thinking about Sven; about how he'll be affected if I commit suicide. I'm hoping it helps him more than anything, though. When he grows up and learns what happened to his older sister, he'll feel that his condition — whatever it is — isn't so bad. He'll know life is only as good as his mind. And his mind will always be good because he doesn't know what bad is. I don't think he'll ever be clever enough to be depressed. I spent part of this morning lying on my bed wishing I had his condition.

Besides, Sven will get more attention from Mum and Dad if I'm dead. It'll all work out fine for him. There's no need for me to worry about my little brother. There's certainly no need for me to be going back over the thoughts I've had going through my mind all day anyway. I need to shut it off; can't wait to shut it off. I'm sure we're doing the right thing. It'll be better for everyone when I'm gone.

I look at my digital watch. 23:47. Almost there, the last minutes of our lives ticking away.

As the bus turns down the canal road, Ciara twists her head so she can look at me. She doesn't say anything, she just smiles, then turns her head back so that she's staring out the window again. So, I do the same; stare out the window. Only this time I try to take in what I'm looking at, rather than slipping back into my thoughts. It's tough to make much out in the dark, but the street lamps are lighting the way a bit, shining onto the calm water of the canal.

The bus pulls over, allowing a few more passengers to get on board. A couple of them climb the stairs and sit behind us. I wonder if that's why we've been so quiet on this bus journey; because there are others around us. But I bet it's more to do with the fact that we're just trying to soak in our last minutes alive. Maybe we've said all we have to say anyway.

I wonder what Ciara is thinking. She doesn't have a little brother; doesn't care for her mam or her dad. She's probably thinking about Debbie. Or maybe Miss Moriarty. I don't ask her though. I just continue to run my fingers through her hair and down her cheek. Until I feel wetness. I stop, then tilt her head towards me.

She's crying.

23:45

Greta

I SIT ACROSS FROM VIVIAN, BOTH OF US LEANING OUR ELBOWS on our thighs in the quiet of my sitting room while we wait on Terry to get some clothes on. My fingers are fidgeting with each other as I try to get inside Ingrid's mind. I've probably been a terrible mum to her over the past few months. Sven's taken most of my attention.

It's beginning to dawn on me that we left her alone to face secondary school. I don't even know what subjects she's studying there; have no idea what any of her teachers' names are.

'Jeez, I just hope they're out flirting with boys,' I say to Vivian. She nods her head. The thought of Ingrid flirting with boys would have been my worst nightmare a few hours ago, but now it seems to be my biggest hope. That's how worried I am. I have no idea what Ingrid and Ciara intend on doing tonight.

'Right-ee-o,' Terry says as he plods down the stairs. He always says 'right-ee-o'; especially during his show. It's almost like a shitty catchphrase he clings to. He claps his hands once and then stands between Vivian and me.

'So, we know they visited Harriet and before that your former child minder, Vivian... remind me of her name again?'

'Debbie. Debbie Martyn.'

'Yes, Debbie. So what does this tell us? I wonder if they have been visiting older girls to get their perspective on boys. Maybe Ingrid — or Ciara, it could be Ciara — has got her first boyfriend and perhaps they just went in search of advice.'

I nod my head slowly as I soak in the plausibility of Terry's theory. Then I look up at Vivian. She's still staring into her lap.

'Vivian, what do you think?' I ask.

She looks up, her eyes heavy.

'Sorry, but eh... could I have a drink? My throat's a bit parched,' she asks.

'Sure thing, a glass of water?' Terry says.

'Eh... do you have anything heavier... a red wine by any chance?'

My eyes meet Terry's.

'Sure thing,' he says, making his way to our kitchen.

'What do you think, Vivian? Has Ciara mentioned any boys in her life recently? Ever heard of this Stitch or whatever his name is?'

She shakes her head.

'I... I don't really... I mean... I don't even know when I last sat down and spoke with Ciara. It's been ages. Way too long.'

'Don't worry,' I say making my way towards her so I can rest my hand on her shoulder. 'I feel the exact same way about my relationship with Ingrid. I guess we're both guilty of feeling our girls have grown up enough to look after themselves.'

She looks up at me. I'm not sure if her eyes are glazed

from emotion or from alcohol. I wonder how much wine she had before I called over to her.

'Here y'go, Vivian,' Terry says, swooping back into the room.

'Is this Merlot?' she says, sniffing into the glass he just handed to her.

'It's red. S'all I know,' Terry says.

I'd normally laugh at something like that. But I just stand back upright and fold my arms.

'Terry, I hope you're right. I hope the girls have just been trying to get a perspective from girls older than them about boys. And that they'll knock back on that door in the next few minutes. But the one thing that's niggling me is the note Ingrid wrote in Harriet's book. Why would she do that? It's sticking in my mind... it almost seems... I don't know... final.'

'Don't be silly. What do you mean final?' he asks me.

I dip my chin into my neck and begin to fidget with my fingers again.

'I don't know,' I say. I don't want to say out loud what is troubling me. Mainly because I can't make sense of it.

Terry sits on our sofa, then claps his hands again.

'She wants to ring the police, don't ye, hun?' Vivian says, swirling her glass.

'Sure the police will laugh at us,' Terry says. 'Don't children have to be missing for twenty-four hours or something before they'll look into it?'

'That's what I told her,' Vivian says.

I rub my face with my hand and then blow out my lips.

I keep seeing the note she wrote for Harriet in my mind; her cute little handwriting.

I love you Harriet

She never says those words, let alone write them. She has never told me she loves me; has never said it to her dad, to her little brother. It's just not how we talk to each other.

'Something's not adding up for me,' I say. 'I'm going to call the police.'

I pace out of the sitting room, into the hallway and pick up the phonebook to search for the local station's number. Terry joins me by the time I've found it and I begin punching it into the phone.

'Are you sure you're not overreacting, Greta?' he says.

I just stare at him as I hold the phone to my ear.

'Rathmines Garda Station, how may I help you?'

'Hi… my name is Greta Murphy. I have a thirteen-year-old daughter who has gone missing with her best friend. Her name is Ingrid Murphy, her friend is Ciara Joyce.'

'Okay, ma'am,' the voice says. 'And how long have these two girls been missing?'

I hold my eyes closed, then sigh a little out of my nostrils.

'They left here at about twenty-past seven this evening.'

'This evening?' the voice says back to me. 'Just over four hours ago?'

'Uh-hmm,' I say as I begin to nibble at my thumbnail.

'Ma'am, I understand your concern right now, but we suggest you only involve the Gardaí should your child be missing over twenty-four hours.'

'But I'm… I'm going out of my mind right now. I know something is wrong, I can feel it in my bones. Call it mother's intuition or whatever—'

'Ma'am… I am sorry you feel this way. But trust me; ninety-nine times out of a hundred, young people find their way home after we've received a call like this. What I propose you do is wait at home. Make sure somebody is there when your daughter arrives. There's no need for everybody to go out and search; somebody needs to be at home when your daughter gets there.'

I bite at my thumbnail again, then feel a rage burn up from my insides.

'That's it? That's all you're gonna do for me? Give me some obvious advice?'

Terry takes the phone from me and rests his other hand around my shoulder.

'Officer, this is the girl's father — Terry Murphy... y'know, off the radio? We'll eh... take your advice on board. Thank you very much.'

Then he just hangs up. As if everything is okay.

'Right-ee-o,' he says, squeezing my shoulder a bit tighter and leading me back into the sitting room. 'Ingrid and Ciara are clearly up to something. But I bet it's all very innocent. This is all we have to do: Vivian, I suggest you go home and wait up until Ciara arrives home. Somebody needs to be there. Greta, you need to do the same here. It's more than likely they'll arrive home soon. The Gardaí have said this is the only thing we can do right now.'

I watch as Vivian downs the rest of her glass, before handing it to Terry.

'What are you going to do?' I ask my husband.

'Well... I have an important interview in the morning. I'm going to go back to bed. Don't wake me up when Ingrid gets home; I'll deal with her tomorrow.'

I switch my stare from Terry to Vivian and then back again.

'That's it? That's all we're going to do? We're just going to wait for them to come home?'

'It's all we can do,' Vivian says, reaching her arm to my elbow. And then she winks at Terry before turning on her heels and strolling down our hallway and out our front door.

Terry leads me to the sofa and sits me into it.

'Just relax, Greta… throw on a movie or something.'

I stare up at him and then find myself nodding my head.

'Okay,' I say. 'I'll just wait here until she comes home.'

I take the blanket that hangs on the back of the sofa and drape it over me as Terry kisses me on the top of my head. Then I pick up the remote control and begin clicking through the channels.

Her hand trembles as she tries to place the key into the ignition; failing six times before finally finding the slot.

'You're a fuckin idiot, Helen. A fuckin idiot!'

She stares over at the house she's just left as she shifts into first gear, sees Louise and her mother staring out at her. They watch as the bumper scrapes off the road, sparks darting in all directions as the car pulls off.

Helen eyeballs herself in the rear-view mirror, then shakes her head.

'A fuckin idiot!'

The speedometer's dial begins to shake as it pushes upwards; the car now doing seventy miles per hour in the narrow streets of a tight housing estate.

By the time she's reached a stretch of main road, the speedometer is inching towards one hundred. Then Helen forces her foot on the brake, the car coming to a noisy, sudden stop; parts of the bumper cracking and flying free.

And then she slaps herself in the face with both hands.

'A fuckin' idiot! C'mon, Scott, talk to me. Give me a sign.

Are there or aren't there two girls out there about to kill themselves?'

She's startled when she hears a rattling on her window.

'Officer, officer… you okay?'

A man with square-framed glasses is staring in through her driver's side window, his nose practically pushed up against the glass.

She waves her hand up at him. 'I'm fine.'

'You sure?' he says. 'Did you have a crash? Would you like me to ring an ambulance for you?'

'I said I'm fine!' she shouts.

The man holds both of his hands up, then slowly backs away from her.

Helen pivots her head around, looks out the back window, the front windscreen, each of the windows either side of her. It's dark. Almost pitch black, save for a tiny street lamp about fifteen yards away that seems to only light the pavement directly beneath it. There are no other cars on the road, no sign of anybody but the silhouette of the man who had knocked on the window walking away from her.

She breathes in through her nose, then pops the breath out of her mouth. She repeats this over and over; each time the sound of the pop growing in volume and frustration.

'Nobody's gonna kill themselves are they? The calls weren't fucking suicide calls; they were distraction calls, Helen. You fuckin idiot!' She slaps both of her hands on top of the dashboard. 'As soon as I heard suicide I let my heart overrule my head.'

She grunts loudly, before a cringe runs down her spine. Then she slaps her hands on top of the dashboard again and screams, an eerie shriek that echoes all the way around the car and back into her ears.

'Fuck you, Alan Keating!' she says. 'Fuck you, Tommy Smith. Fuck you, Scott Brennan!' Then she gasps in some air.

'No... no... I'm sorry, Scott. I didn't mean that, honey. I didn't mean it.'

Her shoulders begin to shake. She wipes a tear that had rested on one of the bags under eyes, and then looks around herself again. The night is dead. Eerie. Creepy. Until car lights shine in the distance, coming towards her. The lights slow down, then a horn beeps.

Helen shifts into first gear, presses at the accelerator and drives off, waving her hand up in the air in apology to the driver behind.

She thinks back through the night as she drives in no particular direction at all; back to when she bluffed her way into Terenure Garda station to meet with Charlie; to when she took him to the Red Cow Luas HQ to view CCTV footage; to when she went to Patrick Tobin's house; to when she went to Brother Fitzpatrick's local pub and ordered him outside. Twice. To when she splashed his face with water. Twice. To when she confronted Tommy Smith in the snooker hall; to when she pinned poor Charlie up against the shop shutters and bullied him into lying to his SI; to when she sat on his desk and gripped onto his car keys; to ramming that car up the back of a Land Rover; to entering the house of an innocent school girl and telling her mother she was there to save her from killing herself.

She stops the car near the canal, its lights reflecting off the calm water. She's often thought about ending her own life. She wanted to do it straight after hearing of Scott's suicide. It was Cyril who woke her and Eddie up one Monday morning, just gone four a.m.

'I'm so sorry,' Cyril said. Helen knew by the look on his face that something awful had happened. 'It's Scott, isn't it? Isn't it? Scott! Scott!' she yelled up the stairs.

'He's not up there,' Cyril said approaching her slowly. He threw his arms around her, hugged her as firmly as he could.

'He's dead, Helen. Him and two friends. They took their own lives. I'm so sorry.'

She's replaying that moment now as she stares out of the windscreen and almost feels tempted to press down on the accelerator, drive straight into the canal. The car would probably take about twenty minutes to sink fully under the water. Two minutes after that she'd be gasping for breath.

'That'd be a fuckin stupid way to do it,' she mumbles to herself. 'Horrible. At least Scott and his mates did it quick. They were breathing in fresh air one second, the next they were gone. Forever.'

She sighs, then presses the balls of her palms into her eye sockets and wiggles her wrists.

'Wake the fuck up, Helen,' she says. 'Think. Think!'

She switches off the ignition, kills the lights that were shining onto the canal's ripples and then pulls at the lever beside her chair, so that it flicks backwards, allowing her to slouch into a lying position. Then she begins to suck on her lips; a tic she always produces when she's floating deep into her mind.

'It's so quiet,' she says, leaning up to peer out the windows. 'It wouldn't be this quiet if Alan Keating was up to something. If he's pulled something off, there'd be sirens all over this neck of the woods. Think, Helen. Come on. Think for fuck sake!'

She shakes her head with frustration, clenching her hands into a ball.

'Uuugh, what am I doing?' she says, pressing at the lever beside her seat again and pumping it back to an upright position. 'There can't be two girls out there... there just can't be. Why did Tommy Smith run away? It doesn't make sense. Does it? Come on, Scott. You're the only one who can tell me. Please. Give me a sign. Give me a sign, son.'

Her jaw drops open when she feels her phone vibrating in

her pocket. She reaches for it, stares at the screen and notices a strange number. Her finger is trembling as she presses at the green button; almost as if she thinks Scott will be on the other end of the line.

'Hello,' she says tentatively.

'Helen,' a familiar voice says.

She sits upright.

'Charlie... is that you?'

'Yes, Helen. Listen... we've just had a phone call made to the station a couple minutes ago. I thought the right thing to do was to ring you as soon as I heard.'

23:50

Ciara

INGRID TILTS MY HEAD UP SO SHE CAN LOOK AT MY FACE. I think she felt one of my tears when she was running her fingers through my hair. I smile up at her, then shift to sit more upright, resting my ear on to her shoulder. Neither of us says anything; we just stare out the front window.

I wonder what she's thinking about. Probably her parents and Sven. Why wouldn't she? She's going to miss them. And they're going to miss her. They're worth thinking about. Not like my family. I'm not going to miss one thing about my parents. I know they're the reason my head is so messed up. They shouldn't have had me. They clearly didn't want me. That's why I'm depressed. It's why my mam sits at the kitchen island every evening drinking wine and why my dad never comes home. None of us like being with each other. All of us are trying to escape in some way; him by working as much as he can, her by getting drunk. And me. By dying. At least I have the courage to end it all and get away from my crap life. Not like them. Chickens.

Won't be long till we get to our stop. Ten minutes or so. I knew it'd be around midnight when we finally did it. Me and

Ingrid talked all of this through. It'll be over in the blink of an eye. No pain. No suffering. Then somebody will find our bodies. They'll ring the police. The police will ring our parents. There'll be lots of crying; lots of drama. It's the thoughts of that drama that drives me to suicide more than anything. They'll deserve all the pain they'll feel when they're told the news.

I let out a sigh, then lift my head off Ingrid's shoulder and wipe at both of my eyes. I'm really tired. Though it doesn't matter. I'm almost asleep forever. The whole weight of tiredness that being depressed brings will no longer bother me; the whole stresses in school about being the short fat one will no longer bother me; the pressure of passing exams will no longer bother me; being lonely in my own home will no longer bother me.

I twist my head over my shoulder as the bus pulls over at another stop. And my heart flips.

It's not… is it? I widen my eyes a bit. Bleedin' hell… it is!

Stitch. In a grey hoodie sitting on the other side of the stairs. He's leaning his head against the window, looks like he's almost asleep.

My heart begins to thump really fast as I stare at him. Which is weird because I was enjoying how relaxing this bus journey had been. Me and Ingrid were just keeping really quiet and really calm as we headed towards our death. But seeing this bleedin' eejit sitting behind us has made me panic a bit.

I twist my head back around and stare out the front window, wondering whether or not I should tell Ingrid he's sitting six rows behind us. I don't want it to have any impact on her. If he starts talking to her; if he starts apologising for calling her Fishfingers, she might change her mind.

I let out a sigh. There's no escaping him. We'll be getting

off in a couple stops. As soon as she stands up and turns around, she'll see him.

I breathe deeply and then rub my eyes.

'What's up with you?' Ingrid says. 'You okay?'

My head shakes slowly and then I turn to face her.

'Look behind you, Ingrid,' I whisper. 'Grey hoodie.'

23:50

Ingrid

Ciara's taken her head off my shoulder. It's a pity. I was enjoying how peaceful and quiet everything was. The bus was totally silent. Even though I know a few people got on behind us.

She turns around and begins to fidget. Then her breathing changes. Maybe she's getting a bit frightened seeing as we're nearly there. Only two more stops to go. I wonder if she wants to change her mind. Maybe she wants to change her mind. I think I'd be up for that. We could probably do this tomorrow instead.

'What's up with you?' I whisper to her. 'You okay?'

She shakes her head and then sighs a little bit. Something's up. I can always tell with Ciara.

She leans her face nearer to mine.

'Look behind you, Ingrid,' she whispers. 'Grey hoodie.'

I don't know why. But I already know who she's talking about before I turn around.

I twist my neck as slowly as I can and see his face almost hidden behind his hoodie, his eyes closed, the side of his head resting against the window.

I try to breathe as slowly as I can as I stare at him because I don't want him to have any effect on me. Not anymore. Then I turn back around.

'What are the bloody chances?' I say to Ciara. She just stares into my face as the bus pulls in at another stop.

'We're getting off at the next one,' Ciara says. 'Let's just stand up, walk down the stairs, and if he notices you or tries to say anything, I'll shut him up, okay?'

I can't believe he's on this bus. Just as we're about to do this. I nod my head and then Ciara stands up and reaches her hand to me. I grab it and stand up too before each of us tiptoe our way towards the steps.

I'm staring into his face when his eyes flick open. Then he gasps and sits up straight, whipping down his hood.

'Ingrid,' he says.

Ciara holds her hand to my mouth, then takes a step towards him.

'Stitch — you have no right to talk to her after the way you treated her last night. You shut the hell up and let us get off this bus.'

His eyes widen. He looks more shocked than I am. I wish he wasn't so handsome. Ciara doesn't think he is. But I've always thought he was one of the best looking boys in the school. I think it's his bushy eyebrows.

'I just… I just… I want to say sor—'

'I told you, Stitch,' Ciara says, raising her voice. 'Don't try to say anything to her.' She points her hand down the stairs and looks at me. So I do as she wants. I grip the handrail tight and begin to sway my way down the steps. 'Don't!' I hear Ciara shout. Then she follows me down and we wait quietly beside the driver as he makes his way towards our stop.

It seems to take ages for him to pull in. I'm a little scared

Stitch will come down the steps to try to talk to me at any second.

But he doesn't.

The bus pulls over and me and Ciara wave a thank you at the driver before we find ourselves back out in the cold air. We stand and wait until the bus has pulled off and then we hug each other again.

'Wow. That was weird,' I say, resting my chin on Ciara's shoulder.

'I gave him the finger, did you see that?' she says. It makes me laugh.

The last time he'll ever have seen either of us will stay in his head forever; Ciara's finger telling him exactly how we feel about him. He'll have to live with that for the rest of his life if we commit suicide. He'll replay calling me Fishfingers over and over in his mind and feel guilty forever.

'You ready?' Ciara says.

We release our hug and then — at the exact same time — we both stare up to the very top of the Clock Tower.

It's one hundred and fifty feet high. They taught us that at school. I think everybody who lives around here knows that. You can see the top point of the Clock Tower from almost every street in Rathmines. It sticks out like a sore thumb. I don't know how many times in my life I've stared up at one of its four clock faces to make out the time. It used to make me dizzy when I was a kid. I'd stand under it and try to stare up to its highest point. Never in a million years did I think I'd ever stand on its ledge one day and jump off it. But here I am. About to do just that. I think we are anyway. Ciara certainly doesn't look like she's going to change her mind.

I squeeze her hand as we walk to the side of the tower and — as we planned last night — Ciara jumps to reach the ladder that leads us to the fire escape. When she pulls it all the way to the ground I suck air in through my teeth, shiver a bit, and then nod at my best friend.

We don't say anything to each other as we climb the shaky steps.

I've never been up here before. Ciara has. She figured out a couple years ago that this was the way she wanted to end it all. She says we'll be dead before we even hit the pavement. She's thought it all through. This is the best way to commit suicide; no pain, no suffering. Just one tiny leap and it'll be all over. She's stood on the ledge a couple times before. Just to test it out.

The wind seems to get stronger the higher we climb but suddenly the shaky stairs end and Ciara is stretching ahead of me, over a small ridge, and on to a concrete ledge. I can actually hear the ticking of the four clocks beneath us as if they're right next to my ears.

I take one step forward and edge my chin outwards, so I can stare down at the pavement.

Wow.

It really is high. I can feel my heart thump a little bit. I think we're really going to do this.

We both stand in silence, staring down onto the footpath where we're supposed to land as the wind gets a bit heavier around us. Then — out of nowhere — we hear a clanging sound.

Somebody's climbing the stairs.

HELEN'S EYES GROW WIDE.

'What'd the call say?' she asks really slowly.

Charlie puffs a disappointed sigh down the line.

'I'm sorry, Helen, but the Royal Hospital museum has just been stolen; they think there's about three million euro worth of paintings missing. Everybody here is kicking themselves; it's got to be Alan Keating. He played us. The calls were a hoax, a distraction. I eh... I just wanted you to know.'

Helen holds the phone in front of her face to stare at the screen. There's nothing to look at, except for the timing of the call flicking upwards in seconds. Eighteen seconds she's been on this call. Nineteen. Twenty.

She holds the phone back to her ear.

'Thanks for letting me know, Charlie,' she says.

'You okay?' he asks.

'Course I am... course I am,' Helen replies, her thumbnail in between her teeth as she stares out of her side window.'

Charlie sighs again.

'I mean... I know I'm going to be in trouble in the

morning with Newell, but I just I... I thought you should know. We were wrong, I guess. But thank you so much for the adventure. It might be my last night as a cop, but I won't forget it. I'll never forget it. I hope you're eh... still up for that coffee some time?'

Helen nods her head as an answer... her thumb still between her teeth, her eyes still wide.

'Helen?' Charlie says.

'Yes. Yes. Coffee. Of course, Charlie. Any time,' she says.

'Cool. So where are you now?' he asks. 'Did you go straight home from here?'

Helen swivels her head slowly, staring around Charlie's car.

Then she inches her nose a little forward to try and make out any of the bumper damage.

'Yeah... I'm at home,' she says, before twisting the phone screen to her face again and pushing at the red button.

She doesn't scream, doesn't sigh, doesn't slap her palms against the dashboard. She just sits in silence, staring at the subtle ripples in the canal, the edge of her thumb back in her mouth.

Her past is playing in her mind in black and white like an old film reel. She's remembering walking into her bedroom one evening, her stomach flipping, a tiny white stick in her hand. She showed it to Eddie. His eyes narrowed immediately. It was a surprise. A huge surprise. But one they accepted. They'd both talked about not wanting kids — preferring to give their progressing careers all the time and effort they required. But they adored him as soon as he was born. They'd often switch shift patterns at work, just so one parent was always home with their precious boy.

'I'm so sorry, Scott,' she says to the glistening lights in the canal. Then she turns the key in the ignition and inches the car forward, before clicking into reverse and backing all the way to the main road.

She dabs at the tears in her eyes while she drives, unsure where she's driving to. She flitters between thinking about going back to Terenure Garda station and leaving the cop car where she found it — or driving straight home, going to bed and pleading with Eddie to deal with the mess in the morning. But she still can't get the two girls out of her head. No matter how much her common sense is screaming at her.

She drives up the main Rathmines Road, spots the Clock Tower in the distance. Then, as it gets nearer, she stares at the hands of it. Almost five to twelve. What an embarrassment this whole night has been for her. She cringes, then without even noticing, she finds herself back at the canal again; car stopped, headlights shining onto the ripples.

'You're literally driving around in circles, Helen. What the fuck are you doing? Make a decision. Make a fucking decision.'

She looks at herself in the rear-view mirror.

'What if they're still out there?' she says. 'Two girls about to kill themselves at midnight. Where would they be? Where would they go to do it? Come on, Scott... give me a sign. Give me a sign.'

She looks around herself, out both side windows, out the back windscreen. Then, as she tugs at the rear-view mirror, her eyes widen.

'Of course!'

She taps the steering wheel, adrenaline rising in her stomach. 'It's been staring at me all bloody night.'

She shifts into gear and speed reverses into the street.

A loud horn blares from a passing car that has to swerve out of her way. Then she wheel spins on to the main

Rathmines Road and then pushes her foot, as hard as she can, to the accelerator.

She's almost grinning to herself when her phone vibrates in her jacket pocket.

'Hello,' she says, holding it to her ear.

'Hel, where are you?'

'I'm at home, Eddie.'

'You are not at home. I can hear you... driving.'

'Well, I'm going home.'

'You told me you were going home hours ago!'

Helen sniffs her nose as a response.

'I have something to tell you,' Eddie says.

Helen sniffs again.

'Keating carried out a hell of a heist tonight. The Irish Museum of Modern Art at the Royal Hospital.'

'Yep... over three million worth of art, right?'

'How did you know that?' Eddie asks.

Helen sighs. Says nothing.

'Hel... what are you doing? Where are you going?'

'I know where the girls are, Eddie.'

'What the hell do you mean *girls*?'

'It's obvious where they're going to commit suicide. It's been staring at me all night. I shudda bloody known.'

'Hel... Hel!'

Helen shifts into fifth gear, the car now speeding towards the moonlit shadow of her destination.

'Hel!' Eddie shouts again. 'Don't do anything stupid, you hear me?'

Helen sniffs wet snot back up her nose, then lifts the knuckles of her fingers to dab at the tears flooding her face.

'Goodbye, Eddie,' Helen says.

'Wait! Where are you? Where are you going?'

Helen blows out her lips, tears spraying on to the steering wheel.

'Hel! Hel!' Eddie sounds frantic... frightened. Then he gasps. 'I know where you're going... Helen! You stop. You stop right now. That is an order!'

Helen swallows back some tears, then sniffs her nose again.

'Bye, Eddie,' she says, before she tosses the phone on to the passenger seat.

It doesn't take long. She's there within seconds, grabs at her door and shoves it open. Then she runs — in her own unique way — as quickly as she can; not even bothering to look up at the top of the Clock Tower. She's certain the two girls are on that ledge. It makes total sense to her. It all adds up.

She stretches until she can reach the bottom rung of the ladder and yanks at it.

Then, without hesitation, she begins to climb.

23:55

Ciara

I PINCH AT INGRID'S TRACKSUIT TOP AS IT BLOWS IN THE breeze; the two of us standing at the edge, staring all the way down to the footpath.

The Clock Tower looks huge from down there when you're looking up at it. But it always seems higher when you are looking down from up here. I'd know.

This is not my first time on this ledge.

But for some reason, I'm more frightened now than I was when I was last up here, even though my best friend is right beside me.

I guess the last time I was standing here I was doing research or something — testing out whether or not this is the best way for me to kill myself. But this isn't research no more. This is the real deal. Me and Ingrid are going to hug each other for the last ever time in just a few seconds, then we're gonna leap.

I decided this was the quickest way to do it. It'll take us two seconds to hit that pavement. Then our lives will be over; no pain, no suffering, no struggle. I could never imagine cutting my wrists, could never imagine drowning myself. This is the only way I was ever going to do it.

I wrap both my arms around Ingrid and squeeze her as tightly as I can.

She puffs out a sad laugh, then grips me and we hold each other as a quiet breeze whistles around us. Then I hear a clanging sound. It's the stairs.

Somebody's coming.

We both spin around.

'Ingrid! Ciara!'

Stitch is lifting his leg over the ridge between the stairs and the roof's ledge.

'What are *you* doing here?' Ingrid calls out, gripping me even tighter. We take a step backwards.

'No, no, no, no, no,' Stitch calls out, shaking both of his hands towards us. 'Please don't tell me you are both gonna do what I think you're gonna do.'

Shit. I can't believe this. The bleedin' ass hole followed us. Now it's ruined. Our pact is ruined.

'Stitch... you just climb back down those stairs and pretend you didn't see us up here,' I say, taking another step backwards with Ingrid.

'Oh my Jesus, no,' Stitch says. 'Seriously, You are really gonna do that? Jump? Kill yerselves?'

I've never seen anyone look so confused. His whole face has fallen, there are wrinkles on his forehead that I've never seen before and his eyes look heavy, his bottom lip is sticking out like a baby about to cry.

'Because of me? Don't be bloody stupid. I didn't mean to... I'm so sor—'

'It's not because of you. Don't flatter yourself.' I say, interrupting him before he gets inside Ingrid's head. I release my grip on my best friend and take two steps forward, my finger pointing. 'This has got nothing to do with you. Climb back down those stairs and don't get yourself involved.'

'Ingrid… Ingrid, I'm so sor—'

'Shut the hell up, Stitch!' I scream at him. He's not even bothering to look at me. He's staring over my shoulder. Trying to plead with Ingrid. But I won't let him. I take another step towards him.

'Get lost, Stitch. If you wanna stand there and watch us do this, you can live with that the rest of your life. But if I was you, I'd just get lost back down those steps and forget you ever saw us up here.'

He falls to his knees.

'Ingrid. Ciara… don't be stupid.'

'Get lost, Stitch!' I scream, taking another step towards him. I stretch out my leg, push the soul of my trainer against his chest.

He stumbles back, holding his hand to the ledge for balance.

'Jesus no, Ciara,' Ingrid says, grabbing me from behind. She drags me back a little. 'She's right, Stitch. Just go back down… forget you saw us here.'

Stitch gets to his feet, his face still all wrinkled, his mouth still open.

'I'm not gonna let yous kill yerselves. Are ye mad?' he says. Then he takes a step towards us and reaches out a hand.

MIDNIGHT

Ingrid

'Jesus no, Ciara,' I say, grabbing around her arms and holding her back.

My breathing's gone all funny. I thought she was going to kick him off the roof for a split second.

'She's right, Stitch,' I say over Ciara's shoulder. 'Just go back down… forget you saw us here.'

He crawls back to his feet, slowly, and stares at me. His eyes are really wide. So's his mouth. He looks different. It must be the shock.

'I'm not gonna let yous kill yerselves. Are ye mad?' he says. Then he takes a step towards us and stretches out his hand.

'Get lost, Stitch,' Ciara roars. I can hear the pain in her voice. She's angry. Really angry.

Stitch doesn't listen. He takes another step closer.

'Stitch… I said get lost!' she screams.

My breaths are getting sharp. I think I just want to jump. Now.

Get it over with.

Stitch takes one more step closer.

'C'mon, Ingrid, take my hand,' he says. 'Let's all go back down the steps and we can talk—'

'Stitch, I swear to you, we're gonna jump. Now if you want to stand up here and watch us...' Ciara says, releasing from my grip and taking a step towards him. I cover my eyes with my hands, but through the cracks of my fingers I watch them square up to each other, their noses almost touching.

Ciara takes another step forward, forcing Stitch to take a step back. This is a mess. What an absolute bloody mess. I can't believe he followed us up here.

'Ingrid... don't mind this mad bitch, come with me,' Stitch shouts out. Ciara grabs him and then suddenly they're wrestling, their hands grabbing on to each other's shoulders.

'Leave her, leave her,' I scream as I run towards them. I grip on to Ciara's waist and try to grab her backwards. But Stitch has her held too tightly. So I thump at his hands... until he lets go. But then he reaches for me. I turn, force both of my hands into his chest and push him away as hard as I can.

All I can do is watch.

As he falls.

Not a sound coming out of him.

He just swirls through the breeze until he stops swirling altogether.

'Sweet Jesus. Holy fucking Jesus,' Ciara says grabbing me. I can hear her words in my ears, repeating over and over in slow motion. She drags me to the ground and lies on top of me. 'Sweet fuckin Jesus,' she says again, straight into my face. I blink at her. Really slowly. As if I'm a robot.

Then I shake my head. To try to turn back time. To see if Stitch will appear back on the ledge with us.

I crawl to the edge to the ledge and stare down. He's just lying there. Facing up to the moon.

'What'll we do? What'll we do?' Ciara screams as she gets to her feet behind me.

I swallow and then press my hands into the ledge so that I can get back to a standing position. I turn slowly, so that I'm face to face with my best friend again, and a tear drops from my eye.

'Our turn next,' I say. I sound really strange. As if I'm not me. 'C'mon.'

I stretch my hand out to Ciara. She just stares at me, her breathing is still really heavy and panicky.

'We killed Stitch… we have to report—' she says, her arms flailing in all directions.

'We don't have to report anything. We just need to jump,' I say.

Ciara shakes her head. She's in a different state of shock to me. Everything is going really slowly for me… but for her it seems to be going really quickly; her breaths, her head shakes, her hands, her thoughts.

'His parents… his parents are—'

'I know, Ciara… I know. Which is why we need to do this. Now. It's time.' My voice sounds really different. My whole body feels really different. As if I'm no longer alive. Maybe I've just accepted it. It's time to die.

Then suddenly Ciara's eyes return to normal and her head stops shaking. Her heavy breaths become normal, her arms rest down by her side and her whole body seems to slow down. She holds her fingers out to me and I grip them. Then, for some reason, I smile at her. And she smiles back.

'You're right,' she says. 'We really need to do this, don't we?'

I nod my head and then we both turn towards the ledge. But rather than stare down at Stitch, I stare across the tops of the buildings on the other side of Rathmines — as far into the distance as I possibly can.

'On three?' Ciara whispers.

I grip my fingers tighter around hers. And then nod my head.

HELEN'S ALMOST HALF WAY UP THE FIRE ESCAPE WHEN SHE HAS to grip her hands to her knees and bend over. But she doesn't want to stop for long.

She takes in one large breath, blows it out and then continues; the tick-tocking of the four clocks that sit each side of the tower rising in volume the higher she climbs; the wind starting to swirl, blowing her leather coat behind her like a cape.

She heaves herself over the ridge, then — after scrambling to her feet — she stares across the ledge.

At nothing.

'You're an idiot. A fucking idiot, Helen,' she says, grabbing a fistful of her orange hair. 'Course they're not up here. They don't even exist. They never existed. You've been chasing ghosts all night.'

She inches forward to the edge of the ledge and stares down at the pavement; down to where Scott landed. And Ingrid. And Ciara.

Then she wipes her face, smudging snot and tears across her cheek.

'I can't believe it's been twenty-two years,' she says, sucking back up her nose.

She stares off into the distance, over the rooftops of Rathmines, zipping her leather coat up fully so that the collar is fastened tight under her chin. It's not the first time she's been up here. It took a year after Scott and his friends died for her to stoke up the courage to visit the scene. Even though hundreds of people had laid flowers at the foot of the Clock Tower in the aftermath of the suicides, Helen couldn't bring herself to visit. She kept her head low every time she left the house because had she looked up, the tower could be seen hovering above the rooftops of the terraced houses of her estate. The sight of it repulsed her. It still does. But one night, just before Scott's one-year anniversary, she found a strength within her to sneak out of the house and make her way to the exact spot they landed on. She circled her foot around it, then stared up to the highest point of the tower.

Seconds later she was heading to that point; grabbing on to the ladder that led to the fire escape stairway. She stood on the ledge, staring down at where she had just been circling her foot. She thought about leaping herself. But froze. Eddie kept coming into her mind. She adored him. Even more than she did when Scott was alive. He went out of his way to ensure she got counselling, went out of his way to make sure she had the best mental health support she possibly could have. He saw to it that she got a job back in the station when she was ready. Even though he knew she'd never be the same person again. She wasn't only heartbroken from Scott's suicide. She was mind broken. And neither her heart nor her mind would ever mend.

Even though the doctors insisted she shouldn't return to police work, Eddie conjured up some position at the front of the station for her — doing admin work. It meant he could keep an eye on her all day long. He knew she was capable of going off the rails at any point — especially if she didn't take her medication — and it was annoying to him that she would poke her nose into investigations every now and then. But at least she was still there, still near him, still existing.

She places her hands into her coat pocket and inches closer to the edge; the toes of her Converse trainers hovering over it, only the weight of her heels keeping her alive. Then she closes her eyes and sucks in a deep breath.

'Hel!'

She twists her head, sees Eddie clambering over the ridge. He has both hands held up and his palms out as he inches slowly towards her.

She wipes at her face, then darts at him.

'Oh, Eddie,' she says wrapping her arms around his head and neck. They squeeze each other as tightly as they possibly can. 'I'm so sorry. So sorry.'

Eddie brings one of his hands to the back of Helen's head, taking a fistful of her orange hair. Then he yanks it back a little, so that her head tilts and he can stare into her eyes.

'It's not you who needs to apologise. It's me. *I'm* sorry. I'm sorry for telling you to go home and watch your soaps. I'm sorry you found out about this case. I'm sorry I haven't been checking up on you as much as I should…. It's just been such a manic night, a manic investigation and… and…' He holds a hand to his face, to cover his tears. He hates crying, does Eddie. Only ever cried in his own company after Scott's suicide.

The two of them shake their heads, then they just grab each other closer again.

'I just want to know…' Helen sobs on his shoulder, 'what happened to them. What the hell went on that night.'

'Sweetie,' Eddie says pushing his wife away again so he can stare into her face. 'How many times do I need to tell you?'

'I know. I know,' Helen says, shaking her head. 'I will *never* know what happened.'

Eddie purses his lips.

'You can't keep punishing yourself. We have to accept that we will never know what happened. We'll never be able to get inside their heads.'

Helen takes a deep breath, then blows it out through her lips; tears spraying either side of her.

'I should have known as soon as suicide was mentioned in the station earlier that you would've been affected by it. I was too bloody concerned with Alan Keating that I... I...'

'Don't blame yourself, Eddie,' Helen says. 'You'd think twenty-two years later that I'd be able to hear the word suicide and not have it trigger me. I just... I'm not sure I'll ever get over it. Not in this life.'

Eddie wraps his arm around the back of Helen's head and pulls it towards him, so that her chin rests on his shoulder.

'Well... we're going to get away from this life,' he whispers. 'On the way over here I made a phone call.' Helen opens her eyes. 'I spoke with Dickinson, told him I would be handing in my resignation first thing in the morning. I'm done. I'm retiring. And you and I...'

Helen takes her head off her husband's shoulder, bringing her nose to touch his.

'We're moving to Canada?' she says, unable to hide a joy that bubbles up within her. She laughs as she says it, spraying tears onto Eddie's face.

Then Eddie kisses her forehead.

'We're moving to Canada,' he says.

Helen wraps her arms as tightly around her husband's waist as she can and uses all her might to lift his feet a few inches off the ground.

When she releases, allowing his heels to rest back down to the ledge, he laughs.

'It's the right time,' he says. 'To hell with this job. To hell with chasing around after ass holes like Keating and looking like a mug. I'm done. We spent the last twenty-two years chasing my dream of becoming a superintendent. Now — for the *next* twenty-two years — it's all about you. All about us. A new life.'

He brushes a strand of hair away from Helen's face and the two of them grin at each other as wide as they possibly can.

'C'mon,' he says, gripping Helen's hand. 'Let's get back down to earth.'

They make their way to the steps and clunk down them with their arms wrapped around each other.

'I'll book the flights in the morning,' Helen says. 'When do you think we can leave?'

Eddie puffs out a laugh.

'I'm supposed to give two months notice, but Dickinson said he'll do his best to shorten that for me and ensure I get the full pension too.'

Helen squeezes her husband into her hip. It seems strangely eerie that Eddie would inform her of her new life at the exact same spot her old life ended. But she's super excited. This is the giddiest she's been in twenty-two years.

'Okay then... well, I'll book the flights for two months from now anyway. It'll give us a chance to say goodbye to everyone, to get the house on the market.'

Eddie releases his grip on his wife, then jumps down to the pavement before holding his two hands aloft. He catches Helen as she leaps towards him and they wrap themselves in a tight embrace again.

'Did I get you into a whole load of trouble?' Helen asks.

Eddie sniffs out a laugh.

'Not much more than usual. Nothing I can't handle.'

They smile at each other again, then Helen leans her head

onto her husband's shoulder, offering one more apology with body language rather than words as they stroll onto Rathmines' main road.

'I'm parked over here. Where's your car?' Eddie asks, pressing at his key ring, making his headlights flash.

Helen squints her eyes a little, then holds her hand over her mouth.

'What?' Eddie asks as Helen takes a few steps onto the road.

Eddie follows her, tracking her line of vision down a line of parked cars until he sees what she's staring at; a cop car, its headlight smashed, its bumper hanging off.

'Oh sweet Jesus,' he says.

The End.

DID YOU...

…miss all of the clues to that twist ending?

Well, watch this short interview with author David B. Lyons
in which he talks you through each and every one.

Get ready to kick yourself!

www.subscribepage.com/thesuicidepact

It is estimated that 1.3 million people will commit suicide this year.

That means one person will die from suicide in the time it takes you to read the words on this single page.

If you suffer with depression, please reach out and talk to somebody.

Here is a list of helplines from certain regions of the world.

Ireland: *Pieta House* 1800 247 247
United Kingdom: *Mind* 0300 123 3393
United States of America: *ASFP* 1-800-273-8255
Canada: *The Lifeline* 1-833-456-4566
Australia: *Lifeline* 131114
New Zealand: *Lifeline* 0800 543354
India: *AASRA* +91 22 2754 6669

Or — from anywhere in the world — visit:

www.befrienders.org

READ MORE FROM DAVID B. LYONS

THE TICK-TOCK TRILOGY
   Midday
   Whatever Happened to Betsy Blake?
   The Suicide Pack

THE TRIAL TRILOGY
   She Said, Three Said
   The Curious Case of Faith & Grace
   The Coincidence

ACKNOWLEDGEMENTS

This was far from an easy write. So a massive, *massive* thank you to my wife, Kerry, and daughter, Lola, for living with a forty-year-old who was trying to live inside the head of two depressed thirteen-year-olds for a few of months. Your patience is a virtue. You both inspire me every day.

This particular novel is dedicated to my mam – Joan. She's off-her-head hilarious in that unique way only Irish mothers can be.

Thank you so much for never being one of those parents who said "sure what would ye wanna do that for?" when their son tells them they want to write. When I was transfixed with writing in school, you always encouraged me. When I told you I wanted to quit my insurance job to go back and study journalism, you didn't question my decision.

When I recorded you and the neighbours up in the local club one evening as research for the first (and only) sitcom I wrote, you never said, "what t'fuck are ye doing?"

When I quit writing music and football articles for national newspapers and websites in order to study literature you never said "but you'll be earning feck all money, son".

You always trusted that I was making the right decisions for myself.

And that's the sorta shit great parents do.

Thank you for being a great parent.

I guess I gotta thank my sister Debra too... who did in fact ask "what the fuck are ye doing?" on multiple occasions during my life. She still asks it often.

Genuine thank yous (like *proper* genuine ones) go to Barry O'Hanlon, Hannah Healy and Margaret Lyons who read a very early draft of this book and gave me priceless pointers on where it needed improvement. Your opinions really helped shape the arc of this novel, moreso than any other you have read for me — and I'm indebted to you for that.

Thanks also to the wonderful Rubina Gauri Gomes who was the first person to read the finalised last draft of *The Suicide Pact*. I knew this was a good book when she texted me a Chris Pratt GIF with his mouth wide open in shock.

Shout outs also go to Susan Hampson and Livia Sbrabaro who gave me huge encouragement and fantastic feedback having read a pre-edited version.

And finally, I owe a huge thanks to the fantastic Maureen Vincent-Northam who edited this book thoroughly with her razor-sharp eye.